I0721326

Cover Design: Jay Aheer

Photo by Wander Photography

Editing done by Jenny Sims Editing4Indies

Proofing Julie Deaton by Deaton Author Services

Proofing by Judy's proofreading

Interior Design by Christina Smith

Cooper
My name came with big skates to fill.
At the top of my game, I had everything I wanted, or so
I thought.
Being traded to Dallas was not what I was expecting,
but neither were the divorce papers I was served.
Now I'm a single dad in a city that isn't my home.

Erika
Handed my biggest client when I was twenty-two made
my dreams come true.
Over time, our work relationship changed.
We grew closer, leaning on each other for support.
He was my rock, my best friend.
Then one drunken night changed everything,
and I saw what was in front of me all along.
I just hope that when the dust settles, we won't regret it.

SOMETHING SO, THIS IS, AND ONLY ONE FAMILY TREE!

SOMETHING SO SERIES

Something So Right
Parker & Cooper Stone
Matthew Grant (Something So Perfect)
Allison Grant (Something So Irresistible)
Zara Stone (This Is Crazy)
Zoe Stone (This Is Wild)
Justin Stone (This Is Forever)

Something So Perfect
Matthew Grant & Karrie Cooley
Cooper Grant (Only One Regret)
Frances Grant (Only One Love)
Vivienne Grant
Chase Grant

Something So Irresistible
Allison Grant & Max Horton
Michael Horton (Only One Mistake)
Alexandria Horton

Something So Unscripted
Denise Horton & Zack Morrow
Jack Morrow
Joshua Morrow
Elizabeth Morrow

THIS IS SERIES

This Is Crazy
Zara Stone & Evan Richards
Zoey Richards

This Is Wild
Zoe Stone & Viktor Petrov
Matthew Petrov
Zara Petrov

This Is Love
Vivienne Paradis & Mark Dimitris
Karrie Dimitris
Stefano Dimitris
Angelica Dimitris

This Is Forever
Caroline Woods & Justin Stone
Dylan Stone (Formally Woods)
Christopher Stone
Gabriella Stone
Abigail Stone

ONLY ONE SERIES

Only One Kiss
Candace Richards & Ralph Weber
Ariella Weber
Brookes Weber

Only One Chance
Layla Paterson & Miller Adams
Clarke Adams

Onlye One Night
Evelyn & Manning Stevenson
Jaxon Stevenson
Victoria Stevenson

Only One Touch
Becca & Nico Harrison
Phoenix Harrison
Dallas Harrison

Only One Regret
Erika Markinson & Cooper Grant
Emma Grant
Mia Grant
Parker Grant
Matthew Grant

Only One Mistake
Jillian & Michael Horton
Jamieson Horton

BOOKS BY NATASHA MADISON

The Only One Series
Only One Kiss
Only One Chance
Only One Night
Only One Touch
Only One Regret
Only One Mistake
Only One Love
Only One Forever

Southern Series
Southern Chance
Southern Comfort
Southern Storm
Southern Sunrise
Southern Heart
Southern Heat
Southern Secrets
Southern Sunshine

This Is
This is Crazy
This Is Wild
This Is Love
This Is Forever

Hollywood Royalty
Hollywood Playboy
Hollywood Princess
Hollywood Prince

Something So Series
Something Series
Something So Right
Something So Perfect
Something So Irresistible
Something So Unscripted
Something So BOX SET

Tempt Series
Tempt The Boss
Tempt The Playboy
Tempt The Ex
Tempt The Hookup
Heaven & Hell Series
Hell And Back
Pieces Of Heaven

Love Series
Perfect Love Story
Unexpected Love Story
Broken Love Story

Faux Pas
Mixed Up Love
Until Brandon

ONLY ONE
Regret
THE ONLY ONE SERIES

ONE

Cooper

WITH A HEAVY heart, I pull up to the daycare. Putting a smile on my face, I look in the back seat at my girls. "You guys ready for school?" Looking at me with big smiles and crystal blue eyes that match mine, Emma and Mia, dressed in pink skirts and white tops, couldn't be more princess if they tried. I'm hoping at least one of them might want to skate.

I get out of the SUV and open the back door to unbuckle Emma, who is four. "Sit tight until I unbuckle Mia," I instruct her as I slide my phone into the back pocket of my blue jeans.

"Okay, Daddy," her sweet voice says. Walking around the SUV, I open the passenger back door. Mia is trying to unbuckle herself, her patience very much like mine.

"Can I help?" I ask, and she looks up, nodding. She's wearing her short strawberry-blonde hair in two tiny pigtails to be like her big sister. The only reason she is ting me help is that it gets her out.

I grab her in my arms, putting her on my hip, walking around the car for Emma. I pull open the door and hold out my hand. "Thank you, Daddy," she says, smiling up at me. I notice her pigtails are a little off, but at least I tried.

"I have to grab your bags." I walk to the passenger side and grab their pink backpacks. "Do you want to put them on and walk into school?" I have to ask because I made the mistake of assuming last week, and Mia was fit to be tied.

"I want that," Mia says, pointing at her bag. I look around, making sure no cars are coming before putting her down. I squat down in front of her and put the bag on her shoulders. "I'm a big girl, Daddy," she says with a huge smile, and all I can do is nod, swallowing over the lump stuck in my throat.

Emma grabs her bag and puts it on herself. I grab their hands as we walk into the daycare. Once I punch in the code to open the door, I hold up my hand to the secretary as I walk first to Mia's class. "Give Daddy a kiss." I crouch down, and she comes into my arms. "I'll see you in two days," I say. The ache in my heart is the same as when I knew I wouldn't see them every day. I fight back the disappointment and pretend it's fine, even though it's not fine. Nothing about this is fine. I'm the first one in the family to get divorced, and it's killing me.

"Okay, Daddy," Mia says, not understanding what any of this means. She walks in to her teacher and waves at me.

The routine with Emma is a little different. She clings to my side, and I squat down in front of her. "Give me a kiss." She wraps her arms around me. "I'll FaceTime you tonight."

"Okay," she says softly. "Will you come tuck me in?"

Everything in me breaks. "Not tonight, honey, but in two days, you get to sleep over for five days." I try to be upbeat. "Now, give me another hug." She hugs me, and then her teacher comes to get her, and I watch her walk into the room. I peek into Mia's class on the way out the front door. I make no eye contact with anyone as I head back to my SUV with my head hanging.

Once I get in, I take a deep breath, calling the one person who has been by my side since, well, forever.

"Good morning, sunshine," Erika says, and I can hear her moving around. I look at the clock and see that it's just past eight, so I know she's getting ready for work.

"Hey," I say, my voice low as I put my head back on the headrest. "I just dropped the girls off at daycare."

I hear her stop moving. "Are you okay?" she asks, knowing that I'm not. "Do you want me to come with you?" I close my eyes. She's not only my agent but also my best friend. We've grown up together, and she knows me better than I know myself, which used to piss off Julianne.

"Nah," I say. "You have work."

"I can catch up later." I get a FaceTime notification and know that it's her calling me. I accept the call and see her face fill the phone. Her long brown hair is tied on the top of her head as she sits cross-legged in the middle of her bed in a sports bra and yoga pants. Her cheeks are pink, so I know she just worked out, and she's holding a protein shake in one hand.

"You look like shit," she blurts out, and I laugh. I bring the phone closer to me to see what she sees. In blue jeans and a T-shirt with a baseball hat, I'm in precisely what I wear on my days off. It hasn't changed since I was sixteen, and it's not going to change. Except for the addition of circles under my eyes since I didn't sleep much last night.

"You are always so uplifting and motivational," I say, and she throws her head back and laughs. Nothing can beat when she really laughs. It's full of heart and makes you want to join in.

"I'm my own eat, pray, love." She takes a sip of her protein shake. "What time are you due at your lawyer's?"

I look at my silver Rolex watch she gave me when I signed with Dallas four years ago. She even had *Every Minute Counts* engraved on it. "Twenty minutes."

"Are you sure you want to do this alone?" she asks, and I nod. "I can be there in fifteen minutes." I shake my head and smile at her. She really is my fucking rock. "Then we can go back to wherever and do some shots."

I laugh at her, knowing that if I really needed her, she would cancel everything and stay with me. "It's all done. All I have to do is sign the papers." The divorce was a shock. I'm not even going to pretend it wasn't. Were we happy? Fuck no, not even fucking close, and only Erika knows that I was slowly dying inside. But I made a promise, and I was going to stick to that promise. No matter what, I was going to stand by my vows until the bitter end.

"Call me if you need me," she says. "Whenever." She puts the phone down, and I can see her starting the shower. "I'll have my phone on me all day."

"Thanks, kid," I say, and she laughs. She gave me that nickname when she met me. I was only eighteen when I was drafted. It made me laugh, and it just stuck with us. When she wants to bug me, she calls me kid.

"I'm older than you by four years," she points out. "I'm already in my thirties."

I roll my eyes. "Whatever. You look like you should still be in school." She puts her face close to the phone. Her green eyes are lighter in the sun.

"Do you see this?" She points between her eyebrows. "That's a wrinkle." She looks like she just graduated high school.

"You have lost your mind," I say, and she shakes her head. "Be safe," I advise before I hang up and put the SUV into drive.

The green trees never really change color in Dallas like they do in New York City. Not only was it my home but it was also the first team that picked me in the draft. They were doing a rebuild, and I got fucking lucky to start my career with my family behind me, literally.

My grandfather was none other than Cooper Stone, who I was named after and compared to every fucking day. My father, Matthew Grant, was also a first pick in the draft, but the glitz and glam of Los Angeles was his downfall. New York snatched him with a condition, a chaperone, which happened to be my mother. From the way they tell the story, he fell for her the minute he laid eyes on her and made her his. When he decided to retire, he took on the role of general manager of the team. Just because he was the GM and my father didn't mean he took it easy on me. In fact, he rode my ass harder than anyone. My game just got better and better as the years went on, and when I turned twenty-one, I met Julianne at a bar in Dallas when we were there for the all-star game. I knew she was trouble, but I was smitten with her Southern talk. She quickly moved in with me, and then we found out she was pregnant with Emma, and there was no way I wasn't going to marry her.

Every single time she could, she would bitch about New York. She hated the weather, she hated the smog, she hated the people, and she hated my family. She. Hated. Everything.

When she got pregnant with Mia, she said she was leaving. She couldn't stand being in New York, so I made the painful phone call to Erika and asked her to trade me. I cried like a fucking baby when she called me back and said Dallas was taking me. It was where Julianne wanted to go, and I wanted to make her happy. Happy wife, happy life, or at least that was what they said.

My father was my biggest supporter after Erika, who knew how much I hated moving. She was the one who called me almost every hour to make sure I was okay. When we moved here, Erika was the only friend I had. Nico, the team owner, was the best, and I knew Manning, Miller, and Ralph, who included me and helped me settle in, but Erika was the one I turned to for everything.

After Mia was born, it was all downhill. I dreaded being home. I dreaded even talking to Julianne, and I guess she felt the same since she had me served with divorce papers after I skated off the ice during practice four months ago.

Julianne refused to talk to me, and all communication had to be done through the lawyer. I didn't know who was more pissed, Erika or me. Erika was out for blood. She had me hire the best divorce lawyer she could get. I honestly only wanted to make sure I had my girls when I was home. Because of my travel schedule, I made sure I had the girls when I was in town. Julianne tried to play hardball, but she underestimated me.

Our prenup was iron-clad, so she didn't get anything extra. The house was to be sold, but I gave it to her and the girls. It was enough that their parents broke up. They didn't have to suffer because of it. My main thing was that their routine stayed the same, and nothing changed on their end.

Pulling up to my lawyer's office building, I park in the underground parking garage. Getting out, I walk over to the waiting elevator. Pressing twelve, I look down at my phone when it pings, and I see that Erika sent me a text.

Erika: You got this.

I'm about to answer her when the elevator doors open, and I step out. The secretary is already standing. "Mr. Grant," she says, "right on time."

I nod at the woman and follow her down the hallway. She leads me to the same conference room that I was in when I first came here with Erika. My lawyer, Debra, sits at the table on her phone and looks up when she sees me. "Mr. Grant," she says, and I smile. "Are you ready?"

I clap my hands together. "Let's do this."

TWO

ERIKA

I SEND COOPER the text and put my phone down on the seat beside me. My stomach is a mess as I think about what he must be going through.

I put on my glasses and make my way to the office. The sports radio plays in the background, but I'm wondering if I should go over to the lawyer's office anyway. I keep checking my phone as I stop at Starbucks to get my morning coffee and another one for my assistant.

Pulling up to my assigned parking spot, I always smile when I see my name, Erika Robinson. Getting out, I grab my black Chanel purse and make my way toward the door. The sound of my black Louboutins click. The sun is even at it's peak yet, and I can tell it's going to be hot as balls outside today.

The cold air hits me as soon as I walk across the marble floor toward the elevators. I smile at the security guards as I pass their desks. I press twenty-five and wait for the doors to close. The phone in my hand has not made a sound as I look at my reflection in the stainless-steel doors. My black pants fit me like a glove, and the white wraparound shirt with bell sleeves is tied around the side in a big bow, leaving the sashes hanging on the side.

The elevator pings, and when the doors open, I step out. The TRI Star Sports Agency logo decorates the wall right in front of the receptionist, who smiles at me. "Good morning, Erika," Marlene says in her usual chipper mood.

"Good morning," I smile, "You look lovely this morning." She just shrugs and smiles shyly. I know she has been working out for the past two months in the hopes of getting the UPS driver to ask her out.

Walking past her, I come to the open space where cubicles, ringing phones, and people's voices fill the room. I look over to the corner and see that Trevor's door is open, which means he's in, and so is Francis's. I note on my silver and gold Rolex that it's exactly nine o'clock. Walking toward my office, I smile at everyone I make eye contact with on the way there.

Francis, Trevor, and Becca started this agency, and it's grown to one of the best out there.

Francis and his team take care of the baseball and golf players. Trevor and his team take care of the football players. They also split the basketball players.

Becca used to take care of hockey until she stepped away from it and handed me her clients. She still works some, but she married the owner of the Dallas Oilers, and they have three children, so she is happiest at home. The staff here has grown to over two hundred, and it continues to increase every year.

"For you," I say as I hand one of the cups of coffee to my assistant, Shauna, who smiles at me. When I took over for Becca, she was just starting here, and I gave her the same shot Becca gave me. I can't do anything without her by my side.

"You are too kind." She smiles at me, and I walk into the office and stop when I see the flowers in the middle of my desk. "They just arrived."

I put my coffee down on my desk and set my keys and purse on the corner. The huge bouquet of pink and white tulips sits in a glass vase with a card sticking out. Grabbing the white card, I sit down and slide the card out with my finger.

Erika,

If I forget to tell you. Thank you for being by my side.

Kid

I throw my head back and laugh, shaking my head. "Those from who I think they're from?" Shauna asks, leaning against the doorframe.

"An inside joke," I say, slipping the card back inside and tucking it in my desk drawer. "Anything going on I should know about?"

Getting up, I carry the flowers over to the round table that I have to the side of my office. I look up and see the picture I took of Cooper the day he got drafted. When Becca handed me her clients, they were all established except for Cooper. He was my first buildup. He got drafted first, so there was nothing I could do about his salary, but the rest was all the two of us. He was ready to do whatever I recommended, and trust me, I suggested everything, including him being on *The Bachelor* in his spare time. None of my other clients holds a special place like Cooper does.

When I was in my last semester of college, I was recruited to do an internship here, and it was the best decision I ever made. I was at the top of my class to graduate with honors with a master's degree in marketing.

I knew I wanted to work in a fast-paced environment. On my first day here, I knew this was where I wanted to be. I fell in love with the hustle and bustle. Becca was the one who trained me. Being taken under her wing was everything. She was who I wanted to be, cutthroat and zero fucks given if you did anything to her clients. Her stepping down was a surprise to everyone. I thought I would have to fight more to keep her clients.

I didn't think anyone would take me seriously. Hell, I had just turned twenty-three. I'd been here for a year, and even though they met with me and communicated through me, I still had the big dog behind me. But Becca had trust in me, which made them have trust in me.

That is not to say I didn't stress for the first six months of my job and worry I would fuck up. I kept a calm façade, but inside I waited for the other shoe to fall. I'm happy to say it never did. There were certainly fuckups over the years, but nothing I couldn't handle.

Moving back to my desk, I grab my phone and send

Cooper another text.

Me: Are you divorced yet?

Cooper was my first client, and we were friends, but when he called me devastated that he had to leave New York and got traded to Dallas, we really became close. I was his only friend here, and I knew that coming here and leaving his family was killing him. I was his confidant, and he knew that anything he told me wouldn't go anywhere. I sat with him at least twice a week while he told me how much he struggled. I didn't understand why he wasn't sharing it with Julianne, but when I finally spent time with her, I got it.

She was only worried about one person—herself. She didn't give a shit that he was miserable. He lost weight, and his game suffered. To her, as long as she was happy, that was the key. I tried to be her friend, but she made it clear I wasn't of her kind. Whatever the fuck that meant. So I faked that I was happy to see her when I did. I did it for Cooper and the girls, but the minute she blindsided him with divorce papers, I was ready for fucking war. She did him dirty, and for that, I hated her even more.

My phone rings, and I jump at it, thinking it's Cooper but see a 631 area code.

"Erika Robinson," I say, looking out the window, the sunlight coming in.

"Erika Robinson," the male voice says. "Max Horton."

I lean back in my chair. "Mr. Horton," I respond, chuckling. Usually, it's Max, but that is when I've seen him and I've been with Cooper. He's switched hats, and so have I. "Good to hear from you."

He laughs. Max was one of the best to ever get on the ice. He had this long history with Matthew, Cooper's father. The history got more complicated when Max married Cooper's aunt, Allison. "Cut the shit with the mister."

I laugh. "Fine," I say. "But I draw the line at calling you Uncle Max."

It's his turn to laugh. "In time, you'll cave and call me that, too."

"Wanna bet," I counter, knowing there is no way I will call him Uncle Max. I'm close to Cooper's family, closer than I am to my own, but that is only because they don't need me for anything. My parents grew up paycheck to paycheck. I am their only child, and I busted my ass to put myself through college, only to have them coming to me every six months for a small loan. Three years ago, with Cooper and his support, I finally said no. I was then called a hoity-toity bitch.

"I bet you a signed jersey that by the end of the year, you will call me Uncle Max," he teases.

"But what do I get if I win?" I ask, rolling my lips. "A Max Horton jersey goes for, what, five hundred bucks these days?"

"Fuck that," he says, and I let out a great big laugh. "You almost had me."

"That," I gloat, "is a great poker player." I tap my manicured finger on the desk. "What can I do for you?"

"I'm wondering if you had time to sit down with me. Michael is ready to look at things."

I close my eyes and raise my hand in the air. "Music

to my ears," I say, instead of mentioning that it's only because I just signed Dylan Stone.

"If it was up to me, I would have signed with you last year," Max says. "But you have to let your kids finally make the decision."

"Well," I say, getting up and walking to the window. "Better late than never."

"I'll touch base with Michael and see when he's going to be free," Max says.

"Sounds like a plan," I confirm, looking out the window at the cars driving by.

"Say hi to my nephew for me," he says, and I smile.

"Will do," I say and hang up the phone with him. My phone buzzes in my hand, and I see that Cooper just sent me a text.

Cooper: I'm officially a divorced man.

THREE

Cooper

I WALK OUT of the lawyer's office, and my chest hurts. My body feels like it weighs a thousand pounds, and my shoulders feel like I'm carrying the weight of the world.

I take my phone out and text Erika, knowing she's probably freaking out. I know if the roles were reversed, I would probably be hiding in the parking lot, making sure she was okay.

Cooper: I'm officially a divorced man.

Just typing the words, I stop next to my SUV and bend over, thinking I'm going to get sick. I breathe in and out and unlock the door, sitting in the heat while the air conditioner kicks on. I don't move my SUV. Instead, I just sit here numb with my head against the headrest. The phone rings, and my eyes peel open as I look at the display on the dashboard.

Dad is written in the middle. My hand comes up, and I press the connect button.

"Hey," I answer, my voice monotone as I look at the screen and suddenly wish he was here. My father is the strongest man I know. He also has this crazy love for his family that even if I tried to explain, I knew I couldn't do it justice.

"Hey yourself," he says, breathing out softly. "Where are you?" The only ones who knew about me signing today were Erika and my father. I couldn't deal with everyone else knowing. The disappointment I had in myself was just too much.

"I just got into the SUV," I say.

"How did it go?" he asks, and I laugh bitterly.

"As good as it was going to go, I guess. The paperwork was already prepared when I walked in. The lawyer just explained that everything we asked for was accepted. Julianne is going to allow us to continue the custody agreement we have. I have the kids two weeks in July and another two weeks end of August."

"That's good," he says. "How're you feeling?"

"Like a complete and utter failure," I confess.

"Cooper … why the hell would you feel like that?"

"Because I let my kids down." I think of my girls growing up without me. "Because I let myself down. Because, at the end of the day, I couldn't make it work."

"Would you feel better if you stayed with Julianne and ended up hating her?" he asks, and I look at the dashboard.

"What makes you think I would end up hating her?" I ask him the loaded question. "So what that she hated everyone I loved. So what that she made me feel like a stranger in my home. So what that she hated doing anything with me."

"When you spend your life with someone, it should be with your best friend," he says. "Someone who will hold your hand when shit gets rough and helps you when shit is going down. Someone who protects you and would die for you."

I close my eyes, knowing he's right. "But I was there for my girls." It's the first time I ever admitted that I wasn't there for anyone but them. It should hurt less, but it doesn't.

"Are you not going to be there for them anymore?" I can hear him tapping his finger on the desk.

"Of course I will," I say without skipping a beat. "Always. How can you even ask that?"

"Don't you think the kids would have picked up on how miserable you were if you stayed with Julianne?" He is the only one who has balls enough not to sugarcoat things. Even Erika has her moments, but she knew that divorce was a delicate subject for me.

"I mean, I never thought of that. I was never rude or nasty to her in front of the girls. Fuck, I moved to fucking Dallas for her," I declare angrily. "I gave up so much to make her happy."

"And that, right there," he says, "should be reason enough for you not to doubt your decision."

"I mean, I can't really doubt it," I remind him. "She served me divorce papers when I skated off the ice. I didn't even have my gloves off, and this guy was there with a manila envelope." Just thinking back on it makes my stomach burn. It took Manning, the captain of the team, to talk me down from driving over to the house. He called Erika, and she came right over, and the two of them talked me down.

"I will never say a bad thing about Julianne," my father says. "But the best thing for her to do was to let you go. Having the two of you growing apart in front of the girls wasn't healthy. Each of you resenting the other. Besides, don't you want your girls to know what unconditional love is?" I don't bother saying anything to him because I know he's right. I know I would never disrespect their mother to them, but would I be a different person? I close my eyes, thinking I would be so miserable that they would probably hate me in the end.

"I'm the first one in the family to get divorced. Fuck, it was supposed to be forever." My voice gets low. "I'm a disappointment."

"One," he says, his tone getting a touch louder, "you aren't the first one to get divorced." I tilt my head to the side and wonder who the fuck else got divorced. "Grandma got divorced."

I roll my eyes. "That doesn't count."

"That counts tenfold," he replies. "It's because of that we all know what unconditional love is." I know he's right.

"And two, you are not a disappointment. Jesus, it's not like you went out and killed someone! You got divorced."

"Yeah, and my kids will be in the category of divorced parents," I remind him, getting a touch angry.

My father laughs at me. "I was in the category of divorced parents." I can see him shaking his head. "And I turned out semi-okay." His laughter makes me chuckle. "Honestly, Cooper, the best thing to ever happen to me was my father leaving. I can't imagine the man I would have become without having Cooper by my side." His voice gets really soft. "Divorce is not the end of the world. The main thing is your girls see that you are there for them no matter what. That if they need you, they can count on you. And maybe one day you'll find a love that's really forever." I don't say anything to that. I swallow down the lump that is forming. "As long as your girls are happy and loved, you can't ask for more. They need the best dad there is. Regardless of if you are married to their mother."

"You're right," I admit. "As long as the girls are okay, nothing else matters."

"Exactly," he says. "And it works out that Julianne accepted you would take them when you would be in town, and when you travel, she has them."

"Yeah," I agree, laughing. "Erika came up with that one. Julianne wanted one week on, one week off."

"Well, there is a reason Becca handed her the keys to the kingdom, and it wasn't because she has a pretty face."

"She works hard," I say, proud of her. "And it shows."

"We are coming down this weekend," my father says, and I smile big. "If it was up to your mother, she would be there today, but Franny and Vivi dragged her to LA for a girls' week trip."

"And you let her go?" I ask, laughing. My father is never far away from my mother.

"I'm on the plane going to her," he admits. "She left last night." I can't help the laughter that rips through me. "So she got a six-hour head start."

"Does she know you're coming?" I ask, my chest feeling lighter the more I talk to him.

"She should know better," he says. "Your sisters are going to complain, but that's what you get when you take my woman away from me." That is what I want. What I strive to have. That is what I dream of, but hey, I got two gorgeous girls out of it. I can't say no to that.

"Thanks, Dad," I say, feeling so much better than I did when I walked out of the office. "For everything."

"It's my job. The four of you are my life. Your brother not so much these days." I laugh, thinking about Chase and his refusal to do anything with hockey until he got a degree in medicine.

"He's a good kid," I say finally. "Tell Mom I say hi, and I'll see you guys on Friday."

"I'll text you when I have the details. I think even Uncle Max is also coming down." I laugh, and I don't know why I'm surprised that everyone is coming down this weekend. This is what we do. When one needs help, we rally.

"Sounds like fun," I confirm, a little excited they are going to come down. "Love you, Dad."

"Love you more," he says and disconnects the call. I pull out of the parking lot and see the sun shining high in the sky. The phone rings, and I see that Erika texted me a couple of times.

Erika: But how are you feeling?

Erika: Silence must be a full-blown pity party.

I laugh at the last text. After I park my SUV, I get out and walk toward the elevators, pushing twenty-five and putting my key in the keypad. The elevator only moves when it recognizes the key, and the door opens a couple of seconds later. The sunlight fills the condo, and it should since the whole back wall is floor-to-ceiling windows.

Tossing my keys on the counter, I walk over and grab the orange juice from the fridge. Pouring myself a glass, I clean up the counter where the girls left their breakfast. I hang the pictures they made me this morning on the fridge, and I'm going to the bedroom to make their beds when I hear a knock on the front door. I smile to myself, knowing exactly who it is. To be honest, I'm surprised she lasted this long without coming over.

I open the door, and there she is, my rock. "Knock knock," she says, holding up a bottle of Macallan whiskey. "I'm here to collect the rent." I laugh as she walks in. When I was looking for a place to stay, she didn't even hesitate to offer me her condo. Even though I rejected it, she wouldn't take no for an answer.

"I have to give it to you," I say, closing the door behind her and then walking to her and putting my arm around her shoulder. "You are totally slacking."

She gasps and pushes me away from her. "How am I slacking?" I grab her again.

"One, you weren't lurking in the parking garage," I

tease as we walk side by side to the kitchen.

"I was giving you space," she replies, walking out of my reach. "And making you sort shit out before."

"Well," I say, putting my hands on my hips. "Don't do that shit again."

She rolls her eyes and shakes her head. "What would you have done?"

"I would have been sitting in the lawyer's office waiting for you," I say, and she opens her mouth and closes it.

She shrugs. "Well, I guess I'm a shitty friend. Instead, I gave you space and bought you booze." A smile fills her face. "You're welcome!"

FOUR

Erika

"Well, I guess I'm a shitty friend. Instead, I gave you space and bought you booze." I smile when I see his eyes are lighter than they were this morning. "You're welcome!" I walk to the place where I used to keep the shot glasses and see a pink sippy cup beside it, making me smile even more. "Do you want a shot glass or the sippy cup?" I ask over my shoulder and see him staring at me.

"Definitely the sippy cup," he jokes and walks over to his phone. "Pizza?"

"It's not even eleven." I grab two shot glasses, and then he tilts his head and takes off his baseball cap, tossing it onto the white marble island. When I bought this condo, I had plans to live in it. It was right next to the office in the heart of downtown, so I thought it was the perfect move for me. What I thought would make me a career woman. I lasted a full month before the novelty wore off, and I realized I wanted a home with a backyard and a pool and grass. Fuck, I wanted to walk on the grass at the end of the day. So I used this as an investment property and rented out the condo to people I knew or were referred by the management.

"You are going to pour shots of whiskey." He points at me, and I nod.

"That is correct." I point at him while I open the bottle of Macallan whiskey I ordered three days ago, knowing it was his favorite, pouring one shot and then the other. I look at my matching Rolex. "It's five o'clock somewhere."

"I got you a whole pizza with your fruit," he says, shaking his head and coming over.

"Why do you have to be such a hater?" I ask, holding up the shot and wondering if this is a smart idea.

He takes the glass from me. "You know I don't drink when the season has started."

"These are different circumstances," I remind him. "It's been a crazy year."

"Fuck if I know." He holds the glass up. "To better days."

"I don't want to toast to that," I say. "My year has been great so far." He laughs.

"Okay, so I'm going to toast to better days," he says. "What do you want to toast to?"

"To brighter days," I say, and he rolls his lips.

"It's the same thing, Erika," he points out, and I shake my head.

"Better and brighter are two different things." I grab

my phone. "Let me look up the meaning."

"Whatever," he says, clicking the glass to mine and taking the shot. "Aren't you going to take it?"

I look at the amber liquid. "I hate whiskey," I confess.

"Then why the fuck did you bring it?" He laughs, walking over and putting the glass down on the island.

"Because I know you like it, and this is me trying to make you feel better," I say as he glares.

"I didn't even want the shot," he says, folding his arms over his chest.

"Fine," I hiss out. "I'll take it." I bring it to my lips and swallow it in one gulp, the burn stinging me all the way down to my stomach. I cough as I try to breathe and run over to the sink in case it comes back up. "The shit I do for you," I say, turning on the water and putting some in my hand to sip it. I point at the bottle. "That's fucking disgusting."

"It's not disgusting," he defends, walking to the fridge and grabbing me the sparkling water I love. "You want to know what's disgusting?" He walks to me, leaning over me to grab a glass. The heat from his chest is on my back, then it's gone in a second. He unscrews the bottle of water and pours a bit for me. Handing me the glass, I reach for it and bring it to my lips. "Tequila."

I gasp. "Tequila is not disgusting," I say, and if I admit it to myself, it is disgusting, but after a couple of shots, it's fine. I laugh. "Remember when you drank Don Julio from the bottle last summer?" I point at him, and he grimaces.

"I thought it was going to go down smooth," he says,

leaning on the counter beside me. "It did not."

"It has to be chilled." I take another sip of the cool water. The bubbles are popping on my tongue. "I told you that."

He shakes his head, and I just look at him. "You okay?" I ask softly, and he just shrugs.

"Not entirely," he says. "But I'm feeling much better."

"Was it the whiskey?" He laughs, and I slide over to him. I put my arms around his shoulders, and even with my heels, I still have to get on my tippy-toes to rest my head on his shoulder. "Do you want to watch one of those stupid movies you like?"

"*Battleship* is not a stupid movie." He crosses his hand over his chest and places it on mine on his shoulder. "Thanks for coming over, kid," he says with a smirk.

"Anything for you," I say with a smile.

The doorbell rings, and I know it's the pizza. He walks to the door as I turn and grab the roll of paper towels and the bottle of water. He comes back in with two pizza boxes, and the smell fills the room. "Are you having more whiskey?" I ask, and he shakes his head. "My plan was to get you drunk enough to forget about it," I inform him. "That bottle cost me a lot of money." I walk over to the island and sit on one of the stools, and he sits next to me. Slipping off my shoes, I tuck one leg under the other. "What did you get?" I look over at his pizza.

"The carnivore," he says, opening his box, and I see it's cooked perfectly. The pieces of meat look really crispy.

"Can I have a piece?" I look up at him, and he laughs.

"You do this every single time," he says, taking a piece and putting it on the paper towel and handing it to me.

"It's not my fault your food looks good all the time," I reply, grabbing the piece and biting it. The garlic sauce hits my tongue, and the sausage just explodes. "Next time," I say, chewing. "I want that one." He shakes his head at me. "You can have some of mine," I tease, knowing he hates pineapple on his pizza.

"I'll pass," he says. "Spoke to my father." I look over at him, stopping mid-chew. I know how close he is with his family, and being away from them is hard on him.

"He's on his way to LA," he shares, and I groan. "My mother and sisters are going for some retail therapy."

"Don't remind me," I say, and he looks at me weirdly. "I'm so bummed I had to cancel."

He puts down his piece of pizza and looks over at me. "You were going to LA?" he asks me, shocked.

"Yeah, they invited me last month," I confirm, grabbing the pizza and taking a bite. "Why didn't you order fries?"

"Hold on a second." He puts his hands up. "You were going to LA to shop with my family?"

"Again, yes," I say. "But then I canceled."

"Why?" he asks, and I shrug. I'm not sure I should tell him the truth, even though I know he will see right through me. When I lie, I never look at him in the eye, and he knows it.

I pick off a piece of pineapple, avoiding his eyes. "Who wants to sit around in a plush robe in the morning and order room service and then buy clothes that I'm never going to wear?"

"You canceled because of me?" he asks, his voice going low, and I look up at him. Seeing the softness in his eyes.

"Well, yeah, I wasn't going to leave you alone to eat good pizza and watch a crappy movie." I lean my shoulder into him and blink away the tears. "I just don't want you to feel like you let anyone down." I look over at him.

"How did you know?" he says, looking at me and then away. "I just told my father this."

"Because family is your biggest thing. Anyone who knows you should know this."

"Yeah, my father said the same thing. I'm just worried about the girls …" His voice trails off.

I turn and face him, trying to spin his stool so he looks at me, but he's heavy. He laughs when I grunt and then turns to face me. "You are the best dad I've ever met," I say. "And the girls are going to flourish when both parents are happy."

"I know," he admits. "I can't believe you canceled your trip."

"Me either," I say. "Did I mention plush robes?"

He laughs, and I know he feels better. He turns to look back at his pizza. "Remember when you took a week off one year and didn't change out of your robe?" he asks, laughing.

"I like robes," I defend, turning back to my own pizza. "Remember when you went on vacation in Florida and decided it wasn't a good idea to wear sunscreen and came back looking like Sebastian the crab."

He throws his head back and laughs. "I'll never do that again." He looks over at me. "Thanks, kid."

I don't say anything. All I do is smile and eat my pizza. We spend the day watching the stupid movies I know he loves. He walks me to my car, and I take my time driving home.

I pull into the five-car garage and smile at my two-story house. It's big enough for a family of five, but it has the big backyard I craved, and for that, I was willing to pay the extra money. I walk up the stone pathway that leads to my big brown door and see a huge cardboard box addressed to me.

"What the hell?" I say, opening the front door and turning off the alarm. I dump my purse and take off my shoes before turning back to get the box.

It's so big I can only bring it in the front hallway. I close the door and walk into my home office to grab a letter opener.

I slice the box down the front, and when I open it, a white envelope with my name on it sits on top. White tissue paper conceals it. I turn it over and take out the card.

Hope this makes up for it.
Kid

I slide the sticker off the tissue paper and find a plush white robe. "Oh my god," I say, grabbing it and then finding another one under it. There are five robes all together with a note at the bottom. I take it out, and I can't help the laughter that escapes me.

Couldn't pick just one.
C

to do at a home. We could have done it at my house."

"Maybe Sunday at lunch, then," I say, and she doesn't even care. If I would have told Julianne that, she would not have allowed it. When my family used to come down and visit, she would have one meal with them. One. That was her cap, and she made sure she chose the shortest dinner. If it was up to her, she would not have even come.

The minute the girls see Erika, they forget I'm even there. She buckles Mia in while she talks to Emma and shows her the pink drink she got both of them. She spends the whole ride looking in the back and asking them questions.

I pull up to the restaurant at the same time as my parents do, and the girls squeal when they see them. I don't even have time to put it in park before they are opening the back door. "Where are my babies?" my mother says.

"Right here," I say, making her laugh. I look over and see that my uncle Max is parking the car with my aunt Allison and my cousin Michael in the back seat.

"Uncle Max came?" I look over at my father.

"He had a meeting with Erika today," he says, and I look over at Erika.

"You didn't tell me," I remark, shocked that she knew he was here.

"Because it's none of your business who I meet with." She grabs her purse and gets out of the SUV. She goes to my father, and he gives her a side hug and a kiss on the cheek. She scrunches up her nose at Mia, who leans in and rubs her nose with hers. I get out of the SUV in time to see her share a big hug with my mother, and Emma wraps her arm around her also.

"Hey there, big guy." My uncle Max slaps my shoulder. "You don't look so bad," he says, and I glare at him. "You look about a hundred and twenty pounds lighter."

I roll my eyes when my aunt Allison slaps him away. "Too soon," she scolds and then gives me a hug. "How is my favorite first nephew?" I laugh when I have to bend to hug her.

"Shit, you grew." I look over at Michael and see he's almost as tall as me, but he bulked up. I give him a hug. He's going to be drafted this year, he and my cousin Dylan. Dylan is going to go first. There is no denying that. When my uncle Justin opened up his hockey camp for underprivileged kids, Dylan was one of the kids who got a spot. He then fell for Dylan's mom and adopted him. There was no stopping him back then, and he just got better because he was born with it. He was going to kill it, and I couldn't be prouder of him.

We turn to walk into the restaurant, and I hold the door open for everyone. Erika is the last one to walk in. "They closed down the restaurant," she says. "We're safe." With a laugh, I put my hand around her shoulder.

"It's not a good time if we don't get kicked out of a place," I tease, and she just shakes her head.

We sit next to each other with Mia on her left side and Emma on my right. She takes off her white jacket, leaving her in a silky pink top. "If you did that not to get dirty." I shake my head.

"I don't care if she took my jacket to wipe her face. I was getting hot," she admits, grabbing a piece of bread and buttering it for Mia and then asking Emma if she wants a piece. Dinner is crazy chaotic, and when I look over at her, she has Mia in her lap facing her with her head on her chest.

"We should get going," I say, looking at Erika, who nods her head. "It's been a long day when you get up at four in the morning."

We kiss my parents good night, and I drop her off at her car. Erika kisses the girls and tells them she will see them tomorrow. I want to ask her to come back to the condo with us, but I know she has a forty-minute drive, and I don't want her staying out that late. "Text me when you get home."

"Go away," she says, shutting the door and walking over to her SUV. I wait for her to get in and drive away before I leave. The condo is five seconds from her office and four minutes to the arena. All of our heads hit the pillows by the time nine o'clock comes.

My parents get to the condo right in time for my mother to cook breakfast and take the girls so I can get ready for the game. "You really need to get a house," my father says when I walk out of the bedroom. "I mean, this would be okay if you were alone."

"I know, I have a couple of houses to check out next week." I kiss the girls goodbye and walk out of the condo.

The drive to the arena is stupid. I should have just walked, but I know the girls are coming to the game tonight. I park my SUV at the same time as Manning, the captain, gets there. He gets out of his SUV and nods at me. "Coops," he calls out to me. "You look better."

"How shitty did I look before?" I ask him, and Miller, the assistant captain, slaps my shoulder.

"Horrible," he says. "Worse than Ralph did when he got another newborn."

I open my mouth, thinking back to last year when Ralph and Candace welcomed another child. Candace is my brother-in-law's sister and the social media expert. "He fell asleep getting dressed once," I recall as we walk into the arena. The journalists are already lined up to take pictures.

We nod politely to them as I open the door and walk down the blue carpet.

"Boys," Nico, the owner, greets us. "We have a big one tonight," he tells us, but every game is a big one. When Nico inherited the team at twenty-seven, he was the youngest owner. No one thought he would do anything with the team but he proved them wrong. Our team is not ready for the Cup just yet, but I give it a couple of years, and I think we have a decent shot at it.

I change out of my black suit and put on my track pants, then go to hit the bike. I do a couple more cardio exercises, and when it's time to hit the ice, I'm bouncing on my skates. I glide out when the doors open, looking at the corner to see if the girls are there. I see their heads jumping up and down when they see me as they hit the glass.

"Daddy," I hear Emma say when I get close enough. Both girls have their hair in ponytails and are wearing

Dallas jerseys with my name on the back.

I look behind them, expecting to see my mother or father, but Erika is standing there with them. She is wearing tight black pants and a white shirt with an oversized brown sweater. Her hair is in a ponytail like the girls. "Why aren't you wearing my jersey?" I ask, and her eyebrows pinch together. She's never ever worn a jersey to any of the games. "You could match the girls."

"You aren't my favorite," she says, smiling.

I throw my head back and laugh. "Liar." I grab a puck and shoot it over the glass. "Who else will carry you over their shoulder while you sing 'Runs the World'?"

"One time!" she shouts, holding up a finger. I skate away to do some drills, then come back over and bend to kiss the glass where the girls are.

"I'll see you guys later," I tell them, and Erika holds out her hands for the girls. I see they are wearing black tights just like her, and the three of them are wearing the same sneakers. If anyone were looking at us, they would think we're a family. I guess, in a strange way, we are. There is nothing I wouldn't do for her.

"You ready?" Manning asks as we stand in the hallway to get on the ice, and I nod at him.

"Press is going to be all over your ass," he says, and I know he isn't wrong. This is the first game since the divorce, and even though it was mentioned in the news, I haven't had to talk to the press yet. "The boys will have your back, and the minute you don't want to answer questions, you just walk away." Manning went through his own divorce a while ago, but no one fucked with him because he never gave any interviews unless it was after the game. The press has been watching me for what feels like my whole life. Knowing they are waiting for me to fuck up only pushes me harder.

"Grant," my coach says, "you're on with Miller and Manning." I nod my head. We walk out of the hallway, and I get on the ice starting at center. The national anthem plays, and I shut it all down.

I skate in a circle, waiting for the puck to drop. I bend, getting ready for the puck to drop. The referee stands there with his legs open wide. "Clean game, boys," he says, and I look over at other centerman nodding my head.

The puck drops, and I win the faceoff, sliding the puck toward Manning, who takes the puck and moves it up. I skate past the centerman going to the blue line and looking to see that Manning passed the puck to Miller, who skates into the zone with it. He moves it toward the net and takes a shot on the net. It bounces off the pad of the goalie, and I pick up the rebound, sending it over the pad and into the net. The horn blows loud as I turn to smirk at Miller and Manning.

"Fuck, that felt good," I say to them as we skate to the bench, and I take a second to look up to the box at my girls. My father high-fives my uncle Max as they celebrate. "Let's do that again."

SIX

ERIKA

I SHOOT OUT of my seat when he scores the goal and yell. He is on fire tonight. This is his second goal. "Look, Daddy scored again," I tell Emma, who is sitting in the seat next to me.

I look over at the luxury box I own, seeing that it's finally full. To be honest, it's only full when his family comes to visit. The rest of the time, I give away the tickets to people in the office.

"Who is number forty-seven?" Franny, Cooper's sister, asks from in front of me. "He looks like he needs someone to talk to." Franny, Vivi, and I spent the day shopping. She didn't have anything to wear to the game tonight, which was bullshit, but I had fun hanging with them.

"That is Brad Wilson, and trust me, he has his share," I look over at her, and she just smirks. "Forget about it," I say, and she shrugs. She wears her black jeans and matching black tank top with a jean jacket and a scarf. "He's the biggest player out there."

"Good," Franny says. "Which means I don't have to deal with the needy."

"Heaven forbid you actually catch feelings for someone," Vivi goads. "If you want to get with her, you have to do it with an ice cube as a heart."

"Exactly," Franny confirms.

"Auntie." I hear a soft voice beside me. "Can I sit on your lap?" Mia asks, rubbing her eyes, and I know what that means.

I hold out my hands, and she climbs onto my lap, sitting with her back to my chest. Her shoes are the same as mine. Something I picked up while we were shopping today. I see Emma is sitting with Karrie, who just smiles at me. "Are you hungry?" I ask Mia, who shakes her head. She never used to come to the games since Julianne hated the thought of it. She would usually send Emma with him, and I would have her all night long and wait for him to finish, but never Mia. When they got separated, I started bringing them to the games on Saturday nights, and she loved it.

I look at the ice and see that Cooper is back. He moves along the board, looking at Manning passing it to Ralph, who then tips it to Brad. Cooper sneaks in there, and I see that no one is watching him. Brad looks like he will take the shot, but instead, he passes it to the side where Cooper is waiting and tips it into the open net. The goalie was not able to slide back in time.

The whole place goes fucking nuts. People jump to

their feet as the siren goes off, and I know with Mia in my lap, all I can do is put my hands up in the air and clap. "Daddy just got a hat trick," I say, and she looks around at the people and claps her hands. "Three goals." The hats fly onto the ice, and Mia looks at me.

"I want to throw a hat," she says, and I look at her.

"Let's go buy a hat"—I get up with her and put her on my hip—"and when you see Daddy, you can throw it at him."

"Okay." She claps her hands with glee. I walk up the steps and look at Emma.

"We are going to buy a hat to throw at Daddy. Do you want to come?" I ask, and she nods her head and gets up and holds her hand out for Karrie.

"I guess I need a hat, too," Karrie replies, getting up, and Emma slips her other hand into mine.

"Where are you going?" Matthew asks as soon as Karrie gets up, and I have to roll my lips. You would think after being around them for the past eight years, I would be used to his caveman-like tendency, but it still makes me laugh.

"The girls want to get hats to throw at Cooper," she says, as he gets off his stool to follow her, and she glares at him. "I think I can handle getting hats."

He smiles and kisses her lips. "Bring her back to me."

"You don't have to," Max says, grabbing a chip and tossing it into his mouth. "He got her chipped a while ago when she tried to run from him." Matthew glares at him. "Was I not supposed to tell her?"

"Allison!" Matthew shouts to Allison, who is sitting

with Vivi and Franny. "Where is your husband's leash?"

"She's the one who wears the collar," Max chides, winking at Allison whose cheeks turn pink, and I almost die when Matthew pushes him. My mouth opens in shock as Michael just grimaces.

"You guys are gross," he announces, shaking his head.

I can't help but laugh, and when we walk out of the family box, we make our way over to the store. The girls grab two hats, and then they want a stuffed toy, and then they see a jersey with pink on it, and they want that and a flag and two foam fingers.

I put the bag on the couch when I walk back into the room and see that it's the end of the second period. Mia gets a burst of energy, but ten minutes into the third period, she climbs back onto me, puts her chest to mine, and lays her head on my chest. "You tired, baby girl?" I ask, and she nods her head. "You want to go home to bed?"

"Auntie Erika," Emma says. "Can we go home?"

I nod my head and look over to see Karrie watching me. "I'm going to get the kids home."

She gets up. "Do you want me to come with you?" she asks, and I just shake my head.

"You stay and enjoy the game. It's not every day you get to watch him live," I remind her, while the girls kiss everyone goodbye.

Matthew grabs Emma and comes with me to the SUV. "You know I do this all by myself when you aren't here," I say, and he just looks over at me. "There is a security guy in the parking garage."

"Well, then I can see for myself," Matthew says, and when we get to Cooper's SUV, I reach into my purse for his spare key.

"Here," I say to Matthew. "Can you give him the keys to mine?"

We buckle the girls in, and he watches me drive out with them. Emma is dragging her feet when we finally get home, and Mia is already asleep by the time I open the door. "Get into your jammies," I tell Emma. "I'll come tuck you in."

She runs down the hallway as I dump the bags of stuff I bought. I kick off my shoes as I carry Mia into the bedroom. The only thing that shows you that it's her room is the clothes she has on top of the bed. I undress her, and she barely stirs when I tuck her under the covers and kiss her softly. I walk back to the other bedroom and see Emma getting into bed.

"Can you lie with me, Auntie Erika?" she asks, and I smile while nodding at her. I get onto the bed with her, taking her in my arms. She turns in my arms as I spoon her, and I fall asleep at the same time she does.

Someone leans over me, and I open my eyes. Cooper's aftershave hits me right away as he leans to kiss Emma. "Hey," I say, blinking my eyes a couple of times as he stands.

"I didn't mean to wake you," he murmurs in a whisper.

"No, it's fine," I say, getting up. "What time is it?"

"Just after midnight," he replies as we walk out of the bedroom, and I see that he's still wearing his suit. He shrugs off his jacket and tosses it on the couch. "Sorry

I'm so late … my family."

"You don't have to apologize," I say, walking to my shoes. I grab them, sitting on the couch.

"You aren't leaving," he declares, and I look over at him. He's in the fridge, grabbing a takeout container. "It's too late. Why don't you just stay here and we can head to your house tomorrow for lunch?"

I think about it. "I need to start cooking at nine."

"The girls wake up at six. I think we can make it to your house at nine." He laughs. "You hungry?"

"No, I ate a bunch tonight." I shake my head, still debating if I should just go home. I lean back on the couch and curl my legs under me. The beep of the microwave makes him open the door and grab a plate. He walks over to the couch with his meal and sits down.

"What's with the bag of Dallas stuff?" He motions with his head to the two bags I put on the island.

"The girls wanted to throw hats at you. So we went to buy hats. How did the game finish?"

"We won," he says, and I smile at him.

"You played good, kid," I say softly. "How was the press?"

"Fine. One tried to ask, but I gave them a look."

I laugh at him. "What look?"

"You know," he says, taking another bite of his chicken, and I look in his dish. "The look."

"I have no idea what you're talking about." I grab his fork and pick a piece of carrot and eat it.

"It's the 'don't mess with me' look." He stares over at me. It looks like he's angry, but then he has to go to the bathroom.

"Are you giving me the look ?" I shake my head. "You look constipated."

He grabs a piece of carrot on his fork and holds it out for me. "It's a scary look."

"If you say so." I rest my arm across the couch and lay my head on it. "You played good tonight."

"It felt good. It's almost like I'm back," he says softly. "I haven't felt this good in a long time."

"Your game was never suffering," I point out to him.

"I know. That was the only thing I could control," he says, leaning forward and putting his plate on the coffee table in front of him. "It's almost as if I was another person, and I'm me again."

"Thank god," I joke with him. "The old you was an asshole. I like this you better."

He gets up and holds out his hand for me. "Let's get to bed." I grab his hand. "So you want to sleep in the master bed, and I sleep with Emma?"

"Nah," I say, stopping at Emma's door. "You can starfish tonight." I'm about to walk into the bedroom when he grabs my hand, stopping me.

"Thanks for tonight," he says, bringing me to him. With the soft light from the moon coming in, I can see his eyes are just a touch darker. His arms go around me, and he rests his chin on my head. I wrap my arms around his waist.

"You did good out there, kid," I reaffirm, and his chest moves as he laughs. I look up at him. "Makes my job easy." He bends his head and kisses my cheek.

"Night, kid," he says and then walks away from me.

"I'm the oldest thing in the condo," I remind him, and he takes his shirt out of his pants and starts unbuttoning it. "Even the Macallan is older than you."

"Will you ever let me get the last word?" he asks, his shirt open, and I see that he's hitting the gym hard these days.

"Maybe," I say, walking away and closing the door, making sure I'm the one who gets the last word. I lean my back against the door as the picture of him with his shirt off lingers for a bit longer.

SEVEN

COOPER

I GET OFF the bus, and the cold air hits me right away. "Why is it so cold in Edmonton?" Ralph asks, and I laugh. He pulls his hat down even lower. I pull my cashmere jacket closer to me as I walk to the waiting plane.

"Didn't you live here?" I ask, and he nods. "You should be used to it, then."

"My blood is thinner," he says, and I laugh.

We are on the last day of our road trip and due back home in five hours. We won the games on the road, and I scored five more goals.

"I can't wait to get back home," Manning says, walking up the stairs to the plane. "And the heat."

We left Dallas on Monday, and I was riding high from the weekend. Sunday morning started with Mia climbing into my bed and then running back out to grab the hats they bought for me and throwing one at me, getting me in the eyeball. Erika and Emma followed suit, throwing more hats at me. She ushered them out of the room, and I fell right back to sleep. When I finally opened my eyes, it was ten thirty, and I rushed out of bed to find a note on the counter.

Took the kids so you can sleep. See you soon.

I dressed in shorts and a T-shirt, arriving at her house at eleven-thirty. The food was already in the oven, and the girls were dressed to lounge by the pool. That was exactly what we did when my family got there. We chilled and relaxed by the pool, and the girls fell asleep in the SUV halfway home. Thank god she packed them pjs and had them change when I was at her house. Thinking back on the day, I don't think I ever smiled so much.

I grab my phone and see my father has sent me a text.

Dad: Call me when you land. I have to talk to you.

Dad: Nothing urgent or wrong.

I shake my head and text him back.

Me: Next time, just say call me when you have a second.

I put my phone away and lay my head back on the headrest and sleep most of the way home. I get into my SUV and call my father right away.

"Hey," he says, answering right away. "Did you just land?"

"I did," I confirm, grabbing the seat belt and putting it on. "What's up?"

"Well, first off," he says. "I have to say how great it was seeing you last weekend." I can almost see him smiling. "And the girls. Cooper, you have nothing to worry about." I smile.

"It was a great weekend," I admit. "And it was great having you guys here. I just wish there were more times like that."

"I know, son," he says, and his tone changes. "I'm calling you with good news." I can tell by his voice that he's excited about whatever this news is.

"We picked the dates for the family vacation," he announces, and I close my eyes, dreading what is going to come.

"By family vacation, do you mean …?" I ask, knowing it's what I think it is. Every single year, we all get together for a family vacation. All of us. We pick a beach destination, and everyone shows up. There aren't any ways around it. If you know this family, you show up. One year, my uncle Mark's family showed up, and we pushed one hundred people.

Last year, they chose Mexico, and we had seven houses side by side. It was insane, and also, if I'm honest, one of the best times. Julianne stopped coming three years ago when she got pregnant and then would go on vacation with her mother and sister while I went with my family.

"I mean all of us," he says. "All million of us."

I laugh. "We might get there one day," I agree. "Send me the dates, and I'll ask Julianne if I don't have the girls."

"We found the houses," my father says. "Side by side. I was going to have you guys stay with us, but your sisters said you needed your own, so I got one for you and the girls."

"Thank you," I say, laughing. "Franny and Vivi just

don't want to be woken up at six o'clock. I'm going to see if Erika is free."

"Sounds good, I'm so excited. All the family together for two weeks."

"I'm going to remind you of this conversation when you wake up one morning, and there is vomit on the side of the house, and you have to wash it off."

"Ugh, don't remind me," he says of that one year Michael and Dylan snuck off to get drunk at sixteen with Alex, and the guys threw up, and she laughed at them. "It's Max's turn next time."

"Okay, send me the dates, and I'll get it fixed on my end," I say, and he hangs up and sends me a text with the dates.

During the divorce, Julianne wanted to do one week on, one week off, but I couldn't bear not to see the kids, so I convinced her for two days each, but we also decided that we would take the kids for a two-week vacation. I drive away from the airfield and call her to get it out of the way.

The dread fills me as one ring turns into two, and then she finally answers on the third ring.

"Hello." Her voice sounds like she ran to the phone.

"Hey, it's me," I say, and I wait for the little butterflies to start or to feel anything for her, but nothing comes.

"Yeah, Cooper, I have this thing called caller ID," she grumbles, and I shake my head. There she is, the woman who makes me want to gouge my eyes out.

"My father just called me and gave me the dates for the family vacation in late June, early July," I start to say. "I was hoping I could have the girls for the full two weeks."

"I was thinking of taking them for the last two weeks of July anyway," she states. "So I think it should work."

"That sounds good," I confirm, wondering where she's going. I want to know, not for her but for my kids. "I'll FaceTime the kids tonight after dinner, and I'll pick them up tomorrow night."

"The girls told me that your parents came down." I don't say anything. I didn't really tell her. I dropped the girls off at daycare Monday before leaving. To be honest, the only time I talk to her is when she picks up the phone when I FaceTime, and even then, she lets the girls answer. We communicate via text when it has to do with the girls and daycare, but other than that, we have nothing to say to each other. If we didn't have kids, I don't think I would even think of her.

"They did," I say, not sure why the fuck she cares at this point. It's not like she went out of her way to get to know them. "Came down Friday and left Monday."

"They had a good time," she replies, and I can feel there is more she wants to say. "The girls said that Erika slept over," she notes, and my body goes tense.

"And?" My voice comes out cold.

"It was just a surprise, is all," she says, and I'm livid.

"A surprise," I say, laughing bitterly. "You didn't give a shit when I had to live with Erika after you served me with divorce papers. Blindsiding me." My tone curt. "I don't know why you would suddenly start to care."

"Whatever, Cooper," she says, her voice eating at

my stomach. "Send me the dates, and I'll put it on the calendar." She doesn't even say goodbye before she disconnects.

I toss my phone onto the passenger seat as the anger leaves my body. When I get to my condo and unpack my shit, I see it's almost six. I grab my keys and head out, stopping to get food on my way over. Only when I pull into the driveway do I think that I should have called her to make sure she was home.

I get out and carry the food with me. Looking around the neighborhood, I see a couple of kids outside playing on their bikes.

Pressing the doorbell, I look down, and I hear her footsteps. "Coming," she says, and a smile fills my face when she opens the door. She stands there in a cropped tank top, showing off her toned stomach and matching loose shorts. Her hair is tied on top of her head as a smile fills her face. "Hey, I didn't know you were coming over." She holds the door, watching me. "What a nice surprise," she says softly, making me happy that I came over here.

I hold up the bag in my hand. "I brought you dinner."

EIGHT

ERIKA

H_E HOLDS UP his hand, and a smile fills his face. "I brought you dinner." He stands there with blue shorts and a Dallas shirt. His hair is pushed back, and his blue eyes look like they are sparkling.

"Then you may enter," I say, moving out of the way for him to come in. He walks in and bends to kiss my cheek. His woodsy smell is all over me. "When did you get back?" I ask. I knew he left on Monday, and he did text me on Wednesday, but it was just a picture he took on Sunday.

"About an hour ago and then," he says and then looks at me, and I can see he has something on his mind. "I don't know, I just …"

"I might need wine," I say, knowing there is more to the story than that. "Do you want to eat in or out?" I ask. "Not to sway your decision, but I did start the fireplace outside and put on this week's episode of *Sister Wives*." I hold up my hands as if to weigh the decision.

He shakes his head. "I can't believe you still watch that show," he teases, walking past my winding staircase that sold this house for me and into my big kitchen.

I put my hands on my hips and stop in the middle of the way. "You are a damn liar if you tell me that you don't watch it anymore." I walk past him over to the massive fridge and pull it open, seeing it's half empty. I grab the open bottle of white wine and a glass, then head over to the sliding patio door. "I have beer and stuff outside."

We walk out and go to my covered lanai on the right. The brown wicker sofa with comfy beige cushions is L-shaped. It faces a stone-covered wall that has the fireplace on the bottom and the television on top of it. "What did you get?" I ask him, setting the wine down on the table in the middle, and then sit and curl my feet under me. I grab the throw blanket I have out here and wait for him to answer me. "It better be something good. I'm starving."

He sits next to me. "Before you complain, I'm going to add that you were not cooking yourself anything when I got here. So …" I glare at him as he takes out two containers. "Grilled maple salmon." I smile and clap my hands happily because he knows it's my favorite. "With mashed potatoes and a side salad." He pulls out two more containers.

"You're my favorite," I say, and he hands me the container. "But if you ask me that publicly, I will deny it until the bitter end." He laughs, and I look at him, grabbing his own. "I forgot forks." I start to get up but he beats me to it. I watch him walk inside the house, and my heart feels weird in my chest.

"You know what you need?" he says, coming out and closing the door behind him. He sits down next to me, handing me a fork. I take the plastic lid off the meal. "A dog." His eyes light up, and I look over at him.

"You know what you need?" I counter him, pointing the fork at him. "A house, and then you can get your own damn dog." He throws his head back and laughs.

"I do need my own house," he admits, grabbing his own meal. "And maybe a dog."

I look at him as I take my first bite of salmon. "You better not even think that I'm going to watch that thing when you go away. There is a line in this friendship, Cooper Grant, and pets are it."

"You would do it for me." He is so full of himself as I glare at him as he chews his own mouthful. "Because you love me, and I would do it for you."

"Love … hate … it means the same," I say, and he chuckles. "Now, not that I don't like when you come over and bring me dinner. Especially after not seeing you for a couple of days." My stomach is suddenly getting tight, thinking that I haven't seen him since Sunday. "To what do I owe the pleasure of your company?" I ask, and the food suddenly doesn't look appealing to me.

"Do you think I loved Julianne?" he asks softly, and I look at him.

"What do you mean?" I question and see that his eyes are on his food, so I know his mind is going a million miles a minute. "You had to have loved her to create two amazing little girls," I say and set my food on the table. "But were you in love with her?"

"Yes," he says. "That was me in love with her."

"I think at one point you truly loved her," I answer him honestly. "But people grow apart."

"I was trying to remember the last time I felt something for her." He looks over at me. "We lived together for five years. We had two children, and for the life of me, I can't remember the one time I felt something for her."

"It's because of all the bad stuff that happened," I remind him. "It just didn't go bad overnight."

"Oh, don't I know it," he says. "I know we weren't meant to be together, and I truly want her to be happy. I just …" He rubs his hands over his face. "I called her today, and for the life of me, I couldn't remember a time I liked her."

"I'm sure there were moments that you will remember." I scoot closer to him. "But maybe you're just so over her bullshit that you can't see it." He laughs. "I mean that in the nicest way." I put my hand on his shoulder. "She always gave you a hard time about your family."

"She said they meddled too much, and I can see it, but they are my family. It's the way they are."

"Then she didn't like that you had to train year-round," I remind him. "She didn't like the way you dressed. She didn't like when you didn't shave. She didn't like how you laughed at certain things. She didn't like your hair at one point. I mean, the list was endless with everything she wanted you to change. Toward the end, she hated everything about you. And you hated everything about her."

"You're right. I just, you know with my family, I thought once you find the woman, it's like bam, it's over. I'm just asking myself what I did wrong."

"You are asking the wrong person." I hold my hand up like I don't know. "I'm over thirty and single. My last relationship was over three years ago," I say, and he gags, thinking back to the guy.

"That guy was a douche." He shakes his head. "Like there was nothing good about that guy."

"Well, he cheated on me," I admit for the first time, and he looks over at me, shocked. "Yeah, the idiot forgot we shared the fitness app, and then I saw that his cardio was on another level at four o'clock in the morning." I get up, walking over to the fridge I have outside and grabbing a bottle of sparkling water. "The next day, I asked him how he slept, and he said like a baby, and he woke up at six."

I look over at Cooper, his mouth hanging open. "Why didn't you tell me?"

I shrug. "Because you would have blown it out of proportion."

"Oh, this coming from the woman who basically said *finish her* when I got divorce papers." He points at me.

"She served you divorce papers during a fucking practice!" I shout at him. "In front of everyone."

"Yeah," he says softly. "Well, today, she was not okay with you sleeping at my house."

"She was upset I slept at your house?" My heart beats in my chest as I close my mouth and think about the words that come out of my mouth. There is so much I want to say right now. "We lived together for two months after she kicked you out."

"I know," he agrees, holding out his hand for my drink. I get him a bottle of water, walking to the couch and handing it to him. "Trust me, I know. That is what I told her."

"Did it bother you?" I ask him. "Her thinking we were together."

"I don't give a shit what she thinks about us," he says between clenched teeth. "We're best friends, and she's always had issues with it."

I look at him, shocked myself. "What?" I ask him.

"She got over it eventually," he adds, and I shake my head.

"You never ever told me." I put my hands on my hips. "And here I was, thinking she liked me."

"What was I going to say? Hey, Julianne wants to know if we have feelings." I shake my head. "Then you dated one of her friends' brothers."

"Who was gay." I point at him, and he laughs, bringing the bottle of water to his mouth. "That was not a fun situation for me. He wanted me to do him." He spits water everywhere and chokes. "I'm not lying." I bring my water to my mouth. "Then she set me up with her dentist, who stared at our waitress's ass while in front of me, and he was mid-conversation."

"Remember that guy you dated?" He starts laughing. "The one who said he was in finance, and you found out he lived with his mother."

I slap his arm. "His mother lived with him," I remind him, and he just laughs. "It's very different, and he was in finance."

"As a bank teller," he says. "When we went on that double date, he kept talking about all the stock trades he did."

I hold up my hand. "Okay, enough of the walk down memory lane." I sit down next to him. "I've dated five guys my whole life," I admit, holding up my hand. "Five." I shake my head. "How sad are we?" I ask, and he puts his arm around my shoulder.

"We aren't sad." He kissses my temple. "Everyone else is sad, and we are perfect."

I laugh. "Yeah," I say, looking at him. "Now, let's turn on some *Sister Wives*. I don't get it," I note, grabbing my food. "I would never be able to share my man, but this show is just so intriguing."

"You won't share your man?" he jokes with me, and I glare at him. "I'll watch this with you, and then I get to pick the next show." And I groan. "You'll like it, I swear."

"Your taste in television sucks," I say. "Your taste in music sucks, too." I fold my arms over my chest. "Actually, you have good taste in one thing only."

"Oh, yeah," he says, amused. "And what's that?"

I lean into him and hit his nose with my finger, smiling. I'm happy he's smiling. "Having me as a friend."

NINE

COOPER

"I DON'T KNOW what the fuck you guys are doing out there," the coach says, "but you guys need to take your heads out of your ass." I look down at my skates. We are between the second and third period and down by two goals. "You guys know how to win, so let's go out there and show them. This is your ice. This is your home." He turns and walks out of the room.

"We need to get back faster and support Mika," Manning says of the goalie. "Those two goals were our fault and not his." Everyone nods and stays silent.

We walk back down to the ice, all of us silent, and when we take our place on the ice, we are ready for war. We push harder, skate harder, and fight harder, and with two minutes to go, we tie the score.

"Grant." He calls my name, and I jump over the board, skating into the neutral zone. Manning skates up the side and passes it to Miller. He gets the puck and skates into the zone, going to the corner and passing it to me. I let it sit on my stick for a second before looking over to see Manning in his sweet spot. I pass the puck over to him, and he raises his stick, bringing it back. The puck flies through the bodies, and the goalie has no time to even react. Manning has the hardest shot in the whole league, and it's times like this that it works in our favor.

The crowd is going crazy, and I can even feel the floor vibrate. Fuck, it's times like these I love what I do.

He skates over to me. "Good play," he says, smiling.

"Good shot." I point at him as we skate to the bench, high-fiving everyone, and with a minute to go, they pull their goalie.

Miller gets it on his stick and sends it down the ice to score the empty netter. The horn whistles, and we get off the bench and skate to Mika. We congratulate him and then skate to the middle, holding up our sticks to thank the fans.

Going back to the dressing room with a win is always a good time. The press is there, and one of them comes straight for me as I take off my gloves.

"Hey, Cooper," he says, the camera behind him. "Good play out there to tie up the game," he starts, and all I want is to take off my things and jump in the shower. "You are on a seven-game point streak."

I look at him and smirk. "I didn't know that."

"Your game is only growing stronger and stronger. What do you think the chances are of you guys getting the Cup?"

I put my hands on my hips. "I'm sure everyone wants

the same thing. We have a good bunch of guys. Only time will tell, I guess."

"Thanks for your time," he says and heads off to interview Manning.

Fifteen minutes later, they are ushered out so we can shower and get moving. I grab my towel going to the shower, and when I come back, half the room is already gone. "Where the fuck did everyone go?" I ask Manning, who slips on his pants.

"It's Saturday night. People want to party." He laughs, shaking his head. "Why don't you have big plans?"

I laugh. "I usually have the girls when I'm home, but Julianne's mom is in town, and they wanted to spend time with her." I shrug, missing them. "Why aren't you going out?"

"As a matter of fact," he says, grabbing his white shirt while I slip on my black dress pants. "We are going out to dinner."

I look at him, shocked. He never goes out, and if he does, no one knows about it. "You, Mr. I Don't Go Out And Talk To People?" I point at him, and he laughs.

"Yeah, aren't you coming with us?" he says, and I tilt my head to the side, confused by his question.

"Why would I come to dinner with you? Um, I'm not going to be the third wheel." I slip on my own white shirt and buttoning it all the way up. "That's fucking sad."

"You won't be the third wheel. It's a team thing. The invites were sent out to everyone." I look over at him and vaguely remember the team dinner that Nico was putting on. I also remember saying no before even reading the details. It's not that I didn't want to. It was just when it came in, I wasn't even in the right mind to want to go out with everyone.

"Shit, I said no because I thought I had the girls." I shrug. "Next time," I say, grabbing my Rolex and putting it on. I grab my belt and put it on and then grab my suit jacket. I tuck my tie in my pocket, opting to leave the two top buttons open.

"Doubt anyone will care," he says. "It'll do you good to get out."

I sit down and think about it. "Yeah, why not. I was going to go home and watch television," I agree, slipping my phone into my inside jacket pocket. I think about texting Erika, but I know she's forty minutes away, and I would feel guilty about her driving so late. Manning and I walk out together, and I follow him to the restaurant.

I can hear the music from inside when I close my SUV door. The parking lot to the restaurant is full. I look over at Manning. "I must be really fucking old if I dread going in there." He points at the restaurant, and I laugh. "If my wife wasn't in there, I would turn around without thinking twice."

"I'm not as old you are, and even I think I should go home," I say pulling open the front door to the restaurant.

The sign at the entrance says closed for a private party. The hostess is standing there with her blonde hair curled and perfect and smiles big. "Welcome."

"Hey." I smile at her, while Manning just nods at her, his hands in his pockets as he looks around the place. "We're here for the party." I point with my thumb while

Manning just walks past her, making me laugh. I put my head down and follow him in.

The place is packed, and I look around to see the team is here. The tables are packed with my teammates and their family members. The bar against the wall is full also. I look around and see Nico talking to a couple of people. "Remind me never to do this again," Manning says and then spots his wife, Evelyn, sitting at a table with Miller and his wife, Layla. "You coming?" he asks.

"Yeah, I'm going to get something to drink," I say, looking at the bar. "Say hi to some people." He nods and walks away toward the table.

Nico spots me right away and comes over to me. He holds his hand out to shake mine. "Cooper, great to see you here," he says, smiling.

"Thanks," I say, looking around. "Not sure it was okay since I said no."

"Hey," he confirms. "You are welcome anywhere.

"How are things going?" he asks, and I nod.

"Good," I respond, and he just looks at me. When he found out I was served papers at practice, he was furious. He made it known through his lawyers that they crossed the line. No one is allowed to enter the building without having a written approval of management. "I'm doing better."

"You look better. There is a fire under your ass," he jokes. "I like it."

"Me, too. I'm going to get some water."

"You need anything," he offers. "You don't hesitate to call me."

"I know." I look at him.

"I told your father I would take care of you like you were my own," he reminds me, and I nod at him. "See you later."

Walking to the back of the bar, I see some of the guys from the team. "There he is," Mika says when he sees me, clapping me on the back. "The one who saved the game." He holds up his glass of beer.

I laugh and shake my head. "Nah, just in the right place at the right time." I lean against the bar and hold up my hand and order a water. I turn and see her walking toward me, but she doesn't see me.

She looks over her shoulder and laughs at something. Her hair is loose, and she is wearing black leather pants with a black long-sleeve shirt that ties at the waist. A champagne lace thing under the top peeks out. The whole outfit is sexy, but the sky-high shoes she is wearing make it extra sexy. I smile as I see the men turn to catch a glimpse at her, and she doesn't even notice.

She is coming close to me, and she finally sees me, the shock fills her face. "Holy cow," she says, coming to me and putting a hand on my arm and leaning in to kiss my cheek. "I did not know you would be here." The smell of her perfume hits me right away. "Good game."

"What are you doing here?" I ask, looking around, and it suddenly dawns on me that she might be here with a date. It's closed for a private party, so she has to be here with someone. My stomach flips, wondering who it could be. "Are you here on a date?" The words escape my mouth before I can stop them, and she throws her head back and laughs at me.

"A date?" she repeats and then steps closer to me when someone bumps into her. My hand goes around her waist to protect her. "I thought we had this conversation the other night. I've decided I'm going to be single my whole life and end up living in a house with cats." She laughs, and the bartender comes over and hands me a water.

"What can I get you?" he asks her, and she smiles at him.

"I'm good, thank you," she says to him and then turns back to me. "What are you doing here?" she asks, and I shrug.

"The girls are with Julianne, so I thought why not." Smiling at her, leaning in to whisper in her ear, "I almost didn't come in when I heard the music blaring."

She throws her head back and laughs. "Of course you did."

"It was so loud," I say and look around. "And I can still hear it but less."

"Because it's the outside area," she says. "I was just out there with Becca. Which is why I'm here. We had a business meeting, and then she dragged me here."

"Well, then it's my lucky night," I say, and she smiles up at me.

"If you play your cards right, it might get luckier," she teases, and I just shake my head.

"And why is that?" I ask.

"I won't steal any of your food since I'm full," she says, and I laugh. She grabs my hand. "Come on, let's get some food in you."

We walk over to the table where everyone is sitting. Candace gets up and comes over to me, kissing my cheeks and giving me a hug. "I'm so happy you are here."

"Thanks," I say to her, my eyes looking for Erika as she sits in one of the empty seats. "It's good to be out."

I walk to the empty chair beside Erika, and the waitress comes over and takes my order. I put my hand around her chair and lean back, taking in the conversations going on. She leans over. "Why are you so quiet?"

"I'm just …" I start to say as the waitress sets my plate in front of me. "I'm good."

I sit up and look around the table seeing everyone with their plates in front of them, except Becca, who smiles at Nico. "That looks good," Erika says, and I laugh.

"I thought you were full," I remind her, cutting a piece of the steak and holding it out for her.

"Are you giving me your meat?" she jokes with me, and I can't help but laugh at her stupid joke.

She leans in and takes the little piece. "No more," she says, chewing and then orders a glass of sparkling water.

"How are you getting home?" I ask when we walk out of the restaurant an hour later.

"I have this thing called a car." She laughs, pushing me. "It comes with four wheels and everything."

"Suddenly, she's a comedian." I roll my eyes, when I spot her SUV. "You want to stay at the condo?"

"Nope," she says, coming to me and kissing my cheek. "I'm going to go home and sleep in my king-size bed." She turns and walks away from me.

"Will you text me when you get home?" I ask as she unlocks her SUV.

"Nope," she says, laughing as she gets in the SUV. I wait for her to drive toward me, and she stops the SUV and rolls her window down. "It's going to be fine. It's forty minutes."

"Fine, I'll call you in an hour and a half and wake you up," I threaten and glare. "Talk to you soon." I turn, walking over to my SUV.

"You're a pain in my ass," she says. She picks up her phone and presses something, and my phone pings. "There, I shared my location with you. You can follow me like you do your Uber orders." She rolls her window back up, leaving me laughing by myself, and I do exactly that. When I see she parked her car, I text her.

Me: Good Night
Erika: Fuck Off

TEN

ERIKA

THE SOUND OF the front door lock makes me open my eyes, and I wonder if I heard properly or if it was in my dream. I lean up on my elbow to see if I heard right, and then I hear the front door open and close. "Oh my god," I say, throwing the covers off me and looking down at my shorts and tank top. I glance around quickly to see if maybe there is a robe to cover myself, but I don't see anything, and I also don't wait. I rush to the door when I hear footsteps, and I almost turn and run back to get my phone when I see him walking into the house. He's wearing track pants and a Dallas shirt, his arms looking unusually huge. His Dallas baseball hat is on his head.

I stand at the top of the staircase, putting my hands on the railing. "What the fuck?" I say, rubbing the sleep from my eyes. "You are so lucky I don't have a gun," I threaten, turning and walking back to my room. I look over at the clock and see that it's just before 10 a.m. Usually, during the week, I'm up at six and on the treadmill for an hour, and then I do the bike. But on Sunday, I rest. It is a holy day, after all. When I bought this house, I wanted two things. One, a pool and grass and two, a big master bedroom. Well, the master bedroom was okay in size, but I knocked down the wall with the spare bedroom, giving me a giant master bedroom and seating area. I get back into my king-size bed, going in the middle where I sleep.

I hear him laugh as he yells, "Does that mean you're coming down, or do I come up?"

"That means go away!" I shout back and bring the covers up to my chin, and I hear the squeak of his shoes on the stairs.

"I brought coffee," he says, and I sink deeper into the bed. It took me over four months to find the perfect blankets for my bed. I wanted to feel like I was sleeping in a cloud. That is how I described it to every person who sold linen. It took lots of test drives before I got my exact bedding. That and the eight pillows I sleep with surrounding me.

"What kind of coffee?" I mumble, opening one eye to see him walk in. I notice him look over at the new couch set I just got for my room. Two massive captain chairs with fluffy cushions face the bed. One of them has the clothes I was wearing last night on it.

"Do you even use these chairs?" he asks, and I stare at them.

"No," I say. "But look how pretty they are. They make the room look so cozy."

He comes over and sits on the bed. "Good morning." He holds up the white cup of coffee with the green logo on it.

"It's ten o'clock on a Sunday," I say. "Why are you even here?"

"I got you breakfast, too." He holds up the white bag, and I know something is up.

"What do you want?" I ask, and he laughs.

"Why do you think I want something?" he says innocently, and I get up to grab the cup of coffee.

"Are you going to deny you want something?" I ask, sitting up in the bed, bringing the coffee to my mouth. The vanilla hits my tongue right away.

"I brought you croissants," he bribes, and I glare at him.

"You definitely want something," I accuse him. "If you have cake in the other one, I'm going to think you want my kidney or something."

He laughs, taking the hat off his head and tossing it as he scratches his head. His hair is longer than what I'm used to seeing him with, but I think that's because Julianne hated his hair long. I, on the other hand, love it longer. He even has scruff on his cheeks. "I have lemon cake."

"Get out," I order, pointing at the door. "Leave the cake."

"Come on." He gets up onto the bed next to me.

"No," I say, trying to get away from him as he puts his arm around me and pulls me to him. "It's Sunday." He sits with his back on my plush headboard that was custom-made. "And you have your dirty shoes on my covers." I settle in his arms and look up at him, his eyes closed. "What is it?" I ask, scared that he might actually need my kidney.

"I have three houses to go visit," he admits, and I groan.

"And?" I'm waiting for the rest.

"Will you come with me?" he asks softly. "And if you say yes, you have thirty minutes to get dressed."

"Ugh, fine," I say, drinking the coffee. "I guess I owe you for when you came looking with me."

"You made me look at twenty-five houses," he reminds me.

"Over three months," I counter. "That's eight houses a month."

"Well, from what Zoe sent me." He mentions his aunt, the realtor. "These were the best and the good news," he says excitedly. "They are in your neighborhood."

"Oh, goody," I say sarcastically. "Will this not let you randomly walk into my house?"

"Maybe," he says, and his hand rubs my arm. "I might have to borrow sugar."

"It's not funny, I thought someone was coming in to rob me." I sit up, my arm tingling from his touch.

"You thought someone was coming into your house to rob you using the code for the door?" He shakes his head and gets up. "And how were you going to defend yourself?" He puts his hands on his hips, and the sound of buzzing fills the room. I roll my lips, and my eyes go big. "What is that noise?"

"Um, you can leave," I say, putting my hands under the covers to locate the buzzing sound, knowing exactly what it is.

"Oh my god," he says with his mouth hanging open. "Was that in bed with you?"

I roll my eyes at him. "Where else would I use it? I was restless, and this helped."

He laughs. "I'm sure it did."

"If you want me to come with you, I need to get dressed," I say avoiding his eyes.

"You dirty, dirty girl," he teases me, and I groan.

"Please, are you trying to tell me you never jerk off?" I fire back, finally locating the vibrator and turning it off.

"Let me see it," he says, smirking.

I point at him. "Too far," I say, tucking it under my pillows. "Too, too far." I get out of bed, putting the coffee on the side table and turning to push him out of the room.

"Go watch television," I say, pushing him out of the door and slamming it shut. The sound of his laughter fills the whole house.

"Do you need an extra ten minutes?" he shouts.

"Do you want me to come visit houses with you or not?" I ask through the door.

"Fine," he concedes. "I'll be downstairs."

I shake my head and walk back to my bed, flipping the pillows over to find the purple vibrator. When I got home last night, I tossed and turned for over an hour before I decided to take care of myself. I fell asleep right after, forgetting to put it away. I tuck it in the side drawer and then go to the bathroom to wash my face and brush my teeth. I comb out my hair, the curls from last night still intact, before I head to the closet.

I slide a pair of black jeans on with a hole in the knee and then walk over to the built-in drawers, taking out my white lace bra and putting on a white silk camisole on top of it. I grab my black jacket and black patent Louboutins and head downstairs. I can hear the television playing, and when I look into the family room, he's sprawled on the couch, watching *The Real Housewives of New Jersey.* "Aha," I say to him, and he looks over at me as I slide the shoes on. "Caught you."

"What the hell are you wearing?" he asks, and I put the jacket over my shoulders. "Where do you think you're going?"

"Cooper, for one, you always go with 'Erika, you look amazing,'" I say, holding up my finger. "And two, we are going to visit million-dollar homes. I have to look the part."

He gets up, shaking his head. "My whole outfit cost forty-five dollars," he says, and I look at him and tilt my head.

"I bought you those sneakers. They were two hundred and fifty dollars." I turn, grabbing my black purse from last night. "Now, do you want me to come with you or not?" He grabs the remote and turns off the television. "And I can't believe you watched that without me," I pout, walking to the front door, and he closes it behind us. I grab the sunglasses from my purse. "It's brighter than a bleached asshole out here," I state, and I can hear him stop walking. Looking over, I see him put his hand on his stomach and laugh out loud.

"Only you, Erika," he says, walking to the SUV and opening the door for me. "Only you can be dressed classy and say something like that."

I grab his chin in my hand. "Only you would expect more from me." I get on my tippy-toes and kiss his cheek, this time coming way too close to his lips. "That would be your first mistake." Dropping my hand from his face, my body feeling off-kilter for a second. "Now, don't make me regret going out on a Sunday." I get in the SUV and look up at him. His eyes are so crystal blue I can see through them.

"Oh, trust me." He smirks at me. "You'll never regret anything with me," he says before shutting the door.

I put my hand to my stomach, watching him walk around the SUV, the whole time wondering *What the hell is going on?*

ELEVEN

Cooper

I PULL UP to the third house, and just from looking at it I know it's the one. It's why I showed it last. I had a feeling it was for me, but I wanted Erika to see it. "This is the last one," I say looking over at her, and her mouth is open.

"It's so pretty," she says, looking at the two-story house. "I mean, the second one was really pretty, and it had a tower," she says, making me laugh. "But this." She smiles big. "There are two balconies on the second floor. The girls will love that." Something inside me settles that she is so happy with the house.

"Shall we go see it?" I ask, and she nods her head. When I showed up at her house this morning, I knew she would come with me. I also knew I couldn't make this decision without her.

I reach for the handle and open the door, and Erika steps out before I do. The two-car garage has a room on top with a balcony. "What are the chances that the girls are going to try to sneak out of that window?" She points at the balcony.

"I'm going to have a state-of-the-art alarm all over the house. You won't be able to open a bathroom door without me getting an alert," I announce, and she gawks at me. "My father did it, and we turned out fine."

"Really?" she questions, folding her arms. "You think you turned out fine?" She tilts her head. "Not sure about that one." She turns to walk up the path, and I go with her. My arm goes around her shoulders. "I love the big windows," she says as we walk past three huge windows toward the large brown front door. She looks over at me, her face beaming. "You ready?"

I take a deep breath. "Yeah, I think so," I say, and she opens the door. We step into the entryway. We must take three steps in, and she gasps from beside me. There is a winding staircase to the upstairs level, but it's the roof. It is all windows so the sun beams down.

"If you don't buy this house," Erika says, stepping into the house and turning around in the center of the room. "I will." I laugh at her. "You need a table right in the middle with a huge bouquet."

"I have a four-year-old and a two-year-old," I remind her.

"Okay, so in ten years, I'll buy you a table and flowers," she concedes, walking over to the left-hand side and seeing the dining room. "Does this come furnished?"

"Zoe said that this is all staged, so I could keep anything I wanted." I see a white marble table in the middle of the room with eight big chairs around it. A crystal chandelier in the middle of the table falls right between two vases of white flowers. Gray carpet matches the curtains that are hanging and tied in the middle. "It's a bit too …"

"Small?" she says, looking at me.

"No, I mean white. But I mean, it's not horrible." She walks to the other side and sees an office. "This can be the computer room," I say, and she nods. "For the girls to do homework and hang with their friends."

We walk around the staircase and come to my favorite part of the house, the family room. "When I was growing up, my parents bought this big house, and it had the family room that was attached to the kitchen with a huge island." I look the other way and see the massive island. "It was our favorite place in the house." I walk toward the kitchen. "It was the meeting area, and when I saw the pictures, I knew that this was perfect." The big white island has eight stools around it.

I walk toward the island, not even caring about the fridge or stove when I stop and see that there is a breakfast nook on the side with floor-to-ceiling windows, showing you the huge backyard. I feel her stop next to me, and she gasps out. "It's crazy, right?"

"This is it," she says, and I smile. "This is definitely it."

"We didn't even see the upstairs." I look toward the staircase, and she shrugs.

"When you know, you know. Can we go and see the backyard?" I grab her hand, then walk over to the door and step outside. A covered lanai fills the whole back of the house. One side with a table, and the other side with a sitting area facing a television and fireplace, just like her house.

"There isn't a lot of grass," she says. "But look at this. It's like a dream." She steps forward, and the pool is massive with stones all around it. A hot tub sits off to one side, and then you see the waterfall from the built-in slide. "I can see two happy girls who will use that slide until they have their own kids." The pictures that fill my mind are of the four of us running around the pool on a Sunday afternoon, and I literally cannot wait to move into this house.

When we finally go upstairs, she steps into the master bedroom. "You don't even have to knock a wall down." She looks around the empty master suite, stopping in front of the fireplace that is in the room. "If you get a bear rug, I'm going to vomit." I can't help but throw my head back and laugh.

I take my phone out and FaceTime Zoe, who answers right away. "Don't tell me," she says before she even says hello. "It's the third house."

"Yeah." I smile, and Erika claps her hands.

"Is that Erika?" she asks, smiling, and Erika walks over to me.

"It's perfect," she tells Zoe. "I hate to say this, but this is even better than my house."

"I know," Zoe says, laughing. "But it wasn't on the market when you were looking." Zoe is also her realtor. "But you get to enjoy it."

"Oh, I will," she says, smiling and looking up at me.

"I definitely will."

"How fast can I get into the house?" I ask, and she laughs.

"The owners are already out of the house. I spoke with the agent, and you can get in there as soon as the offer is accepted," she says. "Let me call the agent and get back to you."

"Let's do it," I confirm and then look over at Erika as she walks around the empty room.

"This is really something else," she says and then walks to the bathroom and then looks over at me. "Holy hell."

I laugh, making my way over to her and look in. "It's very fancy," I say of the white marble flooring that goes up the walls with gray inside. "That tub fits at least two people." She points to the massive tub that faces the window and the glass shower right next to the tub with jets all over the wall. "I hate you," she states.

I put my arm around her. "If you play your cards right," I say, "I'll let you use it."

"If I play my cards right?" She laughs. "I'm here on a Sunday. My rest day."

"Yeah, yeah," I say, and we walk back downstairs.

"You know what you need to do?" she questions, looking around one last time before we leave.

"Besides feed you?" I ask, smirking.

"You need to throw a party," she says, and I groan. "No, listen to me for real."

"Why, why do I need to throw a party?" I ask, standing with my feet apart and my arms crossed over my chest.

"Well, one, for presents." She puts her hands on her hips. "It can be a housewarming party and …" She holds up her hand to stop me from talking. "A divorce party." I put my head back and look up at the window-covered ceiling. "It's all the rage these days. You owe me a party."

"Why can't I take you on vacation instead?" I say and snap my fingers. "My father told me about the family vacation at the end of June and early July." I point at her. "Already confirmed you are coming, and I got us a house on the beach."

"One, you are a liar," she says, her head moving back and forth. "That trip was last week's news, and your father got a house for you."

"Dammit," I mumble. "You spoke with my sisters, didn't you?"

"And your mother," she says. "So don't even, and you didn't even invite me."

"I told my father you were coming, and it slipped my mind."

"Anyway, I can't go," she says, and I have this sudden sadness.

"What?" I ask, my voice soft. "Why not?"

"July first is free agent signings," she says. "It's a busy day."

"Well, they have cell service and Wi-Fi," I share. "Okay, how is this? You come with us on vacation, and I'll throw the stupid party for you."

She moves her head from side to side as she thinks about it. "A big party." I cringe because she knows my big party is like twenty people.

"You invite the whole team," she counters, and I bite my teeth down. "And your close friends."

"You're my only friend," I say, and she comes over to me. Her arms wrap around my waist.

"Smooth," she says. "Really, really smooth."

I pull her to my chest and put my chin on her head. "So is that a yes?"

"Are you going to drink tequila with me?" she asks, and I can tell she's laughing because her whole body starts shaking.

"Abso-fucking-lutely not," I hiss out, and the phone rings in my pocket. Her hands fall from my waist as I grab my phone. I see it's Zoe and answer it right away. "Hey." Her face fills the screen, and the smile is from ear to ear.

"So I just got off the phone with the agent," she says. "He tried to play hardball." She pffts out. "He lost." I laugh. "Congratulations, you got the house." I look over at Erika, who raises her hands to the sky and claps her hands. "I just sent you over the paperwork. Because we did all the paperwork beforehand and the bank has already given you the approval, you can be in the house in seven days," she says. "But the buyers have agreed to let you get things delivered there before you move in."

"That sounds great," I say, and when I hang up the phone, I look over at Erika. "What are you doing next Sunday?"

"Resting," she says, cocking her hip when I just stare at her, but she finally gives in and makes me laugh. "Fine, I'll help you freaking unpack."

TWELVE

Erika

My PHONE RINGS, and I pick it up, seeing Cooper's name. "If you are calling for another favor, you are all tapped out for the month," I say, leaning back in my office chair. From the minute the offer got accepted, he was all in. He was home for the week, so every single day after work we would hit up furniture stores. The girls came with us to choose their rooms and I couldn't wait to see how it would come together. Luckily everything was delivered during the week, so on Sunday we really spent all day setting up the house. His bedroom set was delivered on Monday right before he left on a road trip.

"I've been gone three days," he says, laughing.

"And it's been glorious," I reply even though I've missed him, especially since we are so close to each other. He lives two minutes from my house—two—we timed it. We took the girls for a bike ride from his place to mine and it took us less than ten minutes. "Are you back?"

"No," he grumbles, his voice going low. "That's why I'm calling." I sit up wondering if he got hurt or something.

"The plane had mechanical issues and we should be landing at around six, but I have to get the girls at daycare. I would call Julianne but then I won't be able to see them until next Monday since she is taking them to visit her parents." He stops talking. "Do you think you can get them?"

"Of course." Looking over at the clock and seeing that it's almost four, I say, "I'll get them at daycare and then do you want me to bring them to my house?"

"No," he says, and I can hear his voice is tired. "Just go to my house, it'll be easier."

"This better not be a fucking trick and I get there and there are one hundred boxes to unload," I joke, and he laughs.

"This is not a trick," he confirms. "And I thought with the party being this weekend you would be in a better mood."

"I'm not going to lie." I smirk. "I'm so excited. I just got off the phone with the party planner."

"You hired a party planner?" he shrieks.

"Cooper, what kind of an animal do you think I am?" I say, shocked. "Of course I hired a party planner," I scoff out. "And it's going to be fabulous, you won't have to do anything except get dressed and drink tequila with me."

"I'm not drinking that shit," he hisses. "Okay, we are getting back on the plane. Go get my car and leave yours."

"Okay, I'll leave so I'm not late," I say, getting up. "Fly safe." I hang up the phone and grab my jacket, walking out of my office.

"Shauna," I state while I slip my jacket on. "I have to head out. Which means you get to head out also." She claps her hands. "I'll see you tomorrow."

"TGIF," she says, and I hold up my hand and wave at her. The sound of my heels click the floor as I walk out toward my car. The pink pencil skirt gives very little leg room to climb into the SUV, and I wonder if I should go home and change before I get the girls. But by the time I switch cars and get near them it's already four thirty and I don't want them staying there longer.

I ring the doorbell and they press the buzzer for me to open the door. The woman stands there with a smile. "I'm here to pick up Mia and Emma Grant," I say, grabbing my ID from my purse.

"Yes, Mr. Grant called us before," she replies. "Please follow me." She walks down the hallway and stops in front of a door. She sticks her head in and calls Emma. I stand next to her looking into the class of kids, all playing in different areas when she looks up and sees me.

"Auntie Erika!" she shouts, getting up and running to me. She wraps her hands around my waist and looks up at me. "Is Daddy here?"

"Hey, beautiful," I say to her, bending and swiping my nose to hers. "I came to pick you up because Daddy is going to be late. Go get your bag and we can go get Mia."

"Okay." She skips over to her bag and comes back. "I'll show you where Mia is." She grabs my hand and I smile.

Mia screams my name when she sees me and I squat down and she almost sends me over. "Grab your bag, baby girl," I say and she brings her bag to me. I walk out of the place holding both their hands and get them in the car.

"Are we going to your house or Daddy's house?" Emma asks me.

"I'm taking you to the new house," I tell them and they clap their hands. I get into the SUV and look over to make sure everything is okay. "What do you think we should do?" I ask them. "Do you guys want to help me make dinner?"

"Yeah!" Emma screams first and then Mia follows her. I pull up to the house and smile. He really did well. I get out and let Emma out first and then walk over to get Mia.

"Carry me," Mia says, holding up her hands and I pick her up, putting her on my hip. When we walk in, I slip off my shoes right away and then put Mia down.

"Take your shoes off and go hang your bags," I tell them and they go to the computer room and come back three seconds later. I have a feeling they just dumped their bags in there. I slip off my coat and place it over the banister and then walk into the family room.

When we went searching for a couch, he wanted one thing, big and cozy and that is exactly what he got. The couch is in a shape of a U and the color is a dark gray.

The cushions are so big you sink into them. "Now, what are we going to eat?" I say, walking to the kitchen and seeing it's spotless. I pull open the big stainless-steel fridge and I'm expecting it to be empty but it's full.

"Can we have spaghetti?" Emma asks from beside me.

"We can." I walk over to my purse and get my phone out. I google best spaghetti recipe. I walk back into the kitchen. "Do you want to help me?" I ask and she nods her head. "Mia," I call and she comes over. "Do you want a snack and then watch some TV instead?" She gives me the same smirk her father has and nods.

"Yes, please," she says and I look at the fruit bowl in the corner of the counter.

"I'll cut you some apples and oranges," I tell them, walking over and washing my hands. Luckily for me, I unpacked the kitchen, so I know where everything is. I cut apples and then the oranges and place them in the plastic bowl. I turn on the television and they watch while I grab an onion from the fridge and start dicing it.

I grab a pan and start putting in the olive oil and then adding the onion. I follow the recipe to a T, and thirty minutes later, the sauce is simmering. "I think we should make some cupcakes," I say and they both nod their heads. Walking over, I grab a boxed cake mix and then grab a mixing bowl. "Okay," I say, opening the box, "we need three eggs," and walking to the fridge. "Which means we each can break one."

I hand an egg to Mia who I make sit on the counter on one side of the bowl and then put Emma up on the other side handing her a bowl. "Watch me," I say, cracking the egg and then putting it in the bowl. "Now your turn," I say to Mia. "Gently," I remind her and she hits the side of the bowl and the egg splashes all over her and me. I look down at the white top and laugh. "A little less this time," I suggest, cleaning up the mess and then handing her another egg. "Okay, Emma, you try." She hits the bowl perfectly and I clap my hands. "That was perfect." I look over at Mia. "Okay, your turn, gently." She smirks at me and I lean in to kiss her neck. She hits the side of the bowl and the egg falls into the bowl. Luckily the shells are intact, Emma and I both clap our hands for her. "Let me get the oil." I put it in two cups to give them a chance to pour. Repeating the process for the water also. "Okay, here we go," I say, opening the bag of cake mix and putting it in. "Who wants to help me stir?" I turn and hand each of them a spoon, and twenty minutes later, and lots of licks of the spoon, I'm putting the tray into the oven to bake.

My phone rings and I pick it up seeing it's Cooper. "You better be on your way," I say and he laughs.

"I'll be home in twenty minutes, should I pick up food?" he asks.

"No, I'm making spaghetti and chocolate cupcakes." I turn and whisper, "I will say the girls did double dip, so that's up to you."

"You cooked?" he replies, shocked.

"Goodbye, Cooper." I hang up the phone, turning and putting the water on for the pasta.

I clean up the kitchen while the girls watch some

Disney movie. The water is boiling when the front door opens and I hear his voice.

"I'm home." His voice fills the house and I smile looking over at the girls jumping off the couch and running to greet him. I open the pasta and put it in the salted water, grabbing a spoon and stirring it.

"Look at you." I look over my shoulder and see him walking to me. His suit fits him perfectly and something inside me settles. I turn my head back to look at the pasta before he catches me watching him. I feel him behind me when he bends his head and kisses my cheek. "It smells good," he says, and I laugh.

"Well, time will tell. I did google and this has the best reviews, so." I turn and he looks at my outfit and I look down to see the egg yolk that has crusted over.

"Daddy, Daddy," Mia calls, coming to him and holding up her arms and he picks her up. "I made cupcakes."

"Did you?" He kisses her and his whole face lights up. "Missed you guys," he says, his eyes looking at me.

"Good," I say, turning. "You can set the table."

"Okay, you two," he says, turning, "let's set the table." He takes off his jacket and unbuttons his sleeves and rolls them up.

"Wash your hands before." I point the spoon at him.

He laughs, coming to me and giving me a hug. "Yes, dear," he teases and I push him away. "Thank you," he says softly, standing next to me. "I don't know what I would do without you."

"Oh, don't you worry." I smirk at him, then wink. "I'm keeping score."

THIRTEEN

COOPER

MY PHONE RINGS and I snap it up from the island, seeing it's Erika. "Good afternoon," I greet her.

"Happy divorce party day!" she shouts and I smile thinking how excited she is for tonight. "The party planner is on the way over."

"Where are you?" I ask and she laughs.

"I'm at the spa getting pampered and exfoliated. It's my relax day."

"I thought Sunday was your relax day?" I remind her.

"Well, this week Sunday is my recovery day," she says and then her voice goes low. "How are you feeling?"

"Sore," I reply. We had a game against Washington last night and it was more physical than anything else, but at least we are off until Tuesday.

"How's the wrist?" she asks, and I look down and rotate it.

"I can move it. So I guess it's okay."

"I can't believe you dropped the gloves," she hisses. "What are you, seven?"

I laugh. "He called me a pussy."

"I call you a pussy all the time," she snorts and I laugh.

"It's not the same thing and you know it. What do I need to do for tonight?" I ask, putting my plate in the dishwasher.

"You need to be dressed at six," she says, and I close the dishwasher and pick up a chocolate cupcake that she made two days ago. "I'll be there when I'm done."

"You better be here before everyone else," I say. "I hate parties."

"Relax, I have to go, see you later." She hangs up and I finish the cupcake. Coming home and seeing her in the kitchen, I was shocked she was cooking. Only she would cook spaghetti in a pink skirt and white top. We sat and ate dinner together and it was so good. She gave the kids a bath while I cleaned the kitchen and then left barefoot, with her shoes in her hand.

The doorbell rings and I walk over opening it and see a man dressed in a suit as he smiles at me. "Mr. Grant," he says, holding out his hand. "I'm Geraldo, the party planner." He smiles and slaps his hand. "Are you excited for the big day?"

"Oh, yeah," I respond, looking out and seeing five vans pull up. "Is that for here?"

"It is." He smiles. "Just leave it up to me. Erika and I did a run-through yesterday afternoon," he says and I have to laugh.

"Well, if you need anything, you call her." I walk

back to the kitchen and grab a water bottle and head to the exercise room that I bought with the house. All the equipment was brand new. I get on the treadmill and text her.

Me: Your man has arrived and he's very excited.

Erika: Which man? I obviously have so many I can't keep track.

Me: Geraldo.

Erika: Let him work his magic.

Me: I'm in the gym.

Erika: Good, you need to work out that frustration you have. You know what else helps with that. (winky face)

I shake my head and laugh at her, I run for over an hour, the noise from downstairs gets louder and louder. I avoid even going down there when I get out of the gym and head straight to my bedroom. Heading straight to the bathroom, I climb in the shower when my phone beeps and I pick it up seeing it's from Erika.

Erika: I got you a present. It's in your closet. See you soon.

"What in the world?" I question, walking to my walk-in closet and seeing the big white box.

"This was not here this morning." I grab it and take it out and when I open it there is a note on top.

Wear this tonight. A brand-new start.

I grab the black dress shirt and then see the matching pants. Grabbing the shoebox and seeing the black dress shoes.

The note on the top sticks out. I open it and laugh.

These will have you kicking the girls away.

I shake my head and grab the red jewelry box. Opening it, I see that it's a bracelet that looks like it's braided together. The square clasp has the C engraved.

I hold it in my hand and then grab the note.

Brighter days ahead.

E

I hear the doorbell ring and then look over and see it's six o'clock. I get dressed in the outfit she picked for me. Along with my Tom Ford belt, the bracelet right next to the Rolex she gave me. I walk to the bathroom and run my hands through my hair and then spray on my cologne.

Walking out of my room, I head downstairs and stop when I see the gold balloons placed in front of the stairs.

DIVORCED AF

I laugh and then the door opens and I see Manning coming in holding his wife's hand. "Holy shit," he says, looking at the balloons. "Erika did that?"

"What do you think?" I say as he comes over and extends his hand. "Thank you for coming." I bend to kiss his wife on the cheek.

"She is not single." Manning pushes me away from her, making us laugh.

"Ignore him," Evelyn says. "Your house is beautiful."

"Thank you," I reply and we walk into the family room. Balloons are in the corners. I look over at the kitchen seeing two chefs cooking as five servers walk with trays over to us.

Geraldo sees me and comes in. "Welcome," he says. "Your guests are outside."

I nod at him and wait for Manning and Evelyn to head out before following them. The lights are on low and so are the pool lights, giving the night a glow. Music plays out of the speakers and there are little tables set up everywhere so people can sit. Two bars are set up on either side, one of them with guys already in front of it.

I walk up to them. "Thanks for coming," I say and they smile and shake my hand.

"Can I have a whiskey?" I ask the bartender and look at the napkins and laugh.

Just divorced, free at last.

"This is crazy," I hear from behind me and see Candace there. "I love it."

"Hey." I smile, bending and kissing her cheek.

"I can't believe you are throwing this party without your family," she teases, and I laugh as Ralph comes up behind her.

"The free man," he says, slapping my shoulder. "Look at those balloons." He points at the yard where more balloons are there

Single and ready to mingle.

She's insane, I think to myself.

"I heard we are doing shots." I turn to see Layla standing there with Miller. "Can we get shots?"

Miller groans from beside her. "We said early night."

"You are free to leave," she tells him as she grabs a shot and hands one to Candace and then one to me. Ralph grabs one and then Miller caves and grabs one.

"Going, going, gone," Candace says and I take the shot and grimace.

"Shots suck." Miller does the same face Candace just did, setting down his glass.

"You," Candace says, pointing at me. "Go mingle."

I roll my eyes, turning and seeing that more people have showed up. The guys come to me and all slap me on the back. "Another single one to the pond," one says and I want to shake my head and then I turn and see her out of the corner of my eye. Her hair is down to her waist and curled as she laughs with Geraldo. All I can see is legs, her pink skirt is mid-thigh and when she turns to talk to someone else I see that she is wearing a long-sleeve lace top, but it falls right before the top of her skirt so you can see some skin. She must sense me looking at her because she turns and looks at me, smiling big.

She walks over to me, her pink purse in her hand and her shoes have one strap around the toes, one in the middle of her foot, and one around her ankle. Fuck, I don't think I've ever seen her look so fucking beautiful. "There he is," she says as she gets closer to me. "The man of the hour." Her chest presses into mine, my hand coming up and holding her waist as she kisses my cheek. "You look smashing. Love the outfit." She steps away and all I can do is look at her. "Look at how awesome this is." She turns as my hand falls from her, and I have this need to put it back up. What the fuck was in that shot?

"Mr. Divorced AF," Nico says and I look over to see him and Becca coming out. "This is fantastic."

I laugh and take a gulp of my whiskey. "Trust me, it was all her." I point at Erika who bats her eyes.

A waiter comes over and he has shots of tequilla on the tray, a slice of lime on top. "Tequilla," Erika coos and looks over at me. "You owe me a shot." She puts her purse under her arm as she grabs two shots. Handing one to Becca and then Nico and then takes two more for us.

"I haven't done tequila shots since Mexico," Becca states. "That was a good time."

"To brighter days." Erika puts her glass up and licks the rim of the glass and then downs it and sucks the lime. "Smooth."

"Gross," I grouse when I do my own. "I don't get it." I grab something to eat from one of the waiters who comes by. Everyone is talking to each other and having the best time. Laughter fills the backyard and I look around, admitting to myself it was a good idea.

People come up to me all night long and we laugh and tell stories, the whole time Erika is not far from my side. The cake comes out with a ball and chain that says I'm free.

"You are out of your mind," I say as she takes another shot of tequila with Becca.

"You love me," she jokes. I bring my whiskey to my mouth as I take another gulp. The girls are mingling with the other girls as they dance together. The lights go lower and lower as the time goes on. The guys are all sitting at the table while we watch the girls.

"I have to say this is pretty calm," Nico says from beside me; he is never two steps away from Becca. "And I'm actually full from all the food."

"Me, too," I agree, thinking that there was food here

all night long. Erika comes to me and grabs my hand, pulling me up. "Where are we going?"

"It's customary for the best man," she laughs, "or woman to do a shot with the ex-groom."

"Not more shots," I groan out as we get to the bar and I place my fourth glass of whiskey down.

"One more." She leans into me, holding up a shot of tequila. "Please." She looks up at me and my hand wants to brush her hair back. "Guys, one more shot," she says and the guys come over followed by the girls.

"To Cooper," Erika toasts, holding up her hand and everyone toasts to me. I smile at her and watch her take the shot. I put mine down on the bar and eyeball the bartender who just nods and takes it away.

"This was awesome," Ralph says, giving me a hug. "Thank you so much for having us."

"Guys, I can't thank you enough for coming," I reply and then put my hand over Erika's shoulder. "Now I owe her one less favor."

People start leaving. "This was so much fun," Erika says when Geraldo comes up and tells us that the kitchen is clean and there is food on the counter. He kisses Erika on the cheek and I watch to make sure his hands stay where they should be. "The bartenders are going, but they will leave all the booze on the counter."

"Let's go walk them out," I suggest to her and she nods, the music playing softly. She grabs a chip as she walks to the front door. When the last person leaves, I turn and see her standing with the balloons. Her eyes are so bright.

"Did you take a picture with these?" she asks and I shake my head. She gasps out and runs back to the kitchen coming back with her phone. "Come on."

"No," I say and she pretends to pout. "One picture."

"Yeah," she cheers, and I only see that her skirt looks like it's cut on one side showing you more leg. She snaps the picture and then turns the phone to me.

"You know what we need?" she says, and I laugh as she slips her hand into mine. "Shots."

FOURTEEN

ERIKA

I PULL HIM to the kitchen, his hand in mine. "One more shot," I say, turning and looking at him. When I walked in tonight and saw him, my mouth about dropped. He looked like sex. That was the only thing that came to my mind. I took the first shot to clear my head. I am taking the fifteenth, and my head is still cloudy.

I grab two shot glasses and then grab the brown tequila bottle. "We need salt and lime." I pour the shots, my eyes focusing on not spilling anything. His laughter fills the room.

"You are doing that thing again," he groans, walking to get the saltshaker and two pieces of lime.

"I'm trying not to spill the tequila," I defend and set the bottle down. "You're welcome.

"Okay," I say, licking my hand and laughing when I put some salt on it and then hand it to him. His tongue comes out and licks his hand, and I swear my stomach sinks, or maybe it flips.

"Last one," he vows. Picking up the shots when he puts down the salt, he hands me one, and then I grab a lime. He looks at me. "To you," he says, his voice soft. "For doing this for me. For having my back all the time and for the gifts."

I smile at him, even if I don't want to. "You're welcome," I say and lick the salt, take the shot, and then suck the lime. He coughs beside me, and I can't help throwing my head back and laughing. "Every time."

"It's the most disgusting thing," he says, grabbing a napkin and wiping his mouth.

"Life would be so much better if we weren't best friends," I announce, and he looks at me, smirking.

"What does that mean?" he asks, leaning against the island. My eyes go to the bracelet on his wrist.

"I mean us. It's so easy and carefree," I tell him. "It's like we don't even have to try to like each other. We just do."

"Is that a bad thing?" he asks, the smile on his face huge.

"Kiss me," I command, looking at him. The back of my neck burns. Maybe it's the tequila, or maybe it's the good time we're having. Maybe it's his fucking aftershave, but whatever it is, the words just came out of my mouth.

"I'm not kissing you," he says, shaking his head. I look at the stubble on his cheek, and I want to reach out and touch him.

"Why not?" I put my hands on my hips and step into

him. With him leaning on the island, it's almost like we are the same height. "Don't be a punk-ass, just kiss me." I roll my eyes. "It's just a kiss."

"No way. You're drunk," he says, which is not a no. He just looks at me, and I can see his chest a bit from the open collar of his shirt. I knew he would kill this outfit, and I was not wrong. His ass is perfect in it, and his arms fill it out just enough that you see his form.

"I am not drunk," I deny to him, and his eyebrow goes up. "I'm a bit giddy and happy and carefree, but I am not drunk." I step into him, and my stomach is going up and down. "Just fucking kiss me."

He doesn't move from where he is. My hand grabs his shirt, and I pull him to me. I can feel his breath on my face. "Fine, I'll just kiss you," I say, moving my head to the side and finding his lips. They are as soft as I thought they would be. I think I moan, or we both moan. My tongue comes out and slides into his mouth. His tongue slides in with mine as I lean more into him. My eyes want to stay open, but they can't help but close as I take in the kiss.

His tongue fights with mine, going around and around. His hand goes into my hair as I turn, and the kiss gets deeper. From side to side, both of us craving more, wanting more.

I step away from him, our chests rising and falling as if we just ran a marathon together. His eyes are darker than I've ever seen them. My hand comes up to touch my lips. They still sting from his beard, from his kiss. His eyes are on mine; both of us are shocked by what just happened. "That was …" I start to say, and all the words get lost in my throat and the cloudiness of the tequila is gone, as if someone just threw cold ice water on me. "That was …"

I try to think of words or anything, but both of us just watch each other, and then I don't know if I pounce first or if he does. Either way, his arms are around me, and I've never felt so safe. My mouth finds his again, and this time, I taste the whiskey on his lips as my tongue mixes with his. He turns me and sets me on the counter, his hands going from my hips to my face. I moan into his mouth as I try to open my legs, and he steps into them. My hand goes to his shirt, and I grab it in my hands. "Fuck," he says, letting go of my lips and then sucking softly until he gets to my neck. I slowly untuck his shirt out of his pants when his mouth finds mine again, and it's even better than it was five seconds ago. He pulls me closer to the edge of the island. My hands sneak under his shirt, touching his hot skin. My stomach goes nuts, thinking about him touching me. "Erika," he says my name as his lips leave me, and he leans over me.

My hand comes to his cheek. "Cooper," I whisper, secretly begging him not to stop. I bite his lower lip, wrapping my legs around his hips, and his cock settles perfectly between my legs. I hiss out his name. "Cooper," I say, and he bites my jaw as I scoot closer to the edge. My hands come out to unbutton his shirt as he kisses my neck. "Zipper." It comes out in a pant. "Down my back." His hand rests at the top of my neck as his mouth comes to mine again. His tongue invades my mouth as he slowly unzips my top. If I knew this was going to happen, I would have worn something that could have been ripped off. I feel his hands on my bare back when the zipper finally releases. His touch lights up my whole body. I move my shoulder so the lace shirt falls forward, leaving me naked. I toss my shirt to the side as I fumble with the buttons on his shirt, and I think one goes flying as I finally get them open. My hands rub softly as I push his shirt from his shoulders.

He lets go of my lips and moves the kisses down to my neck, and then he sees I don't have a bra. "Fuck," he groans. "All night, you wore no bra?"

"I paid ten thousand dollars for these," I say, trying to make a joke, but all I can do is reach out for him and kiss him again. His hand comes up, and his hand grabs my perfect B cup breast. I let go of his mouth to take in the feel of his hands on me. He bends as he takes one nipple into his mouth. He bites the nipple and then twirls his tongue around it. "Oh, god," I say, panting.

"Cooper," he reminds me, and I look down at him as he smirks and moves to the other breast. My eyes are on his mouth as his teeth bite down, and it sends a zap straight down to my core.

He moves his head down and moves his nose side to side as his tongue comes out and licks down. My legs are restricted with my pink leather skirt, but his hands come out, and in one swift move, the skirt is around my waist. "I have to taste you," he says, looking at my blush pink lace panties that leave little to the imagination. He squats down in front of me, putting his face right between my legs. "I have to taste you," he repeats. This time, his tongue comes out, and he licks me through my lace panties.

"Take them off. I want to feel your tongue on me." His big hands push them aside, but I feel a snap on the side, and then he rips them off me, tossing the pieces over his shoulder. His eyes watch mine as he sucks my pussy into his mouth. My legs close to keep him there, but then he licks up and down, and one foot sits on the counter as I open my legs more for him to stick his tongue deeper inside me. Putting one hand on the counter behind me, I use my other hand to go into his hair. He moves his mouth side to side as he gets closer to my clit, and then his tongue touches it, and my hips move up off the counter. "Sensitive," I say, and I swear I can see him smirk when he sticks his tongue out again and flicks it right before he bites down on it and my toes curl. "I'm going to—" I moan as his fingers slip inside me, and I want to die. I pull the hair on the top of his head when he fucks me with his fingers, and I come on his fingers and his tongue.

FIFTEEN

COOPER

I CLOSE MY eyes as I feel her tighten around my fingers. I lick her one more time before she finally comes. Her fingers in my hair are pulling, and all I want to do is make her come again. Slipping my fingers out of her, I kiss the inside of her thigh. "Cooper," she whispers, and it's the sexiest thing I've ever heard her say. No, I think the sexiest thing she ever said to me was kiss me. Forget that the whole night I took every excuse I could to touch her. Forget that every time she came close to me and leaned into me to joke or laugh, I wanted to kiss the fuck out of her.

Her hand slides out of my hair and falls on the counter, and I look up at her. She's so fucking beautiful inside and out. I trail kisses along the legs I've watched all night, and then slowly stand up in front of her. Her chest is rising and falling as she gets her breathing under control. Her eyes open when I stand over her, a dark green. The hand that was in my hair comes up, and she grabs my chin and pulls me to her. My tongue slides into her mouth as she tastes herself on me.

I wrap a hand around her waist and pull her to me. Lost in her. So fucking lost I never want to be found. Her hand drops from my face and lands on my chest. I move my head to the side to get my tongue deeper into her. Both of us moan every time one of us tries to get more. Her hands work on my belt, and my stomach quivers when she nearly touches my cock that has been fighting to get out since she asked me to kiss her. He was all for this plan. Fuck, he's been up for her all night. She lets go of my mouth as she trails kisses down to my cheek and then my chin. Her fingers move the zipper down, but all you can hear is the heaviness of our breathing. Her hands move my boxers down, and her fingers wrap around me.

"I need to get up," she says right as I moan, and my head falls back.

I blink and look at her as she pushes away from me and slides off the island. With her hand on my cock, she turns so my back is against the counter. She stands there, her tits teasing me, and I lean down and take a nipple into my mouth. "No," she says, and I look up at her to see her eyes close as she takes in the feel of my tongue. "My turn," she announces, and her hand falls off my cock, and she steps away from me.

She pulls her skirt down to cover her and then moves her hands to the side as she slips the zipper down and the skirt falls in a puddle by her feet. She kicks it away with the rest of the discarded clothes. "Leave the shoes," I say, and she smiles.

"I have to leave the shoes," she says, coming to stand in front of me naked. My hand goes straight for her ass. "I'm going to bend over after, and I want us to be the same height."

"You're playing with fire," I warn, and she throws her head back and laughs.

"Well, then, I guess I have to get ready to be burned." She leans in and bites my lower lip before she slides her tongue back into my mouth. "I can taste myself on you," she says when she lets me go, and then she kisses my shoulder. "Now, let's see if I can return the favor."

I watch her as she licks her way down my chest, sucking in and marking me. I can already see the spot on my pec turn red. "I want to see," she says as she crouches in front of my cock, "if you can taste yourself on me." She looks up when her hands grip my pants and pulls them down along with my boxers. My cock springs free, and if he could talk, he would beg her not to stop. "Holy shit," she says, her hand coming out and gripping the base of my cock. "I knew you'd be packing," she says as she leans in and licks the pre-cum off the tip of my cock. I put my hands on the counter, scared my legs will give out. She looks up at me as she takes my cock into her mouth ever so fucking slowly, knowing I'm about to snap. Her hand moves down on my cock as she takes it to the back of her throat, and I can't help it. My eyes close as I take the wetness of her mouth.

"Fuck," I hiss as her mouth moves over me.

"Erika," I say her name, and she smiles around my

cock. She turned the joke back on me before when she called for god, and I told her my name.

"Trust me," I say, moving my hand to her hair. "I know your name." She sucks my cock back into her mouth, this time going just a touch deeper. One hand works with her mouth while her other hand cups my balls. She swirls her tongue around my cock and then licks the shaft up and down, before sucking the tip back into her mouth and then licking right down the shaft to my balls. Her tongue swirls around them. Her hand jerks me off while she does this. She comes back up, licking, and then takes my cock into her mouth, and I swear she hums when she does it. One hand leaves my hip, and I see it disappear between her legs. "You can play with yourself," I say, and she looks up at me and I see her shoulder move in the same rhythm as her mouth on me. "But only I get to make you come."

She shakes her head in defiance, and my hand grips her hair. "Only I get to make you come," I say to her as my hips move slowly, feeding her my cock. Her eyes close half-mast while she plays with herself, and she sucks my cock. My balls are getting tighter and tighter. "Erika," I say her name. "I'm going to." I try to pull out of her mouth, but her grip on my cock tightens, and I can't move. I also can't stop from coming into her mouth. She looks at me as she swallows me down, taking everything I have to give her, and I swear this primal need runs through me. She moves my cock from her mouth, and I bend down, picking her up and putting her ass back on the counter. I kick off my shoes and throw my pants and boxers right next to her shredded panties. She opens her legs for me, and I see her glistening in the dim light. Her landing strip is wet from my mouth and from her playing with herself. I walk back to her, my hands coming up to cup her tits, and then I suck on her neck.

She puts one foot on the counter and wraps the other around my waist. "Cooper," she pleads with me. I bend, sucking a nipple into my mouth and then nibbling it before moving over just a touch and marking her with the same mark she left on me. The redness is showing right away in her pale skin. The leg around my waist digs deeper into my ass, and I laugh. I move to the side a bit, my hand going down the middle of her chest over her belly button and then sliding over her clit, and then two fingers enter her. "Yes," she hisses.

"Who gets to make you come?" I ask as my hand picks up speed, her pussy getting wetter and wetter. Two fingers in her, and my thumb grazes her clit every so often, and her head goes back. "I'm not going to stop until you tell me," I say into her neck before slipping my tongue into her mouth, and she sucks my tongue like she did my cock. I can feel her getting tighter, and my fingers stop, and she groans out. "Say it."

"Cooper, please," she begs me and rolls her head back as my fingers slowly move back into her. My cock gets ready, my mouth lingering near hers. "Please."

"Tell me, and I'll make you come," I say, and she looks at me with lust in her eyes.

"I want your cock to make me come," she says the words and everything that I was thinking goes out the window. I wanted to take her to bed and lay her out and go gently, but the look in her eye. "Right here."

She doesn't have to tell me twice, my fingers come out of her, and I see her pussy open for me. I grab the base of my cock and rub it up and down her slit. Her right hand leans back on the counter, and her left hand goes under my chin. Her eyes are on mine until my cock aligns with her opening. We both look down as my cock head slips inside her. My eyes move back up to her as I sink balls deep in her. Her head falls back in ecstasy, and I close my eyes and feel her tightness around me. Moving out once, I slam into her and lean down to take one of her nipples into my mouth.

"Cooper," she says my name, and I look up. "Harder," she says as her pussy squeezes my cock. I grip her hips in my hands, and her legs go over my forearms. I pull out and then slam back into her, but I don't stop. I fuck her hard and fast. The sound of slapping skin fills the house. Both of her hands behind her are trying to hold on as I fuck her with everything I have. The moans are coming out of her, and I look at her, watching me fuck her. Her eyes are on my cock, and I look down with her. It's the hottest sight I've ever fucking seen. My cock disappearing into her as I fuck her faster and harder. "I'm right there."

"I know," is the only thing that comes out of my mouth. I don't focus on anything but her. It's primal, it's raw, and it's fucking real. My balls slap her ass over and over again as I try to go deeper and deeper. "Right there," she says, and I know she's going to come. I can feel her pussy getting tighter and tighter around me, and she throws her head back and explodes on my cock. I force myself to wait until she's done coming on my cock, and then her clit glistens, and I move my thumb over to it, and she pushes my hand away. "So sensitive." But I go back and move it side to side two more times before I feel her legs squeeze me, but I'm on the edge. Just as her pussy squeezes me again, I come with her.

SIXTEEN

ERIKA

I THINK I'VE died and gone to heaven. His head falls on my chest as I try to get my breathing back to a normal pace. I can feel his cock still twitching inside me, and fuck if I don't want him to fuck me again. Like. Right. Fucking. Now. Both of us are covered in sweat, and I open my eyes and look down at him. His hands are right beside my hips, and I squeeze his cock while it's inside me. He looks up. "Again?" I ask him, and he smirks.

"Is that a challenge?" He gets up and kisses me as he slowly starts to move while still inside me.

"It's whatever you want to call it as long as you just keep doing that." I move my hips up to meet him as his cock grows back to life inside me.

"But first …" he says. He takes his cock out of me, and I almost cry. "Time to see if the heels work," he says, and I look at him confused because all I can think about is his cock in me. His hands are on my hips, picking me up as if I'm a rag doll. He turns me to face the island, and his chest is to my back. "Open for me." He doesn't have to ask me twice when I bend my leg and place it on the counter and arch my ass to him. I look over my shoulder and see him bite his lower lip before his hand comes up to smack my ass. He moves between my legs, and his cock is the perfect height as he slides into me.

He fills me so full I can't help but moan out. "Fuck," I say, and he slams into me again, and I have to hold on to the counter or I'll fly forward. When he fucked me on the counter, all I could do was hold on for the ride, and what a fucking ride it was. His hand wraps around my chest as he grabs my throat as he fucks me slower than before. My hand curls around his arm, my hand onto his shoulder. His face is right next to mine and he moves in and out of me. I turn my head to the side and slip my tongue into his mouth but I have to let it go because he's going to make me come again. The sound of us panting is the only sound in the room and every second the sound of skin slapping on skin. "Cooper," I say, turning my mouth open and he slips his tongue back into my mouth. "It's so good," I say, my stomach getting tight as he fucks me harder. "More," I say and his hand leaves my throat and he pushes me down onto the counter.

The coldness of the countertop makes my nipples tingle, as he grabs a hold of my shoulder and starts moving into me faster and faster. My hand is gripping the side of the counter, holding on as he fucks me harder than before. I come over and over again, every time begging him for more, every time asking him to go deeper. Until he grabs my hips, and my leg falls off the counter, but it never hits the floor because he's holding me up as he pounds into me, the angle going deeper than before, and he screams my name when he comes inside me again. His chest falls onto my back as he slowly lets my feet touch the floor again. He kisses my shoulder as his chest moves up and down quickly. I close my eyes, and I think I can fall asleep right here in the middle of his kitchen. He peels himself off me, and I want to call him back, but my body is so relaxed.

He slips out of me, and this time, I groan and look back over my shoulder to look at him. "Come on," he says, and I slowly peel myself off the counter. When I turn to him, he holds out his hand to me, and I take it. I take a step forward, and my legs almost give out. He pulls me to him and wraps his hands around my waist, and my legs cross at his back.

"Where are we going?" I ask as he walks toward the stairs, and I wrap my arms around his neck and bury my face into his neck. The smell of his cologne turns me on, and I wonder if he would think I'm crazy if I asked him to do me again, right now.

"Shower," he says. "Then maybe the tub, then I'm definitely going to fuck you in my bed."

"I approve of all that." I smile at him as he places me on the counter. "I think you should, um …" I open my legs. "See if this counter is better than the one downstairs."

"Take off your shoes," he says, turning on the water, "and get ready to do all the work."

He doesn't have to tell me twice as he picks me up and plants me on his cock and sits down on the bench in the shower. While riding him, he tells me he is going to come, and I jump off him and take him into my mouth again and swallow him. I don't even know how long we stay in here.

I put on his shirt as we go down to grab something to eat. Me in his big shirt and him in a towel wrapped around his waist. I grab a cupcake and take a bite, and he stands behind me. His hand moves the shirt lower until he is playing with my nipple. I put my head back on his shoulder and look up at him. His blue eyes pierce into me, and he comes down and kisses me. His tongue slides into mine softly and gently. His finger rolls my nipple and then pinches. His towel falls down by our feet. "This isn't going to help us get food," I point out when he lets go of my mouth.

"Oh, I'm going to eat," he says, pushing the shirt down on the other side. My tits are perkier as both hands play with my nipples, and I swear if he continues, I'm going to come without him even touching me.

"What are you going to eat?" I ask, and I get on my tippy-toes so his cock is between my ass cheeks.

I turn as his hand falls to my side. "I mean …" I take some of the frosting off the cupcake with my finger and bring it to my mouth but rub it on my nipple. "Oops," I say. His eyes get bluer as his mouth goes down, and he makes sure there is nothing left. I repeat it with the other breast, and then I hop onto the counter, taking more icing into my mouth this time. I open my legs for him to stand in the middle as his tongue comes to lick mine clean. His kisses might just be my undoing.

"This is good icing," he admits, scooping some on his finger and moving my legs out of the way. "Let's see how it tastes on you right here." I watch his finger rub over my clit. I try to open my legs wider when he buries his face there. His tongue goes around and around my clit as he cleans the icing off. "I don't know," he says. "I might have to try it again."

He eats me and then slides back into me, and when we go back upstairs, we have to take another shower.

He carries me to the bed, and I finally have him over me. With one leg over his shoulder, he gets so deep into me I just come over and over again each time he pushes into me. I don't know when he slips out of me, but sometime during the night, I feel covers come over me, and I feel him kiss my neck. I want to keep my eyes open and never shut them, but I can't help it, and I fall asleep more content than I've ever been in my whole life.

My eyes flutter open for a second. My whole body feels like I worked out for hours yesterday. I sink deeper into the pillow as I close my eyes again, trying to find the dream I was just having again. My mouth is dry, and I'm about to turn over when a hand grasps my breast. I open my eyes in shock and am surprised when I feel someone at my back.

I look over and see Cooper there with his face buried into my neck. "Oh my god," I gasp as the memories of last night and this morning come back to me. It wasn't a dream. I thought it was a dream, a good fucking dream, and I could swear I was pleasuring myself in the dream. "Oh my god," I say again, and Cooper's eyes open as he looks at me. His eyes are sleepy as my eyes go big when I feel his cock on my leg. "Oh my god." That's the only thing I can say before sliding out of bed and taking the sheet with me, leaving the duvet on him.

"Morning," he greets as he gets up on his elbow. I shake my head and hold the sheet in front of me with a grip so hard my fingers turn white.

"Oh my god." That's the only thing that comes out of my mouth as my heart races in my chest. "What the hell did we just do?"

He laughs and gets out of the bed naked in all his glory. Let me tell you, my body responds right away. My mouth waters as I see his cock in the light again. My eyes roam his body up and down like he's my next meal. The red mark that I gave him right beside his dick last night. I close my eyes to pretend he isn't standing there naked and to tell myself that last night was a mistake. But then I open my eyes again, and I see him. I turn my head, grabbing a pillow and throwing it at him. "Would you cover yourself up, please?"

He laughs and stands there, not moving. "It's going to be fine," I say to myself, and if the sheet wasn't so long, I would pace back and forth. I put my hand on my stomach, ignoring the way my stomach is flipping.

"I don't know about you," he says, smirking and clapping his hands together, "but I feel fucking great."

I glare at him. "It's going to be fine." I put up my hand. "We were both drunk." I point at him and then me.

My head yells that it's a lie, but that is what I'm sticking to. It doesn't matter that I remember every single fucking touch.

"I wasn't drunk," he says, and I glare at him.

"You are not helping, Cooper," I say frantically as I think of losing him because of this. Just the thought makes me want to throw up. I want to go over to him and wrap my arms around him. I want him to tell me it's going to be fine.

He walks around the bed to my side, and all I can do is watch him. My feet feel stuck to the floor. He puts his hands on my face, and I don't move or breathe, for that matter. I look into his blue eyes, and my heart beats normally again.

"Erika," he says softly, and then he bends his head to kiss me. I let go of the breath I was holding right before his lips find mine. His tongue slips into my mouth, and it's like coming home. Like I've been looking for this home my whole life and just found it. I close my eyes, and the hand that isn't holding the sheet comes up and holds his face, his stubble pinching my fingers. But I don't let go of the kiss and neither does he until I forget what I was thinking. Everything is forgotten when he touches me.

He finally lets go of my lips but not of my face. "What was that for?" I ask, my heart speeding up and my hand wanting to let the sheet fall.

"It calms you down," he says softly, his thumbs rubbing my cheeks as he leans in and kisses me again.

"Cooper," I whisper when he stops kissing me, and

his forehead touches mine. "We have to forget this happened," I say, looking into his eyes. I'm expecting him to agree with me. I'm expecting him to tell me it'll be for the best, and we can put it behind us. What I'm not expecting is for the next words to come out of his mouth.

His mouth goes to a smirk. "Not a chance in fucking hell."

SEVENTEEN

COOPER

I KNEW WHEN she woke up that she would freak out, so I was waiting for it. "We have to forget this happened," she says. Her hand clutches the white sheet so tight to her chest, her fingers have turned white. Her hair looks like I pulled it all night long, and I did. Her lips are swollen with all the kissing we did, and you can see little red marks from my scruff. Her face is flushed with the panic she is going through, and her eyes, fuck, her eyes are clear and bright. I could spend all day looking into them, but I have other things planned for her.

I hold her face in my hands, my thumbs moving over her cheeks, making sure she is looking at me when I say my next words with a smirk on my face. "Not a chance in fucking hell."

"Cooper," she tries again, and this time, I lower my lips to hers to kiss her softly, then rub my nose with hers before kissing her again. This time, my tongue comes out to slide into her mouth. Her tongue fights with mine. I pull her to me, my hands on her ass, and her hand finally lets go of the sheet. I pick her up and carry her back to bed. "I guess we can continue for the day." She opens her legs for me, and I slide into her. Her back arches off the bed, and I close my eyes to take her in. "Well, we already did it today, so it technically didn't count. We have until midnight." I laugh at her as I pull out and then slam back into her.

"Is that so?" I ask again as I fuck her. The sound of our skin slapping against each other fills the room with our panting breaths. I pull out of her and bury my face in her pussy. Knowing her clit is sensitive, I bite down on it and then slam back into her, making her come again.

"Well, we have about fourteen more hours," she says from beside me when I roll over on my back. "Then we just clean the slate." I look over at her and see her eyes closing. My hand goes to my chest as it rises and falls, and before I say another word, I can hear her soft snores.

We spend the day in bed and then on the couch and then the counter before finally collapsing right before midnight. I wake up before her, and I slide into her right before we leave. It's fast, it's hot, and it's fucking perfect, just like every other time before it. She avoids looking at me, and it kills me, but I know that she's working through all this in her head.

She borrows a pair of shorts and a T-shirt to wear home. The whole ride to her house is silent. "Have a great day," I say when I put the SUV in park, and she glares over at me. I lean over and kiss her lips softly. Her hand comes up and holds the back of my head.

"We can't do this," she says, shaking her head and reaching for the door handle. "We need a reset."

"We had sex twenty minutes ago," I remind her. "So I guess we can do it tonight, too?" She slams the SUV door in my face.

I watch her walk to the front door, and she never looks back. "She is going to fight this all the way," I mutter to myself before leaving, and if I didn't have to be at practice, I would park the SUV and chase after her. But I know she needs time. She has to work this out in her head.

The drive to the rink is uneventful, and I pull into my parking space. Getting out of the SUV with my protein shake in my hand, I can't fucking help the smile that fills my face. "You look too happy for a Monday." I hear as soon as I lock the door and see Ralph getting out of his SUV with Manning. Both of them are dressed in the same thing as I am—sport shorts, Dallas shirt, and matching baseball caps.

"Yeah," Ralph says. "Why are you all smiles and shit?"

We stop when we see Miller arriving, and he gets out of his SUV with a smile on his face. "See, I'm not the only one." I point at Miller, who gets out and stretches. His outfit is exactly like ours.

"I got laid this morning without interruption." He holds his hands in the air as if he just won a game in overtime. "Full-on four minutes of uninterrupted sex." He closes his eyes. "And it was fucking amazing."

"I don't think I would be celebrating that," Manning says, and I roll my lips to stop from laughing.

"Yeah?" He puts his hands on his hips. "When's the last time you went longer than four minutes without a kid yelling for you?" He stands there waiting for his answer.

"Saturday night and Sunday morning." Manning shakes his head. "Rookie. Get your woman right after the kid falls asleep and get up at the ass crack of dawn."

"Whatever," Miller says. "You say that when your kids climb in bed with you at all hours of the night." We walk toward the door. "Sometimes, I wake up in the morning and I don't even know what bed I'm in or who is beside me."

"So," Manning pushes, looking over at me, holding the door open for us, "is that why you look so happy? You got laid." I walk in and shake my head.

"Can't I just smile to smile?" I ask as we walk into the locker room.

All three of them answer at the same time. "NO."

"Well, I am," I say, not ready to share what happened in the last two days. I walk to my spot on the bench, put my keys away, and then walk to the gym and get on the bike. My mind goes straight to Erika. And the smile I wore before comes back in full force. Watching television while I ride, I look over to see some of the guys coming in and warming up before we have to get on the ice. Some do their workout before and some after; I like warming up and then skating.

The door opens, and I see Nico coming in. He's wearing jeans and a sweater. He looks around the gym, talking to a couple of players.

"Good morning," I hear from beside me and see Nico coming to stand beside me. "How you doing?"

"Good," I say, not lying. "Actually, I feel fucking great."

"I can't believe the season is over, and we start playoffs in a couple of days." He looks at me. "Another year complete. Thought we would end up better in the standings."

"I think the beginning of the year was what fucked us up," I answer him honestly. "Manning having the knee surgery. Mika having a groin injury. We had so many injured. People coming up to play with us, and then people getting sent down. It was hard to build up that confidence we had at the end."

"Well, we face the number one team in the league first round," he says. "That should be fun. We won against them twice this whole year."

"You never know, stranger things have happened," I say, but even I think it will be a five-game series, at best. They just have a better team than we do. If we had another month, it would be a different story.

"Next year," he says, nodding. "Next year, we smash it. Don't forget tonight." He looks at me, and he must see the confusion on my face. "Ticket holder dinner."

"Oh, yeah," I say, grabbing my phone and texting Erika.

Me: Ticket holder dinner tonight. Are we going together?

She gets back to me right away.

Erika: In a meeting. I'll meet you there.

I put my phone away, shaking my head as I warm up on the bike. Then I head over to the treadmill before getting up and walking to get my equipment on. We train hard for over three hours, and when I get back into the dressing room, I sit down and drink some water.

"We leave tomorrow at ten," the coach says. "I know we have a big shindig tonight, but you can sleep on the plane."

I get up and throw my shirt in the big basket in the middle of the room. "You did get laid," Miller says, looking at me. I'm shocked he knows, but then I see him pointing at my chest. I look down to see the marks she left on me. I smirk and just shrug.

"You dog," Mika says. "Was it the blonde at the party?" he asks, and I just look over at him.

"What party?" He laughs, taking off his skates.

"Your divorce party. There were these two blondes." He shakes his head, and I look at him with my mouth open.

"There were blondes at my party?" I look at him and then over at Manning, who just shrugs.

"They came with Wilson," Mika says, and Wilson looks up from his side of the bench.

"They also left with me." He winks. "Both of them."

"So who was it?" Mika asks, and I shake my head and untie my skates, not even going to answer him. I get in the shower and call Erika on the way home, and she sends me straight to voice mail.

EIGHTEEN

Erika

MY PHONE RINGS again, and I look down to see it's Cooper and send it straight to voice mail as my stomach crunches tight. I've avoided him all day, and I have no idea what to do or who to talk to about it. All I can hear is his voice in my head, saying *Not a chance in fucking hell.* Over and over again.

The last two days play in repeat over and over in my head all fucking day long, annoying me to the end of the earth. I was angry for remembering every fucking touch, every fucking kiss, every fucking minute. I thought I needed to get away from him to think, except every single time I started to think about it, it was things that I shouldn't be thinking about. I should be thinking about our friendship. I should be thinking about when I realized he was my best friend. When I met him in New York, and he was not sure he wanted to play for his father. How we sat down and spoke openly, and how from that meeting on, we talked every single day, and if we didn't speak, we would text. The most we've ever gone without speaking was four days. I should be thinking about the fact that we work together. I work for him, and so many fucking lines have been crossed it's not even funny.

I put my head in my hands when Shauna comes in with a black bag in her hand. "Okay, I'm off," she says, and I look over at her and then down at my watch to see that it's just past six o'clock. "Here is your outfit for tonight, and I have a car scheduled for you. All you have to do is text me when you're ready, and I'll send him over."

"I can do all that," I say, getting up and walking to grab the bag from her. When this event was planned out months ago, I decided to leave from the office instead of going home and then coming back to the city. But when we planned this, I didn't know I would have had sex with Cooper the morning of. "Just text me his number." She looks at me and smiles. "Have a great night. Take pictures."

"Thanks, you, too," she replies, turning and walking back out of my office. I tried to come up with an excuse the minute Shauna reminded me about the dinner tonight, but no matter what excuses I came up with in my head, it wasn't good enough. I had clients on the team I needed to show up for, and I knew it. There were no two ways about it. I had to be there tonight.

I was mentally a mess, and I was pissed that the only person I could talk to about this was also the same person I was avoiding. He has been my best friend for the last eight years at least, and I'm scared I've ruined it because we spent the night having sex. I mean the whole night and the day after and this morning, but it's the same thing. So what if it was the best sex of my life. So what that I was myself with him. So what if just thinking about him again makes my stomach flip and my heart speed up. So what if my hands are clammy, and all I can see when I close my eyes are his eyes. It means nothing.

"Hey," Becca says, sticking her head into the office. "I'm going to get ready, and we can head out in about thirty minutes." I think about seeing if I could maybe dip out for the night.

"I'll be ready. I just have to change," I say, smiling. I can do this. It'll be fine. I walk into the bathroom in my office. Unzipping the black garment bag, I see the powder blue top and skirt I had picked out. I slip out of my pants and grab the matching blue skirt.

It fits like a glove when I zip it up at the side, hanging the pants in the garment bag. Taking off my shirt, I see that I still have the red marks he left on me. My hands touch them, and then I shake my head, taking off my bra and grabbing the top. It's one sleeve with ruffles from the shoulder down. I zip the side with no sleeve. The ruffles start from that side and then meet the other one as they ruffle down. Grabbing the blue patent shoes, I finish the outfit. Cleaning up my clothes and zipping back the garment bag, I step out of the bathroom into my office.

I see Nico walking in as he heads to Becca's office. She comes out to greet him and gives him a smile and a kiss.

"Are you ready?" she asks, and her mouth goes open. "That outfit is gorgeous." I smile, grabbing my purse and walking out.

Nico smiles at me and kisses my cheek. "Shall we go?" he says, looking at his watch. "We are late."

My whole body shakes with nerves as the elevator slowly makes its way down to the parking garage. Nico's SUV is waiting for us as I get in the back seat. The phone pings in my purse, and even though I don't want to take it out, I have to.

I look down and see that Shauna has sent me the number of the car service. I text her back a thank-you and let out the breath I was holding. When we get to the arena, all I have time to do is put my phone away before the door is opened. The valet holds out his hand as I smile at him and get out. "Thank you," I say and wait for Becca to walk around the SUV and join us. "Thank you for the lift." I smile at her. When she came into the office this morning to remind me again that she was going, she offered a ride, and instead of saying I couldn't go, I said sure.

Walking into the arena, you can see the ice has been transformed. A blue wooden floor covered with blue carpet has been placed over the ice. Tables are set up all around the place with a stage at one end. I take a step forward, and I see him.

I try to swallow, but my mouth is drier than the desert in the summer. He's wearing a blue suit with a baby blue shirt, and his eyes just pop. He smirks when he gets close to me. "Hi," he greets, wrapping his arm around my waist and kissing my cheek. Actually, it's the corner of my lips he kisses. "I was wondering when you would be here."

I look at him. I can do this. I can pretend nothing happened, I tell myself. "Yeah, Nico gave me a ride." His hand drops from my waist as he stands in front of me, and my body aches for his touch. "This is nice," I blurt the first thing that comes to mind as I look around, and he laughs. And I finally let out a huge breath. "Go away."

He chuckles. "Not a chance." We walk more into the rink. His fingers graze mine like they've done a thousand times before, but this time, my body wants more than just a soft touch.

I spot Manning and Evelyn and stop to chat with them, hoping Cooper gets bored and leaves, but instead, he's right by my side the whole time. My body, at this point, is one tight nerve.

"I'm going to go get something to drink," I tell them and turn, hoping he doesn't follow me. I walk up to one of the bars and smile at the bartender. "Can I have sparkling water?" I ask, and then I feel him beside me.

He stands beside me with his hands in his pockets, his Rolex and the bracelet I got him on his left wrist. A smirk is all over his face. "Are you going to have a glass of wine?" he asks.

I shake my head. "No," I say, avoiding turning to look at him. Maybe if I don't keep looking at him, I can pretend he isn't here.

"Why not?" He turns toward me and leans on the bar. I know I have to look over to answer him, but I'm afraid of what I'm going to see. Afraid my body is going to deceive me.

I take a deep breath and finally look over at him. His blue suit fits him like it always has. His baby blue shirt is open at the collar, showing me his chest, the chest that I spent most of the night kissing or licking and sometimes biting. My stomach flips over when I see his eyes staring at me. My mouth moves before my head can think about the words. "Because it's going to make me forget the things that I shouldn't," I state, standing tall with my shoulders back and my head high. I turn back to the bartender when he comes back with a glass of sparkling water.

"And what's that?" he asks with his annoying smirk. Someone steps behind me, and I have to move forward, bringing me much closer to him. I've stood in front of him so many times before, sometimes even closer than this, but that was before. His smell makes my nipples tighten, and all I want is to touch him. All I want is to have him touch me. My neck burns when I think of it, and then the fear creeps in just as fast. Losing him would kill me.

"That we work together," I remind him, taking a drink of the water. The cold bubbly water hits my tongue like an explosion. I look back at him. "And we are best friends." I swallow again. "And we can't go there." There, I said it. *We can't go there*, my head repeats.

He slowly nods his head. "And what would happen if you drank the wine?" His eyes sparkle and are so crystal blue that all you can do is get sucked into him.

He waits for my answer, and I hate that we are having this conversation with so many people around. But if we were alone, I don't think I could trust myself with him, which pisses me off even more. I'm not a lovesick teenager. I'm an adult, and I should be able to handle this.

"If I drank the wine …" My hands shake just a touch as I look around to make sure no one is listening to our conversation. My voice goes low when I admit, "I would remember what it's like to kiss you." Swallowing down the lump in my throat, I move my eyes around, making sure no one who knows us is here. I look up at him, staring into his eyes. "I would remember what it's like to have you over me."

He stands, and I want to kick myself for admitting that. Maybe I shouldn't have told him, but it's Cooper, and I can tell him anything. He takes a deep breath as he looks around and puts his hands in his pockets, making his arms bulge even more. "Drink the wine; don't drink the wine. At the end of the night, it's all going to end up at the same place."

I cock my hip, annoyed that my whole body is tingling, thinking about what I shouldn't be thinking about. This is crazy. We've been best friends for the past eight years. One night shouldn't ruin this. "And where is that, Cooper?" I ask stupidly.

He leans forward, his smell is overwhelming, and all I can do is see him over me. All I can picture is him all over me. "The night ends with me in you." His words send shivers down my whole body.

NINETEEN

Cooper

I LOOK AROUND, making sure that no one is eavesdropping when I lean into her. "The night ends with me in you." I want to kiss her, but this is not the place.

I'm about to say something else to her when I hear Nico on the speaker. "Can everyone grab a seat?" he says, and I look at her.

"Let's go grab a seat," I suggest, pulling her hand, and she comes with me. She's avoided me all day long, but I knew she would. I waited by the door, knowing she would try to slip in, and the minute I saw her walk in, my heart settled in a way I can't explain. She looked like a deer in headlights when she saw me and tried to get away from me, but I was done with her running, at least for today. I slip my hand in hers, and she looks at me with big eyes.

"People will see," she says, and I have to stop and laugh.

"Do you know how many times we've held hands?" I ask, and she just looks at me. "Or that I've walked with my arm around your shoulder? A gazillion times," I inform her, and we walk to the table as I spot two seats open where Manning, Miller, and Ralph are.

"Can we?" I ask before Candace smiles at me.

"We saved them for you guys," she states, and I side-eye Erika, who glares at me.

Nico gives a speech, and then Manning gets up under protest to give his speech, and the whole time, I count down the minutes until we can leave. When the clock hits eight, I look around the table. "We're going to head out," I announce. "I have stuff to do before we leave tomorrow."

As soon as I say the words, the whole table gets up. "What the heck?" Erika questions, and they all laugh.

"We have been dying to leave," Manning says, grabbing Evelyn's hand. "We just didn't want to be the first ones."

I laugh. "I was dying," Miller says. "I wanted to leave at five fifteen."

We spot Nico, who just nods at us as we all turn and walk out. "I guess this means I don't need my car service," Erika says from beside me as we walk toward my SUV.

"I guess this would mean that if you got into that car service," I say, unlocking my door. "It would just decide whose bed we're sleeping in tonight."

She takes a deep breath. "Cooper," she hisses with her teeth clenched.

"Get in the SUV, Erika," I demand, and she looks up at me. "I'm teetering on the edge of the cliff right now." I step in closer to her and put my hand on her hip, turning my body so no one can see. "All night, I've thought about tasting that mouth, and I've been really patient." I lean in. "But that patience is running out really, really fast. So if you don't want me to kiss the ever-loving shit out of you in the middle of the garage, I suggest you get in the car." I lick my lips. "Or better yet …" I pull her to me, and she can feel my cock. "Don't."

"Fine," she says breathlessly, turning and getting into the SUV. "But this doesn't mean anything. It just means I don't want anyone to know." She reaches out and pulls the door closed and glares at me. I swear all I can do is laugh.

I get in the SUV and buckle my seat belt, looking over at her. "Tell me what's going through your mind," I ask softly, and she turns to look at me.

"That I fucking hate that I can't talk to you about this," she answers, her voice going a touch higher. "I hate that all day the only person I wanted to talk to about this was the only person I couldn't talk to about this." She lets go of a huge breath she was holding. "I need a new best friend," she grumbles. I grab her hand and bring it to my lips, and I'm so tempted to pull over the SUV and kiss her. But instead, I just drive toward where we live.

"You can talk to me about anything," I assure her quietly when I pull up in her driveway.

She leans forward and opens the door. I turn off the SUV and get out. I walk behind her, and when she opens the door, I step in behind her. I shut the door behind me and grab her hand. Turning her to me, I grab her face in my palms, and her hands fly to my chest. "Cooper." That's all she gets out before I take her mouth. Pulling her face to me, I crash my lips down on hers. Her mouth opens for my tongue, and we both give in. She sinks into my arms as she kisses me back with everything she has. I let go of her lips and kiss along her jaw and nip her neck. Her hands slip up from my chest to my face, and then I look at her. She leans in and starts kissing me. I pick her up, and her shoes fall off as I walk over to the stairs.

"Next time," I say as I wrap my arm around her waist, "you wear a dress that allows you to wrap your legs around me." She tilts her head back and laughs, giving me a chance to suck her neck. Once we get into her room, it's all hands on deck. Her hands fly out to peel my jacket off while I try to figure out her top. By the time I find the zipper on the side, she has my pants undone and is sinking to her knees. I close my eyes when I feel her mouth around my cock. She moans, and I swear she enjoys it just as much as I do.

I need to touch her, so pulling her up, I claim her mouth again as her hand jerks my cock. "I need you," she admits softly. She pulls my shirt out of my pants, and my hand finds the zipper again and this time I unzip it, and when I peel her out of it, her tits spring free, her nipples pebble and aching to be bitten and then sucked. I lean down and bite one and then suck it in. The whole time, she jerks my cock.

"I need to get into you," I say as she moves back

toward the bed, and I unzip her skirt and peel her out of it, bringing the panties with it. My shirt leaves my body, and I don't even know how she did it, nor do I care. "Get on the bed," I order, and she turns to climb on the bed. She flaunts her ass in my face, her pussy already wet, and I haven't even touched her. My hand comes up, and I slip a finger in her, and she stops moving. I can't help but bend and slip my tongue into her pussy at the same time as my finger.

"Get on the bed and spread your legs for me." She crawls to the middle of the bed, putting her head on the pillows, and she opens her legs for me. Her pussy glistens, her landing strip begging me to come on it. She watches me take off my pants, but she does this while playing with her clit. "Don't make yourself come," I warn when I can see her hand start to move faster, and she groans. I crawl onto the bed between her legs, rubbing my cock up and down her slit, and my mouth waters to taste her. "One more taste," I say, burying my face into her pussy. Her moans fill the room as I tongue her. I can feel her getting wetter and wetter, and I know she's at the edge. I suck her clit and then bite it, and in one swift move, my cock is buried in her, and she comes. Her hips skyrocket off the bed as I pump into her. Thrust after thrust, harder and harder, her moans get louder and louder. I lean and suck her nipple into my mouth. "Show me how much you missed me," I say, and she offers me her mouth, her tongue coming into my mouth.

"I can show you, but I'd prefer your cock in me rather than in my mouth," she says between thrusts. "Let me ride you."

She doesn't have to ask me twice. I pull out of her, and she smiles as we trade places, but I throw the pillows on the floor. With my back against her headboard, she holds my cock in her hand and takes it in her throat. I watch her swallow me. "Play with yourself," I say, and she looks up at me, smiling as her hand goes to her pussy. "I want you to do everything I say," I command as my hips move, and my cock goes into her mouth. "And then right before you come …" Her eyes close. "You stop and ride my cock." I push her hair from her face. "Put two fingers inside you." I know she does this because she sucks my cock deeper in her throat. "Move them in and out at the same speed as you suck my cock. Nice and slow." She groans around my cock, and I swear I want to come down her throat. "Now slide your fingers up to your clit and move them in small circles." Her eyes close halfway, my hips helping her. "Now put your fingers back inside you." She lets my cock go.

"I'm close," she says, and I smile.

"Not yet." She groans and sucks my cock again. "Move your fingers faster, I can hear how wet you are." Her hand grips my cock like a vise, and I know she's going to snap. "That's it, baby," I praise, and her hips move side to side as she tries to control it.

"Come sit on my cock," I say. Her mouth lets go of my cock, and she holds it up and rams herself down on it. She puts her hands on my shoulders to grip, and she fucks me, slamming down each time. My hands come up to tweak her nipples. "So fucking tight," I say, and all she can do is moan, squeezing my cock. I roll her nipples, and every time I do, her pussy gets tighter. "You going to come on my cock?" She nods and moans at the same time as my hands go to her hips. I lift her up and down, helping her, and she throws her head back and comes, her juices running down my balls. Fuck, she's gorgeous. "Yeah, I'm going, too," I say when she's coming down from her high. She gets off my cock and takes me into her mouth and swallows me right when I come.

I swear I see stars as she sucks me clean. "Holy shit," I say when she lets go of my cock and collapses beside me.

TWENTY

Erika

"I CAN'T MOVE," I mumble as I look up at the ceiling. That was probably the hottest sex I've ever had, and the second hottest was yesterday. His touch makes me crazy, and all I crave is more of his touch.

I look up and see him with his head back and his eyes closed. "I need a minute," he says, and I want to laugh.

I sit up, and look around the room at our clothes scattered everywhere. "This is not what I was expecting." I look at him, seeing his heaving chest still trying to control his breathing. I scoot next to him on the bed, and he wraps his arm around my shoulder, and I look up at him. This man, who knows me better than I know myself, smiles at me. I lean back, and he bends to kiss me.

"Talk," he insists, knowing I have to talk.

"Well, the first thing we should discuss is, um," I start to say, but I can't think when he touches me. "I need a robe." Getting off the bed, I walk over and pick up his shirt, putting it on.

"I don't know how much talking you want to do," he says, not even attempting to cover himself. "But you look fucking good in my shirt."

I have to sit down, and I do it at the foot of the bed. "We need to really talk, Cooper." I grab a pillow and place it over his cock that is starting to rise again. I sit in the middle of the bed, and he looks at me. "We really have to stop doing this."

"Think again," he says, not even waiting a second for me to finish. And I roll my eyes. "Erika, do you really want to stop doing this?" he asks, and my stomach sinks. "Honest to god, you look me in the eyes and tell me that you don't want to do this, and we won't do it." His voice comes out soft. "But you can't deny this thing between us."

"I'm not trying to deny this thing between us," I finally say, and I get off the bed because I have to walk it out while we talk. "That"—I point at the bed—"was the best thing I've ever had."

"You think?" he says and chuckles. "Well, I don't have to think. The last three days have been the best I've ever had. Ever."

"Ugh," I say, throwing up my hands. "Okay, fine, it's the best I've ever had. Are you happy?" I ask him, and he just shrugs. "I'm just …" I start. "We aren't even using protection," I point out, and he looks at me.

"You have an IUD," he points out. "I know because I had to take you to get it installed, or whatever it's called. You made me wait outside, remember?"

I roll my eyes. "Oh my god." I put my hand to my head. "See? This. You know everything about me."

"Yeah, and?" he says. "That just makes it better."

"But like we aren't using protection," I say, and he tilts his head.

"I'm clean," he says, and I don't doubt that he wouldn't be clean. "I haven't had sex in three years," he admits, and it's my turn to be shocked.

"You were married," I point out. "Mia is two."

"And the last time we had sex was when she was conceived and not that I'm comfortable with talking about other people while we're naked, but it was six months before that."

"The last time for me was four years ago," I say. "So I'm clean also."

"Can you come here?" He holds out his hand to me, knowing I'm the one who will have to take the leap of faith. I get on the bed and move over to him.

I crawl over his lap, and he sits up and takes me in his arms. "The best thing about all of this is that we can be honest with each other," he says, and I look up at him. "You ignored me today."

"I didn't ignore you," I lie, and he just raises his eyebrows. "Okay, fine, I ignored you. But I just didn't know how to talk to you."

He laughs. "You talk to me like I'm Cooper. Like you've always talked to me."

I laugh. "Yeah, right," I say, shaking my head. "What did you expect? For me to be like *hey, I had the best sex of my life, but I'm afraid that it's going to fuck shit up.*"

"Well, yeah," he says. "There is nothing wrong with that." I hate when he is the sensible one. "Now I have to leave tomorrow for five days," he says, leaning down and kissing me. "So we have five days of sex to put in the bank." I shake my head, laughing, but I'm not laughing when he pushes me back, and his mouth devours me.

The alarm goes off, and my hand sneaks out of the covers. "What time is it?" I hear him grumble from beside me.

"Five," I respond, shutting the alarm off. "What time is the flight?" I ask him.

"Ten. I have to go home and pack." His finger plays with my nipple softly, rubbing it back and forth. "I'd like another round here and one at home before I leave," he says, and who am I to say no to that.

"I'll call you when I land," he states when we pull up to the office building, and I have this weird feeling in my stomach.

"Okay," I say to him, and he leans over and holds my chin with his finger.

"And you're going to answer," he pushes, and I roll my eyes.

"I'm going to answer," I confirm, and he leans over and kisses my lips softly. "Fly safe," I say, getting out of the SUV and walking away from him. My feet are getting heavier and heavier with each step.

He calls me when they land, and I answer him. He FaceTimes me that night, and even though at the beginning it's a bit forced, it's just Cooper and me by the end. It's the longest five days of my life, and when I get a text that he's landed, I smile.

Me: Welcome home.

Cooper: Good to be home.

I'm putting the key into my door when my phone rings and I see it's Cooper. "Hey," I answer, opening my door. "I just got home."

"Why didn't you come here?" he asks, and I can tell from his voice he's tired. The two games they played in Vegas were fucking rough. They were outshot and outplayed, and by the end of the second game, it was getting physical.

"I don't know," I say honestly. " I just thought you wanted to relax tonight."

"I am going to relax when you get here."

"But you have the girls," I remind him. "And you haven't seen them in two weeks."

"I miss you." His voice comes out softly, and I turn around and close my door. "And I was hoping you could come over, and we could have dinner together."

I get in the car. "I was giving you space," I say honestly. "I didn't want to be all over you when you just got the girls."

I make my way over to his house. "I just," he starts to say, and I park in the driveway beside him. "I," he says when I ring the bell, and I can hear him moving in the house. "I wanted you here."

He opens the door, and my stomach flips when I see him. He still has his dress pants on with a white button-down shirt that is rolled up on his forearms. His scruff is longer than normal, but it's the playoffs, so I'm expecting it to get longer. His blue eyes look tired, but what makes my whole face light up is when the smirk on his face turns into a full smile. His hand reaches for me, and he pulls me inside. "The girls?" I ask, knowing his mouth is going to find mine.

"Eating a snack and watching television," he replies as his mouth comes down and kisses my lips as his tongue slides into my mouth. "Fuck, I've missed this," he says, letting go of me. His hand goes to my cheek. "You look beautiful," he compliments as he looks at me up and down. I didn't even have time to change, so I'm wearing my loose floral skirt and a white short-sleeve silk top with nude high heels, "Nice dress." His hand grips my ass, pulling me into him.

"It's loose," I say, kissing his neck. "You know, just in case someone wanted to pay me a visit at the office, and we would go for lunch," I tease, and he looks at me. "I wanted you to have easy access," I say, winking. "Sucks you didn't come to see me."

"Daddy!" Emma yells for him. I step out of his arms and walk away from him. I look over my shoulder and see him with his hands on his hips, and he looks at me.

"Are you telling me that if I came to see you for lunch …?" he says.

"That we would have used the back seat in your SUV?" I fill in the words for him. "The answer is yes," I say, walking into the kitchen and seeing the girls. "Well, look who it is." I walk to the counter, and Emma claps her hands and rushes to me.

"Auntie Erika," she says, wrapping her arms around

my waist. "I missed you." I kiss her head and look over at Mia, who is trying to climb down from the stool. I walk over to help her and take her in my arms.

She hugs me and kisses my cheek. "Okay," Cooper says when he finally joins us, and I see his cock is still half-mast in his pants. "Dinner is ready," he states, walking over to the stove. I put Mia down on her stool and walk over to him.

"What can I help with?" I ask him.

"Oh, you need to sit down and save your energy. It's going to be a long night for you." I open my mouth, and he steps behind me and holds my hips so I can feel him. My eyes go to the girls to see if they are looking. "A very fucking long night," he whispers, and I shiver under his touch.

"I'll set the table," I say. I turn and go over to get the plates. He walks with me and reaches across to get the cups, grazing my nipples with his fingers, and I just look at him. "Don't play with fire."

"Or else?" he asks, and I look over my shoulder, seeing the girls.

"Or else I'll leave without you seeing what I have under here and go home to my purple friend," I threaten, and his eyes get darker.

"Did you use that friend while I was gone?" he asks, and I tilt my head.

"Did you use your hand while you were gone?" And I can see from his eyes that he did. "I guess that answers your question."

"I'm throwing that thing out," he says, and I laugh.

"I'm not kidding."

"You can but just so you know." I step closer to him. "I have more than one." I leave him and turn to the kids. "Who wants corn?" I ask as I make the plates for the girls.

We sit at the island, and I sit next to Mia, making him sit next to Emma. "Did you guys have fun with Mom?" I ask them, and they nod.

"Daddy," Emma says. "When are we going to the beach?" she asks, and he just looks up.

"We leave soon." He looks at me. "You took vacation, right?" he asks, and I just stare at him.

I avoid answering his question, and he knows it. When he goes up to put the girls to bed, I clean the kitchen. I'm drying my hands when I feel his hands on my hips as he kisses my neck. "Are they in bed?"

"Yeah," he says, and his hands turn me around, and I see he's wearing a shirt and shorts. His mouth falls on mine. His tongue slides into my mouth, and my back arches.

He picks me up and carries me over to the couch. "The girls," I say when he sits down, and I straddle him.

"They'll call me if they need me," he shares, and I bend my head and kiss him. I grind into his cock, and he moves a hand up my legs. "You need to be quiet." He smirks as he moves my skirt higher and slides his cock out of his shorts. My body craves him, and when I move my thong to the side and slide down on his cock, we both moan. My skirt covers that his cock is buried in me. "I missed you," he shares, and I move my hips up and down slowly.

"I missed you, too," I admit as his hands tighten on my hips. "I hate being quiet," I pout, and he laughs. His hand pushes up my shirt, and he covers my tits. "Faster," I say, and he looks at me, pushing the hair away from my face as I pick up speed. The only thing you can hear in the room is our heavy breathing until I look at him. I moan, and his mouth covers mine as he comes at the same time I do.

I collapse on him, my head on his shoulder, and I kiss him. "That was good, but I want you naked."

"Well, the girls are here, so that is not going to happen," I tell him as he rubs my back, neither of us saying anything.

"Why didn't you answer me before?" he says, and I sit up with his cock still in me. "When I asked you about the vacation."

"You weren't really serious about me coming, were you?" I ask. "That would be so weird."

"Not if we don't make it weird. It'll be a challenge since all I can do when I'm around you is touch you, but I think we are two adults. We can handle it." I am about to say that it's a bad idea when his hips thrust up, and I forget what I'm about to say. "We leave in two weeks."

TWENTY-ONE

COOPER

"OKAY, GIRLS, TIME to go!" I shout for the girls while I pick up their luggage and place it outside the front door. Then I grab mine and set it next to theirs.

They come running down the stairs. "Are we going on the airplane?" Emma asks excitedly as I grab their backpacks I packed this morning.

"We are going to see Grandma Parker and Grandpa Cooper," I tell them, and they both squeal.

I pick up Mia and buckle her in, looking over at Emma getting in the booster seat. I kiss Mia's nose and then open the SUV to load it with our luggage, making sure to leave room for Erika's. I get into the SUV and look over to make sure the girls are okay as I drive to pick up Erika.

I pull up and see that her luggage is already outside. Getting out of the SUV, I see her poke her head out and smile at me.

"I'm not going to lie," she says, looking at me. Her hair is piled on her head as she steps out of the house, and I see her wearing a tight one-piece dress with her jean jacket and white sneakers. I put her bag in the back and shut the SUV. She stands next to me. "I'm going to miss the beard just a little." I wrap my arm around her and bring her to me. I was wrong about us going out in five. We actually went out in seven, which was a bitch to lose, but we were proud of what we did. It took me two more weeks to shave off the playoff beard.

"You want me to grow a beard, baby?" I ask softly, bending to kiss her, and she smiles.

"I won't say no if you don't shave the entire trip." She smiles at me, and the past month has been crazy. When I have the girls, she comes over and has dinner with us, and then we usually make out on the couch before she sneaks home. When I don't have the girls, we alternate from house to house. It's the easiest relationship I've ever been in. I lean in again and kiss her mouth.

"Two weeks," I say, and she puts her hand on my face.

"This is a very bad idea," she replies, and all I can do is smile.

"Or the best idea I've ever had," I gloat with excitement in my voice as she walks to the side of the SUV and opens it to say hello to the girls.

"Are we excited to go to the beach?" she asks them, clapping her hands. "Are we going to build sandcastles?"

The girls scream with excitement, and she gets into the passenger side. I slide into the driver's side and automatically reach for her hand. "Um," she says, and

I just smile at her. "Can we talk about this?" she asks quietly, looking in the back at the girls, but they are too busy watching the movie playing on the iPad.

"I'm all about talking," I say, and she glares at me. She's so fucking beautiful. All I want to do is lean over and kiss her.

"We are going to be with your family and the girls for two weeks," she starts. "And I don't think it's a good idea to share," she says. "This."

"I agree." No matter how much I want to hold her hand in public or kiss her lips. I love having this thing between us being just us. "But," I say, and she groans.

"Why is there always a but with you?" She shakes her head.

"We've always been touchy-feely," I point out. "How many times have I walked with my arm around you?" I ask, knowing I've done it at least every single day. "How many times have I walked in and given you a hug?"

"Okay, fine," she relents. "But the kissing on the lips and the holding the hand in the car. We've never done that before."

"So no slipping you the tongue?" I joke with her, and when we pull up at the private airport, I turn to her. "I promise to be on my best behavior," I vow, and she stares at me, knowing I have more to say. "In front of people. But …"

"Here we go with the buts," she says, and I want to take her mouth to stop her from overthinking it.

"But at nighttime, you're mine," I declare. "All mine." I reach for the SUV door. "Every part of you."

"My room might have a lock on it," she says, laughing. "And I might have brought a couple of friends to keep me company."

I get out, standing and looking at her. The sun hits me right away as she looks me up and down. "You're looking good there, Mr. Grant," she compliments, and I laugh. I'm wearing a white polo with blue shorts. "Some might say good enough to eat." She shuts the door, and all I can do is laugh. She opens the door, and I see one guy run over with a luggage cart.

"Hi," I say to him. "Cooper Grant, we have a flight at ten." I look over at Erika, who grabs Mia and puts her on her hip and then holds out a hand for Emma. I move to the side as the guy gets our luggage out. "Look over here," I tell them, taking out my phone and snapping a picture.

"Do you want me to get one with you and the girls?" she asks, and I walk to her and put my arm around her shoulder. "Or we can do this," she says when she sees me holding out my hand and snapping a picture of the four of us. I smile when I look down at it and lean down to kiss her but then kiss her forehead instead. "Smooth." She chuckles as we follow the man with our luggage.

"Is that our plane?" Mia asks, and Erika smiles and nods, kissing her neck. She's always shown my girls unconditional love.

We stop by the private plane, and I watch Emma walk up first, and then I put my hand on Erika's back so she can walk up the steps. I expect her to hand Mia to me, but she walks in with her. I follow them in, and I can see her putting Mia down in one of the captain chairs.

"Mr. and Mrs. Grant," the flight attendant says. "Welcome aboard." I look over at Erika to see if she heard, and I can see that the only thing she cares about is making sure the girls are buckled in okay. "We are going to be leaving as soon as the bags are loaded."

"Thank you," I say, walking over and my hand goes on her waist. "Did you buckle Emma in?" I ask, and my whole body wakes up when she looks at me. Her green eyes are lighter in the sun as she stares at me.

"Where do you want to sit?" I ask Emma.

"I want to sit next to Erika," she answers, and I shrug as Erika moves in front of me, her ass right on my cock, and I hold her hips there. She looks up at me and licks her lips, and it's taking everything, and I mean everything, in me not to fucking kiss her.

"I might need help," she says quietly. "With the lock on the bathroom door."

"I think I can help you with that," I say, and she settles next to Emma. I sit in front of her, and I wish we were sitting side by side.

The kids clap their hands when they look out the window and see that we are moving. "How long is the flight?" Erika asks, and I feel her foot by my leg. I reach under the table in front of us and grab her leg, putting it on my lap, and she just looks at me.

"This is what friends do all the time," I say, and she laughs. The plane takes off, and then the flight attendant comes over and asks the kids if they want anything. Erika is already out of her seat, grabbing the girls' bags and getting their iPads out.

She hands me Mia's and then sets up Emma's before turning to me and walking to the bathroom. I watch her over my shoulder and then get up to follow her. "Leave the door open," she states when I step in, and she is leaning against the counter. "So it doesn't look like we are joining the mile-high club."

I step in front of her, and my hands go to her hips as I squeeze in. "What can I help you with?" I ask, and she just looks up at me.

"I'd really like a kiss," she admits, wrapping her arms around my neck and getting up on her tippy-toes.

"Well, since you asked so nicely," I say, bending my head, and my lips fall on hers. Her tongue comes out right away to kiss me, and she presses her front into me. I'm so lost in her I don't hear the flight attendant clear her throat, and when she calls my name, we both snap apart.

We look over at her as she smiles at us. "Sorry to interrupt, but the girls were asking for candy."

"I was having trouble with the lock," Erika says, and I have to roll my lips because all the flight attendant does is nod.

"I'll be right out," I say, and she turns her head and smiles even bigger.

"Oh my god." I hear Erika say, and her head falls on my chest. "I told you this was a bad idea."

"And," I reply when she looks up at me. "I told you it was the best idea I've ever had." I kiss her softly. "Nothing will change my mind."

TWENTY-TWO

ERIKA

I SIT NEXT to Cooper on the couch with his arm around me as we continue our flight and the girls watch their show. I lay my head on his shoulder as we make our way to the vacation house. "Auntie Erika." I hear Mia call my name as she walks to us and climbs on my lap. "Can you help me?"

I look down at the game she is playing as she settles against my side and I figure out the princess game. "We land in ten minutes," the flight attendant informs us, and I smile at her. When she caught Cooper and me making out in the bathroom, I wanted to crawl into a hole and die, but then I thought of all the shit she must see, kissing is probably pretty tame.

"Let's go, baby," Cooper says, getting up and holding his hand out to me. I keep it in his as I follow Mia back to her seat. The plane lands, and when we get off the plane this time, he carries Mia.

I hold Emma's hand as I walk over to the waiting SUV. "Auntie Erika," she says. "I'm hungry."

"I know, baby girl, I'm going to make you something to eat when we get to the beach," I confirm and look over at Cooper. "Can we stop and get the girls something to eat?" I ask as he buckles Mia into the other side.

"Anything for my girls," he says and winks at me, and although I roll my eyes, my stomach flips from him calling me one of his girls, which is the most ridiculous thing. I close the door and walk around the SUV, and he meets me there. "Hi," he greets, wrapping his arms around my waist and bringing me to him.

I put my hands on his arms, sliding my fingers up the sleeves of his shirt. "Hi," I return. It's been two days since we've been naked with each other, and I'm already itching to feel his body on mine. He bends his head and kisses me softly. "Let's get on the road and get the kids to the beach."

I walk away from him, and he slaps my ass, and I stop to look over at him. "Friends definitely don't slap each other on the ass." I point at him.

"Oh, how wrong you are," he jests, smirking at me as he walks to the driver's seat.

I get in and look over at the girls. "Ready?' I say, and he puts his hand on my leg as we drive. My fingers link with his. We stop and get the girls some food, and when I lean in the back seat, he runs his hand up my leg, brushing against my panties. "Cooper Grant," I scold him, and he bites my ass. I huff, sitting back down while the girls eat in their chairs, and we make our way to the beach. When the GPS tells him to turn left, the girls see the beach and shout. "I can't believe your family found eleven houses side by side," I say, and then he looks over at me. "Okay, fine, I can believe it."

When we pull up to the house that will be ours, I look over and see that no other cars are there. "When are they getting here?" I ask him when I get out, and you can hear the sound of the waves crashing against the sand from here.

"They said sometime around dinner, depending on everyone else. Worst case is tomorrow morning," Cooper shares, and the girls get out of the SUV.

"I'm going to take the girls to see the water on the beach." I smile at the girls. "Can you get the bags by yourself?"

"I think I can do that," he says and then looks at Emma. "Give me a kiss." She kisses him on the lips, and he goes to Mia and asks her the same thing. I'm smiling when he comes to me and asks me for a kiss. I shake my head, kissing his lips and then walking away.

"You're a sly one," I toss over my shoulder. The girls hold my hands as we follow the walkway on the side of the house. "Look at how pretty the house is," I say, looking up at the house that will be ours for two weeks.

The sound of the waves gets louder and louder as we walk past the pool and toward the wooden deck. The wind blows the sand, and when we get to the end of the deck, we see the stairs that lead down to the beach. "Let's take off our shoes," I suggest, kicking off my white sneakers and then helping Mia take off her shoes and socks. Emma is done when I finish with Mia. "Okay, let's go get our toes wet," I say, and we walk down the steps, Mia on my hip and Emma holding my hand.

When I get down to the bottom, I put Mia down. "Okay, we are just getting our feet wet," I tell them, and Emma smiles at me as we walk very fast down to the water. The sand is warm on my toes until we get closer to the water, and the wet sand sticks to my feet. The waves crash onto the shore, rolling up onto our feet, and the sound of the girls' laughter fills the air.

"That's cold," Mia says, running after the water going back and then running back to me when she sees another wave hit. I run to her to make sure she doesn't fall, and all she does is laugh. I don't even know how long we are out here chasing the waves when I see Cooper walking down the steps to join us.

"Be careful," I tell the girls as they run together. I put my hand up to block the sun as I watch the girls. He puts his arms around my waist. "Hey," I say, looking over my shoulder. "How's the house?"

"Nice," he replies, kissing my neck. "Fridge is full, and so is the pantry."

"Yeah, your mom called me the other day to find out what I eat," I say, laughing as the girls call his name.

"Daddy," Emma says. "We are chasing the waves."

The girls run through the water. I know their shorts are getting wet, and we will have to change clothes as soon as we get into the house.

"I think this is a private beach," Cooper says, looking around, and I see that it's just us on the beach.

"I mean, I don't put anything past your father for renting the beach for two weeks," I say, turning in his arms.

"Daddy," Mia calls him. "Can we go see the house?"

"Come on." I hold out my hand to her as we walk back to the house. Cooper has his hand over my shoulder. One hand holds Emma, and my hand holds Mia, and he is right. We've walked like this before. When we get to the steps, he grabs Mia to walk faster, and I walk up with Emma.

"Wash off your feet." I point over at the little faucet on the side of the deck. I turn on the water for the girls and wash off their feet before turning and following Cooper into the house.

The back door leads straight into the kitchen, a white island in the middle of the room with three stools. The girls run to the fridge and open it, asking for a snack. "You need to wash your hands," Cooper states. "And then you need to change."

"You go do that," I say. "I'll cut some fruit." I take off my jacket, and he points at the stairs.

The girls go, and he lingers, coming over to me and kissing me quickly. "We are going to spend all day outside, so the fresh air can get the girls tired, and I can have my way with you tonight," he says, smacking my ass before going up the stairs.

I've cut the watermelon, strawberries, and some grapes by the time they come back downstairs dressed in shorts and Dallas T-shirts. "I made you plates," I tell them, and they climb onto the stools. I run over to make sure Mia doesn't fall. "Eat this, and I'm going to go change," I tell them, and they nod at me. I walk up the steps, poking my head into the first room and seeing bunk beds. Cooper is unpacking their bags.

"Hey," I say, "which room is mine?" He looks up and just smirks.

"I put your bags in my room," he informs me, and I fold my arms over my chest.

"Cooper," I say to him, and he comes to me and grabs my ass with his hands, bringing me to him. "The girls," I remind him, and he puts his head back, and I laugh.

"Fine," he finally says, letting go of my ass and kissing the ever-loving shit out of me. There is no mistaking that this kiss is needy, and if the girls weren't downstairs, I would already be naked, and so would he. "You can move your bags," he concedes, letting go of my lips.

"Thank you," I say, turning and walking away.

"But," he says, and I laugh.

"Of course there is a but." I stop and turn to look at him. "Heaven forbid there would be no buts."

"But," he says again. "If your ass isn't in my bed tonight, I'm going to carry you there over my shoulder." He puts his hands on his hips, and I swear I can feel his touch already. "Are we clear?"

TWENTY-THREE

Cooper

THE SUN HITS my face, and I blink my eyes open as the ocean waves sound in the background. I turn to the side to grab Erika, but the bed is empty. I get up on my elbow and look around the room. The walls are painted gray, and the whole back wall is four doors that face the ocean and open to a balcony. One of the turquoise curtains is pushed aside, and I can see Erika's hair blowing in the wind. I look over at the bedside table and grab my phone, seeing it's just a bit after seven.

We kept the girls up later than I wanted to, but they weren't used to the room and the bunk beds. But the minute the house was quiet, I took her hand and led her to the bedroom, the both of us lunging for the other one. I throw the cover off me and pick up the boxers I took off during the middle of the night when she rubbed her ass against me. I slip on the boxers and smell the coffee.

I walk to the room and see the girls are still sleeping,

and the door is closed, something Erika would have done when she woke up. The stairs creak when I get down to the last step. I walk over and see the mug on the counter next to the coffee maker, and I smile when I know she left it out for me instead of me opening and closing the cabinet doors to find it. I pour some coffee and make my way back to the bedroom, grabbing the blue shorts on the way out. Opening the door, I feel the warm breeze and look over at Erika, who looks up at me and smiles. "Morning," she says as she sits on one of the white Adirondack chairs facing the ocean. I leave the door open in case the girls have to call me.

I lean down in front of her, and a smile fills her face. "Morning," I return, and her hand comes up to hold the back of my head as I kiss her softly. "When did you wake up?"

"About thirty minutes ago," she replies as I sit in the empty chair beside her. "You wouldn't let me go to my bed." She laughs. "You had a death grip on my breast." She takes a sip of her coffee, and I lean over and kiss her again.

"Turn in the chair," I say, and she looks over at me. She is wearing a long button-down pink linen gown that falls to her knees.

"What?" she asks, looking at me.

I get up and turn her chair to face the side of my chair and sit back down, taking her legs in my lap. "There, much better."

"What time is the family getting here?" she asks, and I rub her legs and shrug. "Did you sleep well?"

"Yeah," I answer. "And we didn't even get interrupted." I wink at her, and she shakes her head.

"Daddy." I turn and see Mia coming out, rubbing her eyes as she crawls on my lap. I kiss her as I cradle her at my side.

"Did you sleep good?" I ask and then look over when I see Emma coming outside, rubbing her eyes just like Mia did. She looks at me and then looks over at Erika, who holds her hands out so she can crawl into her lap.

"Morning," she whispers to Emma and kisses her head. "Did you sleep okay?" she asks, and she nods, still rubbing her eyes.

"Can we go to the beach today?" she asks Erika, who smiles at her.

"We better," she replies with a smile. With my daughter on one side and my hand on Erika's legs while she holds my other girl, I could not feel more content. "How about we go in and make breakfast?" She looks at Mia. "And then we can get ready to go to the beach."

"Well, well, well." I hear and look next door and see my father standing there, his hand propped over his brow to shield the sun. "Look at who is lounging around."

"Grampy!" Mia jumps out of my arms, and my mother joins him.

"What time did you guys leave New York?" I ask, shaking my head.

"At the ass crack of dawn," my sister Franny grumbles, rubbing her eyes. "I'm going to bed. Don't wake me up." I laugh at them.

"Why don't I make a big breakfast?" Erika suggests,

slipping her legs out of my lap and putting Emma down. "I'm going to go put my shorts on," she says, and I look at her. "Meet you downstairs."

"Yeah," I say. I want to run my hand up her leg, but I know people are around.

I get up from my chair and look over at my complaining father. "Baby," he calls my mother. "We need to call someone, and they need to put umbrellas and chairs on the beach. We have kids."

"This is going to be so much fun," I say, leaning over the railing. I walk back into the room, and I hear Erika.

"Which swimsuit do you want to wear?" she asks and I peek in the room and see her bent over. Her linen outfit is not hiding anything.

"I'll dress them. You go get dressed," I remark, adjusting myself. She smirks at me.

"I might need help tying my bikini bottom," she whispers in my ear. She walks into the room where she put her clothes but didn't sleep. I get the girls dressed and then walk downstairs, opening the back door and seeing my parents outside sitting down.

"Dad," I call, and he looks over. "The girls are dressed." He gets up, slapping his hands together, turning to walk into the front and I walk outside with them, seeing my father opening the gate, the girls squeal.

"Where are my girls?" he asks, and they jump up and down. They run over to him, and he takes them both in his arms. "I have some surprises for you guys."

"We'll take care of them," my mother says. "Go relax. We have breakfast coming in an hour."

I run up the steps two at a time and find Erika in the room wearing a black bikini. She was not fucking kidding about the ties. Her bikini bottoms have bows at each side, and her ass is showing way too much skin. I walk up behind her and grab her hips. "You can't wear that." I kiss her neck as she laughs. My hands slide from her hips to her tits, and my cock wakes up and wants in on the action.

"Where are the girls?" She moves her head to the side so I can keep kissing her.

"My parents have them, and they ordered breakfast," I say, and my hand goes down her toned stomach and slips into her bottoms. "They told me to relax."

"Did they?" Her hand moves behind her, and she grabs my cock in her hand. "And what did you have in mind?"

"Better if I show you," I say, picking her up and placing her on the chest in the room. Her arms wrap around my neck as my mouth finds hers. It takes me no time to be sliding into her, and when we walk back outside forty-five minutes later, we find no one on the balcony. Looking over, we see them at the beach.

"I'm going to get sunscreen," Erika says. "I'll meet you there." I nod, and I want to bend to kiss her, but she raises her eyebrows and looks around. She brings two fingers to her lips and then places them on my lips before turning and walking inside. Her green bikini is showing under her white beach dress. The black bikini is in the wash.

I walk down the steps, and the minute I step on the

sand, I hear my name. "Cooper Grant." I look over and see my grandfather and namesake. He walks with his hand in my grandmother Parker's hand.

"Grandpa," I return, walking to him. He takes me into his arms and gives me a big bear hug. His hands come up and hold my face just like he did when I was a young boy. His eyes are glistening with tears.

"Look at you," he says, blinking the tears away. He brings me back for a hug.

"Hey," my grandmother interupts. "Let me get a hug." I bend to hug my grandmother. "My baby," she says, and I laugh. "Where are my great-grandbabies?" she asks, and I point at the sea as I hear the girls squeal as they run in and out of the water with my father chasing them and my mother sitting on the sand watching them. "Where is Erika?" She looks behind me.

"She went to get sunscreen for the girls," I say, and she smiles and nods her head, walking toward my father.

My grandfather puts his arm around my shoulder. "How are you doing?" he asks as we walk toward the girls.

"I'm doing really, really good," I confirm with a smile, and it makes him smile.

"Not going to lie," he replies. "You look good."

"I feel good," I say and then look up to see my father coming to us.

"They are going to come within an hour and give us lounge chairs and some umbrellas," he says. "Max just called. They are taking off. Dylan, Michael, and Alex missed the plane, so they are going to arrive tomorrow."

I shake my head. "How did they miss the plane?"

"From what Max said, their heads are all up their asses," my father shares, and my grandfather laughs.

"God, I can't wait to have everyone here," he says. "Now, where are my girls?" he asks, walking away from us to the girls, who yell and scream for him to chase them.

"How is the house?" my father asks, and I just nod.

Fifty-five minutes later, four guys arrive with twenty umbrellas and over one hundred chairs. My mother brings the girls to the house when they complain they are hungry. I spot Erika walking toward us, and then she stops when she sees the girls. She shares a hug with my mother and my grandmother. She turns and walks back to the house with them.

"Let's sit," my father says, and he points at the empty chairs right next to my grandfather, who sits and looks out at the water.

"This is good, right, Dad?" my father says to my grandfather, who smiles.

"Best weeks of the year. We need to pack coolers," he says.

"Nah," my father says. "I hired a beach crew to take care of us every day. They are going to bring water toys, too." I laugh because my father can never do things low-key. "Why are you laughing?" He pushes my shoulder, and I just shake my head. "How are you doing?"

"Good." I look over at him, and I'm dying to tell him about Erika. "I'm having fun." I skate around it, and he just eyes me.

"You're having fun." He repeats my words. "What the fuck does that mean?"

"How soon before it's a reasonable time to start dating?" I ask, and my grandfather looks over at me and laughs, shaking his head. My father just looks at me with his mouth hanging open. "What?"

"How soon before you start dating?" He repeats the words to make sure that he heard them right.

"Yeah," I say. "Give or take."

"I haven't a fucking clue," he admits.

"How did you know Mom was the one?" I ask, and my grandfather puts his head back and laughs.

"Not only does he want to start dating," my grandfather teases, "but he's wondering if he's in love."

"Would you two just please answer the question?" I say, annoyed.

"When I was dating your grandmother," my grandfather starts, "there was a miscommunication, and she took off for four days. Longest fucking days of my life, and I thought I would die."

I look over at my father. "And you?"

"I took one look at her and I knew she was going to be mine," my father answers honestly, and I roll my eyes. "Now, is there something you would like to share with us?"

I avoid looking at him because I'm afraid he's going to see through the bullshit I'm getting ready to tell him. "No reason. I was just curious." I can see him watching me from my side view, no doubt wanting to ask me more questions.

"Well, you know what they say," my grandfather says, and we turn and look at him. "Curiosity killed the cat."

We all laugh. "Good to know," I say and then finally turn and look at my father, and I was right. There are so many questions in his eyes, but I know it's not the time to say anything.

TWENTY-FOUR

Erika

"Everything okay?" Zara asks me when I walk back to the chairs and sit down. Looking toward the water, I see teenagers everywhere as they run in and out of the water with their surfboards.

"Yeah, just checking emails to make sure everything is okay." I smile and look over at her as she sits in the chair right next to mine. Zoe's on the other side of her, and Caroline lies on one of the resort beds that Matthew ordered yesterday.

Every single day, he orders something else, making this beach look like a resort. Chairs and umbrellas are everywhere, and yesterday, they delivered five daybeds and four couch sets. This morning when I got up to have coffee outside, we found the teenagers passed out on them. We then saw Matthew and Max storming the beach to wake them all up and send them to their houses.

Every day, it's a bet to see what else is going to be

delivered. I swear I'm going to wake up one day to find a Ferris wheel on the beach.

I lean my head against the chair and feel the sun hit my face. It's been three days since the start of our vacation, and I, for one, have never felt more relaxed.

The days are spent lounging on the beach with the kids making sandcastles or sand surfing. The girls are getting all the attention from the teenagers. Franny and Vivi especially.

The older kids are busy with the Jet Ski, and most of the time, Michael and Dylan are the ones in the middle of trouble with Alex slinking off in the back so she doesn't get caught.

Dinners are the best. After everyone leaves the beach to clean up, we always meet for dinner. The big group of us laugh and enjoy everyone, then sit on the beach for s'mores and a bonfire. The girls stay up way later than they should, but they crash so hard, leaving time for Cooper and me.

I have yet to even lie down on the bed in "my" room. Even though Mia climbed into bed with us this morning, she didn't notice when I slipped out and went to the bathroom. We've even had a chance to sneak off a couple of times during the day. It's usually us in the bathroom just wanting to touch each other, which is where I just came from.

"I swear those two are going to break limbs," I hear Zara say from beside me, and I put my hand up over my eyes to see that Dylan and Michael are trying to surf side by side. "What the hell are they doing?"

"It's called surf bowling," Zoe informs us. "They said the main goal is to knock the other one off the board while standing."

"Idiots." Caroline gets up and walks over to the shore, and we can't help but laugh. Dylan and Michael sit on their boards, and then they start to paddle when the wave is coming. Dylan gets up first, and then Michael is right next to him. They both try to take the other one out. The two of them fall off their boards and then go under the water.

"As their agent," I say, "I don't recommend anything they are doing." Zara and Zoe laugh, and I see Allison get up and walk over to stand beside Caroline with her hands on her hips.

"Michael Horton!" she shouts with her hands around her mouth, but I don't know if they can hear her over the sound of the crashing waves. "If you get hurt, you better find a friend to drive you to the hospital." He looks up, and he smirks at her very much like Max does. His eyes are just as blue as Max's also.

We all laugh, and she turns and yells for Max, who is sitting down. He gets up and walks to her, followed by Justin, who tries not to laugh. "Where is the third one?" Zara says of Alex. "The three musketeers."

I look over to the side and see Alex shaking her head while she looks at them. "I'm right here," she announces from beside us, and I have to say she's blossomed this year. She was stunning before, but she's breathtaking now. "I play the winner." She also is super tall and fit.

"You are not playing anything," Parker warns from

her chair, looking over at her. "If you get out there, your father is going to drag you back to the house." She rolls her lips. "Especially when he sees the back of your suit."

I turn to look at her, seeing that she's wearing a towel around her waist, obviously hiding the bottom. "It's called a cheeky, Grandma," she informs us.

"It's called locked up until you're thirty," Zara threatens.

"If she goes to Europe," Vivienne, Karrie's best friend and Cooper's godmother, adds with her French accent, "they wear thongs and go topless."

"Shut up," Alex says. "You are lying."

"It's not a big deal," Vivienne states. "It's just breasts. Everyone has them."

"Vivienne," Karrie says, "can we not?"

Alex gasps. "Mom!" she yells for Allison. "If I go to Europe, I get to go topless and wear a thong."

"For the love of Christ." I hear Max groan as he looks over at Alex, and I have to roll my lips as Dylan and Michael both come to the shore. "You aren't going to Europe."

"I'm going to go backpacking in Europe the summer before college," she informs him.

"You can do that if I become Liam Neeson from *Taken*," Max informs her. "And the chances of me becoming him are very, very slim."

"Buzzkill," Alex pouts and drops the towel and walks over to them. "Who won?"

"No one won," Allison tells her. "There is no knockdown surfing."

"Should we get horses?" Matthew comes over and stands beside us. "The girls said they wanted to ride ponies, and the teenagers showed me a video."

"Jesus," Zara says. "Can we be more extra?"

"Do you really want me to answer that?" I finally say, smiling up at Matthew. "If we say no, will you listen to us?"

"No," he answers honestly. "It can be an activity."

"What is?" Max asks, coming to us.

"Getting horses," I reply, and he groans.

"No," he says. "Allison and I did that in Mexico, and the beach was full of shit for two days."

"Pfft," Matthew retorts, grabbing his phone. "Going to add must scoop poop."

Everyone laughs at him when I hear my name being called. "Auntie Erika," Emma says, running to me. "Can you make a castle with us?"

"Of course," I say. Getting up, I look toward the house and see Cooper coming out. I hold out my hand and walk over to the sand, where there are pails and shovels.

Mia runs over to us. "Okay, let's fill the pail," I suggest, getting on my knees in the sand with them. The girls fill one pail, and we walk over and start dumping it.

"What are you guys doing?" Cooper asks, and I look up at him. He's wearing the same shorts he was before, and his chest is bronzed from being in the sun for the past three days.

"We are building a sandcastle," Emma tells him, and he squats next to me.

"You changed your suit," he notes, and I smile,

looking down at my white bikini with pink stripes.

"Someone has a goal to make sure I wash every single bikini twice," I tease, walking over to get more wet sand in the pail. The four of us walk back and forth, and after I don't even know how many trips, I say, "Doesn't look that bad." I tilt my head to the side as the girls look at it.

"You look hot," he says, and I laugh. "Girls, doesn't Auntie Erika look hot?" he asks, and I can see his blue eyes sparkling.

The pail of water in his hand is half full. "Cooper Grant." I point at him. "Don't you dare." I can see him grab the pail, and I run away from him with Emma following me. The sound of laughter fills the beach as he chases us with Mia trailing him, laughing and yelling.

"Get her, Daddy!" she screams, and I run toward the water as the waves crash over my feet and I turn and kick water at him. He laughs, bending down and throwing water in my direction, and I turn to escape it.

"Cooper!" I yell at him, and he finally grabs me around my waist and spins me. I can't help the laughter that comes out of me.

"You got her, Daddy," Mia cheers.

"What shall I do with her?" he asks Mia, who smiles.

"Go dunk her in the water," she says, and I gasp.

"Don't you dare." I look over my shoulder at him. "I just washed my hair."

"Mom!" Cooper yells for Karrie. "Watch the girls."

She gets up off her chair, and the girls clap for their dad as he walks into the water. "Cooper," I warn when the warm water hits my knees. "If you get my hair wet."

He turns me in his arms.

"I'm not going to wet your hair," he assures softly as we walk deeper into the water. "I just wanted to touch you, and the only way I could do that was by chasing you."

I laugh as his hands hold my hips. "Well, then," I say, going around him. My chest against his back. "Squat down," I order and wrap my legs around his waist and my arms around his neck. "Does this help?" I ask him, putting my head on his shoulder. If anyone were looking at me, it would look like he's giving me a piggyback ride. His hands rub my legs, and we just stand here in the water as the water goes up and down. I rest my head on his shoulder. "This is nice," I say, kissing his shoulder.

"It would be nicer if you were in front of me and I could kiss you," he grumbles, and my stomach flips as I think about him kissing me.

"Is that a pout?" I ask him, and he smirks. I move toward him and scrunch up my nose, rubbing it on his cheek. "You can get all the kisses you want tonight."

"Yeah, yeah," he says, just like one of the kids. "Whatever."

I can't help it. Another laugh escapes me, and I don't think I've ever smiled this much in my whole life. During this whole vacation, I wear a smile on my face. In the morning, in the afternoon, and at night, it is as if I can't wipe the smile off my face.

TWENTY-FIVE

Cooper

THE SOUND OF the fire crackling is filling the beach. The teenagers are laughing, and I look over at Erika, who holds Mia in her lap, and I can see Mia's eyes slowly closing. "Okay, girls," I say, and Erika looks over at me. "Time for bed."

I stand, and once I do, everyone else does also. "I'm ready for bed," my father adds.

"That's 'cause you're an old man," my uncle Max tells him.

"You're going to bed, too." He points at him.

"That's what you think," Max declares, slapping Allison on the ass.

"I'm going to be sick," Alex says from beside Franny and Vivi. "They are so gross." She gets up and walks over to the teenagers as they lie on the bed, probably thinking of stupid things to do.

"That's my sister," my father tells Max and pushes

him.

"See you guys tomorrow," I say and hold out my hand for Erika. She puts her hand in mine and gets up, Mia groaning that her legs are tired.

Bending down, I take her in my arms as we walk back to the house. "I'm going to go take a shower," Erika says. "Good night, girls." She kisses Mia in my arms and then kisses Emma on her neck. "Sleep tight." She walks toward the bedroom she is pretending to stay in, and I fucking hate it. She finally gave up and stopped waking up at the ass crack of dawn to sneak out.

"Quick, wash off your feet," I tell the girls, walking over to their bathroom and making them sit with their feet in the tub as I turn on the water. I gave them a bath before we went outside to have dinner. I wipe their feet before turning and going back into the bedroom, handing them their pjs. They crawl into bed, their eyes closing before I even walk out of the room.

I walk downstairs, making sure the lights are off and the shades are closed. Last night, I was bending Erika over the counter when I heard the teenagers, and she ducked down right before we saw a head walk by the window.

I shut the lights off except for the soft one in the corner, then go and sit down. Grabbing the remote, I turn on the television when I stretch out on the couch, waiting for Erika. I hear her footsteps and look over to see her with her hair piled on the top of her head. She wears a beige tank T-shirt that falls just past her ass.

She sees me sitting on the couch and comes over,

bending to kiss me. "The girls sleeping?" she asks as she sits on the arm of the sofa. Her legs point toward me, and my hand reaches out to rub her ankle.

"Yeah, they were out before their heads even hit the pillow," I answer as she leans over and her fingers flirt with mine. "How was your shower?" I rub from her ankle to the top of her foot.

"Lonely," she says with a smile and then rubs my leg, her finger doing little circles and she scoots over to me. "Really lonely." She lies on the side of the couch and bends down to kiss me, sliding her tongue into my mouth. Her hand goes to my face. "I was hoping you would join me," she says right before she kisses me again, and this time, she slides on my lap. Her shirt rolls up, and my hands find her bare ass. She kisses my chest. "I kept waiting." She looks up and smiles when she gets to my cock. Her hand rubs over the top of my shorts, and then she pulls them down. My cock springs up for her. She puts her mouth over the top, looking at me the whole time. "I waited." She takes my cock in her mouth, and my hands hold her arms that are holding her up as she jerks and sucks my cock.

"Come here," I invite, and she climbs back up on me, biting her lip. She bends to slide her tongue into my mouth, her shirt slides up as she kisses me, moaning in my mouth. "Did you touch yourself thinking of me?" I ask, and she smirks at me, coming back and kissing me.

"Maybe. Only one way for you to find out," she whispers, getting off the couch. With one foot firmly on the floor, she throws the other on the side of my head, her hands fall forwards on my chest, lining her pussy right up to my face. I can see the wetness coming through the white cotton as she moves it over to the side. I pull it from her hips, and my mouth licks up her clit. My tongue goes around and around, and then I feel her fall on me and her mouth is on my cock. I lick up and down and then fuck her with my tongue, sucking her clit into my mouth. My hands are on her ass as I make her come with my tongue. She rides my face, taking my cock into her mouth when she is close, to stop from moaning out loud. The thong is in my way, so I rip it off her as my finger slides into her. Her hand continues to fist my cock. "I'm going to …" She lets go of my cock to come on my fingers. Burying her face in the cushion, she moans.

She moves her leg away from me and turns to bends to slide her tongue into my mouth. She straddles my hips, one foot on the floor, the other on the side of the couch as she slides down on my cock. I watch her face as she rides me, her eyes turning a darker green. She bends down to kiss me and then sits up, my hand coming up to cup her tit while she pulls her shirt down under both tits, leaving them out for me to feast on. I lean up and take a nipple into my mouth and twirl it with my tongue. She moves up and down, panting, neither of us saying anything as she rides me.

Her eyes look into mine as I let her do what she wants to do. I suck her neck when she leans forward, putting an arm by my head, her tit coming near my mouth every time she moves on it. I nip it each time, then she slips her tongue back into my mouth as she rides me hard, sitting on the top of my cock and rotating her hips. She gets up, sitting by my side on the couch and kisses me, and lies on me. Her back to my chest, and she slides back down my cock. Her head is on my shoulder as she looks over at me and slides her tongue into my mouth when her fingers meet mine by her clit as we both play with her. She lets go long enough to moan out, "I'm going to come," making our hands go even faster, and my hips rise up to fuck her. I wrap one arm around her waist and another around her tit as I fuck her hard. Her hand goes crazy on her clit until she comes. I fuck her softly until she is done coming on my cock. Before I slide out of her, my cock is still hard as a rock. I take off my shorts, and she trades places with me.

Her head on the arm of the couch, she spreads her legs for me, and I get a quick taste of her before I put a knee into the couch. Her leg goes over my shoulders, and then I slide into her. I slide into her gently at first, bending to kiss her and then bite the nipple out of her shirt. "Cooper," she says, and I just look at her.

"No," I deny. "Not this time." I fuck her slowly, killing me as much as her when I stoop and kiss her. I slide out and in her slowly, ever so slowly, feeling all over her. She rubs her clit as I grab both tits in my hands and pump in and out slowly. Her back arches off the couch, and I pull my cock out and fuck her slit with it. "Put it back in," I order, and she grips my cock and slips it back into her. "Fuck me," I say, and she moves her body back and forth. I lick my thumb and bring it to her clit, and she arches up. My hands go to her hips as I raise her off the couch and eat her pussy. Placing her back down on my cock, she works herself over and over again until she comes. Her eyes open and she looks at me and slides off me. She sits in front of me, bending her head to take my cock into her mouth.

"You are going to come," she says as she jerks my cock with her hand, then slides down to take it to the back of her throat. "In me." She straddles me with my back to the couch. Holding my cock up, she slides down it, and I close my eyes. My hands come up to pinch her nipples and then tweak them. She starts to pant again. "In the shower." She lifts herself up and then sinks down again. "I kept picturing your cock." She closes her eyes as her hand plays with her clit. "As my fingers." She moves faster up and down, and I'm so fucking close. "I thought you would hear me," she admits, moving faster and faster, and I can tell she's about to come again when her pussy gets tighter. "This is so much better," she says and comes on my cock again. She moves up and down, and I can feel my balls get tighter.

She gets off my cock and falls to her knees between my legs, my cock going back into her mouth. But this time, she doesn't stop sucking me, and her hand grips the base of my cock as I come in her mouth. My hips buck off the couch when I shoot my last shot. She sucks up the head of my cock, wrapping her tongue around it as she stands. My hand comes up to play with her pussy.

"Not yet," she says, holding her hand out. "Let's go to bed." I get up, leaving my shorts downstairs. I follow her up to the bedroom, and we spend most of the night with me inside her.

TWENTY-SIX

ERIKA

"HERE." HE LEANS over and holds out a strawberry for me, and I lean down to take it in my mouth. He brings his lips to mine then, making me laugh.

"You are terrible," I scold as I kiss him and taste the strawberry on his lips. His phone rings on the counter between us.

He picks it up, and I see Julianne's name "Girls!" Cooper shouts from the kitchen toward the stairs, where the girls said they were going to go and choose their clothes for dinner. "Your mom is on the phone." I look over at him as he pushes away from the counter and walks to the stairs shouting upstairs. "Girls!" he yells again while the phone continues to ring in his hand.

"Why don't you answer the phone?" I say, grabbing another piece of strawberry. "And then walk upstairs to them."

"No." He shakes his head. "Then I'm stuck talking to

her," he says, and I roll my eyes.

"Answer the phone, Cooper." He runs upstairs, two steps at a time, and his phone finally stops ringing. I hear the girls talking as I put away the snacks they got when they came in a little while ago. Grabbing a bottle of water, I push the stools under the counter as I walk past the couch we had sex on last night. Every single time he touches me, it feels like the first time, but yesterday, it was different. It was hot, it was soft, and it was better than any other time.

Walking upstairs, I tiptoe past the girls' room, hoping that the floor doesn't creak. I hear Emma telling Julianne about the beach. When I get into my bedroom, I close the door behind me. Walking over to the hutch, I fish around for clothes to wear tonight. He places his hands on my hips, and then I feel his lips on the back of my neck. "I need a shower," I say, as his hand wraps around my waist. We've been at the beach all day again. My tan is spot-on, but I have sand all over me from going into the water with Mia. My hair is piled on my head, and I can swear I feel the little pieces of sand when I scratch my head. My hand goes on top of his as I move my neck so he can kiss me again.

"I hate that we can't shower together," he moans, and I push him away before the girls walk back in the room with Julianne on the phone, and she sees us.

"You need to go give the girls a bath, and then you can get in the shower," I suggest.

"Or," he says, holding out his finger, "we can send the girls over to my parents' house and shower together." I roll my eyes. "That is a much better idea than yours." He stands in front of me in another pair of shorts. His chest is perfectly tanned, and I lean in and kiss right near his nipple.

"Daddy." We hear Emma, and I jump back as if someone threw ice water at me. "Mommy wants to talk to you."

"Go." I prod, and he walks out of the room. I want to tell him to put a shirt on, but she's seen him naked. The thought of them together makes my stomach hurt, and I turn and make my way to the shower. I push away the thoughts of the two of them, but nothing I can do will make it go away.

Slipping on my beige linen pants that cuff at the ankle, I look at myself in the mirror. "They have kids together," I remind myself. I shake my head and walk over to the lace bra, putting it on and slipping on the white V-neck short-sleeve shirt.

I let my hair air dry, and when I walk out of my bathroom, the girls are in the bath, and Cooper is sticking his head out of the bathroom. "You look beautiful," he compliments, coming out and kissing my lips like we've done this forever. "You smell like coconut," he says, kissing my neck.

"It's after-sun cream," I reply. "Why don't you go get a shower and I'll watch the girls?"

He smiles at me, his eyes so fucking crystal blue I can get lost in them. I think I am lost in them. He kisses me once and then walks away, smacking my ass. "Hey, that almost got you in trouble today." I point at him. We were at the beach, and I was standing up watching the girls, and he was going to grab me something to drink when he walked away and smacked my ass. He knew the minute he did it that he fucked up. Luckily, no one was looking, or at least no one said anything.

Walking into the bathroom, I get Mia out first, and she wants me to do her hair in a braid, and then Emma gets out after. "My mommy does French braids," she says, and I smile at her, ignoring the pull in my chest. "Do you know how to do French braids?"

"I do," I affirm as she wraps herself in a towel. "Do you want me to do your hair like that?"

She nods her head and gets dressed in a floral sundress, and Mia wears the same one. Cooper comes into the room, and I look up at him. He's wearing beige shorts and a white polo short-sleeve shirt. His hair is wet from the shower, and his scruff gets thicker as the days go on. "Are we ready?" he asks, and I get up to go to him. "Go put your shoes on," he tells the girls and they run downstairs.

He wraps his arms around my waist and pulls me to him, and the pain or whatever it is settles in my chest. "I'm starving," I state, and he kisses me, and we walk downstairs together. We walk out with the girls, and I'm not sure why I'm surprised when I see six picnic tables on the beach and a large grill in the middle. The smell of barbecue fills the air. The girls walk down the stairs, and he puts his arm around my shoulder as we walk to dinner.

The girls run over to his mother, who bends down to

hug them.

"But did you get insurance with the grill?" Max stands beside Matthew as he puts ribs on the barbecue.

"Why the fuck would I need insurance?" He looks at him.

"You aren't used to handling big things," Max says, bringing the bottle of beer to his mouth to hide the smirk. "So in case it blows up."

"Jesus," Evan, Candace's brother and Cooper's uncle, says. "I'd really like to eat tonight," he adds, and I notice all the men are dressed the same. Shorts and a polo. "And if you piss him off." He points at Matthew. "Then he's going to get all hot and bothered, and he's going to burn stuff."

"One," Matthew says, pointing the tongs at him. "I only get hot and bothered for my wife." I laugh and then bury my face in Cooper's shoulder when he groans. "And two, this buffoon is in my bubble."

Max laughs. "Good to know I still get under your skin twenty years later."

He turns and walks away from Matthew, who looks around. "Dad!" he shouts. "I need help."

Cooper Sr. comes over and the two of them discuss what to cook when. "Want to go for a walk?" Cooper asks me, and I smile and nod. He walks toward the girls and tells them we are going for a walk. Emma skips over to me and says she wants to come. Mia calls over to Cooper.

"Family walk," Cooper says, pulling my hand down the beach. He doesn't let it go as we walk down the beach.

"Don't get your feet wet," he tells the girls, who pretend they don't mean to when the water runs over their feet.

We turn and walk back toward the barbecue, and we can see people sitting down. Mia and Emma run to Alex, and she sets them between her and Dylan, who holds out his burger for Emma to take a bite of. "Alex!" Cooper yells. "You got them?" And she nods her head.

"I'm here, too, you know," Dylan says, and I roll my lips as he hands Emma a french fry.

We settle at a table with Franny and Vivi. "Tomorrow night," Vivi says from beside me at the picnic table. "I want to head into town and go to the pub."

"That sounds like so much fun," Franny says.

"Mom!" Cooper yells from beside me, calling his mother who sits two tables over. "The girls are going to the pub tomorrow night."

"What is wrong with you?" Vivi hisses at him. "You have to ease into things like that."

"We'll take the girls," Matthew says. "Your brother is coming with you."

"I don't want to go to the pub," he pouts from beside me, and I laugh at him. "Somehow, that worked out differently in my head."

"I'm sure it did," Franny chides, and Mia comes over to us and says she's tired.

"It was a long day," I say, pushing her hair that fell out of her braid behind her ear as she lies on Cooper's chest. "So much excitement."

We get up, leaving everyone still sitting at the table as we walk back to the house. Emma drags her feet.

We walk into the house, and I walk over to the fridge, grabbing a bottle of water as he walks upstairs to put the girls to bed.

I walk back outside and sit on the patio step. The lights are off, and I can hear laughter coming from the beach. The back door opens, and he steps out. He sits behind me, wrapping his arms around my chest and his legs are outside mine. "Someone might see," I note as he moves my hair to one side so he can kiss my neck.

"We sat like this today," he reminds me, putting his chin on my shoulder. "We always sit like this." He kisses my neck, and I look over at him, and he comes at me with a soft kiss. My heart goes to my throat. I turn and watch the water. "What's wrong?" he asks softly.

"Nothing," I reply softly and look back at him over my shoulder, and it finally gets me that I'm falling for him. Like in love with him. Maybe I've been in love with him this whole time and never knew. Maybe in the end, it was supposed to be us all along. And maybe, just maybe I'm overthinking this whole thing, and I should just live in the moment.

"You keep forgetting," he says, his arms wrapping around my stomach as he pulls me back to him, "that I've known you a long time."

"I know," I grumble.

"And I know when you're lying," he reminds me.

"Have we always been like this?" I ask him, and I look over at him.

"What do you mean?" he questions, and I turn a little, still staying between his legs.

"The touching and stuff?" I ask him. "I don't remember."

"Yes," he says. "It's always been like this."

"Cooper," I whisper, "I don't want to lose our friendship." I ignore the burning in my stomach at the mere thought of not being able to call him or talk to him and especially to touch him. My hand comes up to cup his cheek. "Like the thought of losing you, it's just …"

"You will never lose me," he assures, and I look down, not sure I can look into his eyes. Afraid that what he'll see there will scare him away. He puts his finger under my chin and raises my chin to look at him. "Whatever happens, you will never lose me."

"Yes, but this will change our relationship," I admit. "This sleeping together."

"I think it will change it," he agrees, "but only for the better." Putting his legs up, he makes sure his arms are still around me.

"How can you know that?" I ask, sinking into his arms.

"I have no clue." He smirks. "But I know that I don't want it any other way. "

"Can we promise each other that no matter what happens …" I swallow. "That things between you and me will never change?"

He looks me in the eyes. "I promise you that nothing will ever change between us."

TWENTY-SEVEN

COOPER

"I'M GOING TO head over and drop off the girls," I say from the stool at the counter when I grab the last piece of apple off the plate. We came in about thirty minutes ago, and the girls asked for a snack. Erika was already cutting some fruit and cheese for them.

"It's four thirty." She looks over at me and laughs. "We literally left them at the beach thirty minutes ago." Her hair is piled on top of her head like it always is when we are at the beach. Her white linen button-down shirt is open and over her olive green bikini. Her face has a bit more sun today, and her green eyes are brighter.

"Yeah, and I have to shower." I wink at her, pushing off the stool and walking behind the counter. I wrap my arms around her waist and bend my head to whisper in her ear. "We have to shower." I nip her ear, and her shoulder scrunches up, and the sound of her laughter fills the room. I attack her neck, dipping her backward as she tries to push me away, but my hold gets tighter. I'm not letting her get away from me. I don't even let her go when there is a knock on the back door, and my parents walk in. Instead, I let her stand but put my arm around her shoulders.

"Oh, hey, you two," my mother says with a smile. "Still roughhousing." She shakes her head.

"We came to get the girls," my father announces, looking around the room for them.

"They are upstairs packing," Erika says, pointing at the staircase. "From what I think they understood, they are packing all their stuff."

My father laughs. "Fine by me." He walks over to the railing and shouts, "Girls!"

"I see where you get it from," Erika says of my father shouting up the stairs.

"Dad," I prompt, walking to him. "One night." I hold up a finger.

"I never see them." He looks at me and almost whines. "It's the only time I get to spend time with them."

"Oh, please." I roll my eyes, putting my hands on my hips. "That might work on Mom." I point with my thumb over at my mom, who just shakes her head.

"Let's play it by ear." My mother smiles, walking toward the stairs and going up them.

"Yeah," my father says. "Let's play it by ear."

I look over at Erika, who cleans up and pretends not to laugh. It takes my mother a minute to come back down with a bag packed, the girls running to my father, who bends down and picks them both up. "You were right.

They were trying to shove everything in this bag." She holds up the small backpack, then she looks over at me, and her smile is gone. "Why can't you fix your bed in the morning like Erika?" she says, shaking her head and mumbling, and I look over at Erika whose eyes go big. She hasn't even slept under those sheets, let alone made that bed.

"Say bye to your father and Auntie Erika." My father nudges, and I lean down and kiss both girls.

"I'll see you guys tomorrow," I say and see Erika come out and kiss them both.

"You two have fun," my mother suggests to both of us. "And sleep in." She closes the door behind her.

"Oh, we are definitely going to sleep in." I walk to the back door and lock it. "Now." I turn and clap my hands together. "Let's get in the shower." I hold out my hand for her and pull her behind me as I lead her to the shower in my bedroom. "We haven't showered together in eight days." I look over at her, and she laughs.

"Is that a pout, Mr. Grant?" she asks as I walk past the bed that we didn't make this morning and toward the bathroom.

Dropping her hand, I walk to the shower and turn it on, then walk back to her, pulling down my shorts. My cock springs free and ready. "It is a pout." I walk over to her and kiss her lips and push the shirt over her shoulders, and it falls to the floor. My hand goes to her back when I grab the string and pull it loose and then follow with the same one at her neck. Bending my head, I kiss the top of her breast.

"I can think of something that will turn that pout upside down," she teases, pulling loose the two strings on her hips, and the bikini bottoms fall to the floor also. She walks away from me, going into the shower, and getting on her knees. I follow her in, and she definitely turns my pout upside down.

"What are you going to wear?" she asks when she wraps herself in the white towel. Her hair is already wrapped up on top of her head.

"Shorts," I answer. "Shirt." She laughs. "It's the same thing I wear every day in the summer."

She comes over to me as I step out of the shower and grabs my towel. "I'm going to wear a dress," she says, getting up on her tippy-toes and kissing under my chin. "What time are we leaving?"

"Whenever you want," I reply, and she looks up at me.

"What time is everyone going?" she asks, and I shrug. "Didn't you ask?"

"Nope." I smirk. "Because we're not going to the pub."

"What?" she asks, shocked.

"It's the first night without the girls, and the last place I want to bring you is the pub, so I'm taking you out on a date," I say of the plan I put into motion this morning. "Just you and me."

Her mouth opens at the same time that she smiles. "You're taking me out on a date."

"Yup," I confirm. "I don't know what type of date." I'm honest with her. "I tried to google places."

She puts a finger on my lips. "As long as it's just us, it'll be perfect," she says and turns around. "I'm going to go and get pretty for you."

My eyebrows pinch together. "Erika." I call her name and she turns back. "Too late, you're already beautiful."

"Smooth, kid, smooth." She walks back into her bedroom and closes the door, and I fucking hate it. *This is the last time we do this family vacation and pretend to not share a room*, I think to myself, grabbing my boxers and getting dressed. I put on my blue shorts when the door to her room opens, and she comes out wearing a strapless white bra and lace panties. "I don't have anything nice to wear," she says, and I can see her eyes filling with tears. "Like I have all those clothes at home," she says. "All I have here is vacation outfits, and I didn't pack anything."

I walk over to her and grab her face in my hands. "Baby," I note, using the nickname I sometimes call her. "You can wear a potato sack, and you'd be the most beautiful girl there. We don't even have to go out. We can stay here."

"No, I want to go out. I just want this to be sort of a test run and then when we get back home we do the whole date thing," she counters and I smile and kiss her lips.

"Deal," I agree, and she smiles.

"Okay, I'll be ready in twenty," she states, turning and running back into her room and closing the door. I tie my blue shorts and grab my baby blue short-sleeve button-down shirt. And then walk to the bathroom, slicking my hair back.

I walk back out and her door opens, and I sit down to look at her. She left her hair loose and curled the ends. She is wearing a long, white, loose-layered skirt with pink flowers on it; it goes down to her ankles. Her arms are bare as she wears a white crop top that goes up to her neck. "This is the best I can do," she says, and I get up.

"If that is the best you can do, I really don't know if I can handle you at your best best." I wink at her, and she laughs.

She puts her hands on my wrists. "Can I tell you that this is the best date that I've been on?" she admits softly as her green eyes light up even more. She hasn't put on makeup since she's been here, and she didn't even put any on tonight. This is her, and I have to admit this is the only way I want her, relaxed and at peace.

"Shall we go?" She nods her head. We walk out of the house, and I open the door for her. I look over at her. "Remember, this is new even to me," I remind her, and she laughs.

When I pull up to the parking area, she looks around. "Is this?" Her eyes go big. "Is this the boardwalk?"

"Maybe." I get out of the SUV and walk over to her side, opening it for her. Holding my hand out, she takes it and gets down. She holds her dress up a bit as we walk toward the wooden boardwalk. She puts her other hand to her chest, and I look down at her, and my heart literally fills in my chest.

She jumps up and down. "This is the best day ever! I've never been to a boardwalk before," she says, turning and kissing me. "Thank you."

I grab her hand, and we start walking. As we pass a store that sells frozen custard, she points at it, her eyes taking in everything. "We have to bring the girls here," she adds, and that feeling I had in my chest before starts, except for this time, it feels like it's getting bigger. Her hand stays in mine the whole time, and when we pass one of those stuffed animal places, I stop. "Stop." She shakes her head, laughing, and I look at her. It's always been like this with her, so carefree and full of life. Neither of us are scared to say what we are feeling. I grab the basketball, and she throws her head back and claps her hands, and asks for my phone. "I need proof if you win." I hand her my phone, and she looks at the screensaver of her and the girls when we got off the plane. "Nice." She turns the phone for me to see, and then she enters my password and sees the picture of the two of us I took last night while we sat outside. My arms are around her and her face is close to mine. "Ready?" she asks, and the guy looks at me funny.

"She thinks I suck," I state as I bounce the ball on the ground. "What she doesn't know is …"

"You used to play basketball in high school." She finishes my sentence for me, and I look at her. I'm the one with my mouth hanging open. "You told me this story."

"Well then," I say and throw the ball and get it in. The guy grabs the ball and hands it back to me, and I sink it again.

"One more and you can get the big one," he says. She holds the camera up, and I sink the shot. The sound of her laughing makes me turn around, and she comes to me.

"My hero!" she exclaims, wrapping her arms around my waist as she picks the frog one. "Thank you," she says, kissing my lips, and we walk slowly with my arm around her shoulder as she holds the frog in her hand.

The lights on the Ferris wheel turn on. "Can we go?" she asks, pointing and I look over at her.

"I'll take you anywhere you want to go," I say the words, and I don't add the rest of the sentence, not sure either of us is ready for it.

TWENTY-EIGHT

Erika

"I'LL TAKE YOU anywhere you want to go," he says as he pushes the hair away from my face when a breeze comes through. My whole heart is about to explode in my chest, yet all I can do is tilt my head back and wait for him to kiss me. "Just say the word." He bends his head and kisses me.

"I've never been on a Ferris wheel before," I finally admit when we get to the front of the line. The man takes the stuffed frog and places it on the side.

"You can get that when you get off," he says as he holds the bar open, and I step in.

"You better make sure no one steals it," I joke, smiling. "He had to work pretty hard to win it." I motion with my head, making the guy laugh.

"I got it on the first try," Cooper boasts, sitting on the bench next to me, and the whole thing starts rocking. I put my hand on his leg to stop the moving, and he wraps his arm around my shoulder. "Don't worry. I've got you," he confirms, and all I can do is put my head on his shoulder. "Sorry, excuse me," Cooper says to the man who is making sure the bar is sealed. "Do you mind taking a picture of us?" He hands him the phone, and I turn to smile with him. He hands us back the phone and steps away while he presses the button to start moving the Ferris wheel.

"This is so pretty," I say when we move a bit, and we can see the whole boardwalk. "Are those where the houses are?" I point at the houses on the beach that are lit up. I turn to look at him, and all he is doing is looking at me.

"You're beautiful," he compliments, leaning and kissing me. I get lost in his kiss as the Ferris wheel goes around. The wind makes my hair go crazy. I laugh as I try to push it to one side but then finally give up and just look away from him. His thumb rubs up and down on my arm.

He holds my hand when I step off, and I grab my frog, his fingers linking with mine as we walk down the boardwalk and laugh at things that we each point out. "Can we bring the girls tomorrow?" I ask him when we make our way back to the SUV.

"Probably," he replies, and I look at him. "We have the boats tomorrow."

"Of course we do." I shake my head. "There has not been one day of no activity."

"My father wants to make sure he entices us to come back," he shares, opening the SUV door for me. Grabbing the frog, he tosses him in the back seat and then turns to me, wrapping one hand around my waist and another coming up and holding my cheek. "This has been the best vacation." He kisses me, and my heart skips.

"I've had an okay time," I joke with him, and I try to hide my smile, finally giving in and laughing. "It's been the best vacation for me also," I finally agree softly.

"Thank you for coming with me," he says, rubbing his nose on mine and turning his head. "And for asking me to kiss you."

My hands come up to touch his chest. "I think we need to thank Don Julio for that one." I laugh, and he crushes my lips, and then I throw my head back and can't help the laugh that comes out.

He kisses my neck. "Let's go home," he says, and I get into the SUV and wait for him to get in. His hand comes over the middle console so he can put his hand on my lap. He grabs my hand in his and brings it to his lips as I look out the window. He parks the SUV, letting go of my hand, and I want him to grab it back.

He opens the door, and my stomach flips as I watch him walk around, my hands shaking in my lap. He opens the door and holds out his hand. I slip my hand in his as we walk up the dark pathway to the door. He takes the keys out, unlocking the door but turning, and his hand lets go of mine as he runs his fingers up my arm all the way to the top of my shoulder. My whole body fills with goose bumps. "Tonight," he says in almost a whisper. "Was the best first date I've ever been on." His fingertips touch my neck one at a time until he runs his hand to the back of my head. "Everything with you is always better." He bends his head and slides his tongue into my mouth. I step closer to him, my hands going to his hips. He lets go of my lips, softly kissing the corner of my mouth. "For as long as I can remember," he says, his nose trailing his kisses. "You've always been at my side." I swallow down the way my heart flips and ignore the heat coming up my neck. "Good times." He kisses my chin. "Bad times. Every single time, the only thing I can remember is you being there."

"That's what friends do." My voice is trembling, and his lips brush mine. My hand moves from his chest to his face, my fingers running through his scruff. His tongue slips into my mouth as he walks into the house. He picks me up, and my legs wrap around his waist. He kisses me softly as he walks us back to his room. He doesn't turn on the light, and only the moonlight comes in through the open windows. He sets me down, and I can see his face in the moonlight. Neither of us says anything, but our actions speak words we are both afraid to say. At least I am.

He slowly peels the shirt off me, his lips finding mine. We undress each other, each of us touching softly between kisses. My fingertips graze his chest when he moves to open his pants, and they fall to the floor. I walk over and get in the middle of the bed. He follows me and crawls over me. My legs open for him as he settles between them. He rubs his cock up and down my slit and then comes over to kiss me. His tongue slides into my mouth at the same time he slides into me. My hands move up his back, rubbing his shoulders and then down his arms.

Both of my hands are beside my head as he lets go of my mouth and links our fingers together as he slips out of me and then back into me. My eyes find his as his head rests on my forehead. Our chests rise and fall together as he takes us both over the edge.

The next morning, the sun hits my face, making me open my eyes. I close one eye and look over to see Cooper sleeping. His arm is on my stomach, I watch him, and I know we have to have a conversation. The thought makes my stomach flip over as I slowly slide out of bed, not wanting to wake him.

I look over to the bedside table, seeing that it's just after seven. It's even earlier than when we have the girls. I slip on a pair of panties and a long shirt. Walking downstairs, I get myself a cup of coffee. I open the back door and sit on the step, watching the water crash on the shore. Birds are chirping and flying over me.

The door opens behind me, and I feel him over me. He sits down behind me. "Why did you wake up so early?" he grumbles, and I look over my shoulder to see his eyes are still semi closed.

"I guess I just had a lot on my mind," I reply. For a split second, I think about pretending I'm okay, but this is Cooper. He would see right through me.

"And what is on your mind?" he asks, kissing my neck and laying his head on my shoulder.

"We need to talk about what's going to happen when we get home." I see his eyes finding mine. My heart pounds in my chest, knowing there might be one answer to this, and that is not to be together. It's something I need to prepare for, something I know will hurt me, but I also know it is something that might just have no choice but to happen.

"What do you mean, what's going to happen when we get home?" he repeats what I just said, his eyes finding mine as he tries to figure out where this is going.

"This thing between us can ruin my career," I say, and he just looks at me. "How would it seem that we are together and I'm your agent? People can say that me being your agent could be a conflict of interest for them," I say, and I wish I could get up so I could pace back and forth while we have this conversation. "They can turn it and say I play favorites." I close my eyes, the realness making me sick to my stomach.

"Well, there is only one thing that we have to do," he responds as if it's nothing and without skipping a beat. "You're fired."

I shriek. "You can't just do that?" I ask, shocked, my palms getting sticky and a lump forming in my throat.

"Oh, but I can," he confirms, getting up and looking down at me. "The last thing I will allow to happen is you getting hurt in all of this." He shakes his head. "There is no way in fucking hell that is going to happen," he huffs out and puts his hands on his hips. "So the only thing to do is to fire you." He turns and opens the back door. "Now, can we go back to bed?"

"Just like that." I put my hand up to my forehead as he shrugs.

"Is there another answer?" he asks and waits, and when I don't say anything, he continues. "So that's the answer." Right here, sitting on the deck listening to the water crash in the background, I finally admit I'm in love with him.

TWENTY-NINE

COOPER

"THERE THEY ARE," I say, walking down the front steps of the house and seeing Mia and Emma. They squirm out of my father's arms to run over to me. Both of them are in shorts and a New York shirt. I look at them and then at my father, who just smirks and shrugs. He turns to walk back to the house to get everyone so we can head over to the dock. We were supposed to be outside three minutes ago, but when you have so many people, it's hard to gather them.

"Daddy!" they both shout my name and run over to me. I squat down and open my arms, hugging both of them. I kiss Emma and then Mia.

"I missed you," I murmur softly to them. "How did you sleep?"

"Grandma made pancakes," Mia says. "With chocolate chips." Her eyes go big. "And strawberry."

"Yum." I hear the door behind me close and look over

to see Erika coming out wearing a long white dress, and I know she is wearing her white bikini underneath because when she was trying to put it on, I kept taking it off. She left her hair loose, and she is holding a big straw bag that's overfilled. I get up and walk up to her, grabbing the bag. "What is all this?" I look down at her, and she is wearing her sunglasses.

"Change of clothes for the girls and me," she says, smiling.

"Did you pack me anything?" I ask, smirking.

"God, she isn't your maid," Franny moans, and I look over my shoulder at her. She is wearing sunglasses and a hat on her head.

"Ouch," I say, looking at her. "Is that from the pub last night?"

"I wish," she shares. "It was a bust. There were three people in there, and two of them were working."

"So what did you end up doing?" Erika asks her.

"We came back and had a drinking game on the beach," Vivi offers, joining Franny, but she looks fresh. "Madame here." She points at Franny. "Decided that she was going to challenge Michael and Dylan to a drinking contest."

I shake my head and laugh. "Why would you do that?" I ask, and I can tell she is glaring at me from behind her shades.

"You weigh a hundred and fifteen pounds." I chuckle. "They weigh close to two hundred."

"You know, Cooper," Franny spits. "No one asked you."

"Can we get everyone in the SUVs?" my father yells as Max and Allison come out of their house with Michael following them and Alex. Michael has the same look Franny does.

"You know what I think?" Alex suggests, all chipper. "I think we should stop and get a big breakfast." She turns. "Or like fresh fish."

"Shut up," Michael says to her, pushing her shoulder as he climbs into one of the SUVs and slams the door.

"I'm not going in that SUV." Alex looks at her father.

"You can ride with us," Erika says to Alex, who comes over.

"I heard that I had to see two special girls," my uncle remarks, looking toward us and seeing the girls. "Come over here so I can take a picture."

"Don't listen to Uncle Max," Erika prods, and then my uncle tilts his head back and laughs, holding his stomach.

"You owe me money, Erika." He points at her. "Told you that you would call me Uncle Max."

"Are we leaving?" My uncle Justin comes over, followed by Dylan, who has his glasses on and looks like he's green.

"Is he sick?" Max looks over at Dylan.

"He spent the night hugging the toilet," Justin jokes, slapping his shoulder. "Then got kicked in the balls by his sister who went in said toilet and got scared it was a home invader."

"Right in the nuts," Dylan groans, holding himself. "I saw stars."

"Shut up and get into the SUV." Justin pushes him.

"If you want," Max says. "Your better half is in that SUV sleeping." He points at the black SUV. Dylan walks over and pulls the handle of the door, and Michael's head falls back.

"Dude, what the fuck?" he grunts, his glasses falling off his face, his hat ending up on the floor.

"Why would you lie with your head against the door?" Dylan asks him, picking up his things. "Move into the back," he tells him, and I just shake my head.

"Was I ever that dumb?" I look over at my father, and Erika answers for him.

"Yes," she blurts out, and I look at her. "The day after you were drafted, we met with the sponsors," she points out, and I close my eyes. "You threw up on his shoes." My father laughs and nods his head. "Then there were the NHL awards in Vegas." I hold up my hand for her to stop talking.

"Okay, fine," I concede and put my hand over her shoulder.

"Daddy," Mia says softly. "My tummy hurts." She puts her hand to her stomach, and I look at her.

"Mine, too," Emma adds softly, putting her head on my hip.

"Oh, no," Erika says, reaching over and checking to see if she is hot. "She isn't warm."

"Do you guys want to stay here with me and watch movies? We can have a relax day," Erika suggests to them, and they both nod their heads.

"I'm not going to leave you here with the girls," I

insist, and she looks at me.

"Why not?" She shakes her head. "Go spend time with your family. We can have a chill day."

"Are you sure?" I ask, and I look over at my father, who is watching us.

"Yeah, I think we need a break from the sun," she replies, turning and walking back into the house with the girls.

"What's going on?" my father says, coming beside me.

"The girls aren't feeling well, so Erika is going to stay back with them." I look at him. "I think the New York shirts made them sick to their stomachs." I smirk at him and walk into the house to check on them before I leave. Erika pushes me out the door, and I don't even have a chance to give her a kiss before I have to get into the SUV.

When we pull up to the dock, four boats are waiting for us, and I look over to see a lot fewer people than I thought. "Where is everyone?" I look over and see that it's only the guys.

"The girls decided to do girls' stuff," Max says, making sure Dylan and Michael get on the right boat. The both of them go down to the rooms to sleep it off.

We sit down, and the boat starts to leave the dock, and when we are far enough away, the captain gives us the all clear. We get up and walk over, grabbing the fishing lines and start fishing.

My grandfather goes down and drags Michael and Dylan upstairs. "You like to party like a rock star," he scolds them. "Then you suffer like a rock star."

"Pretty sure rock stars aren't fishing the day after." Dylan stands up.

"I'm pretty sure rock stars have strict rules not to be woken up before six p.m.," Michael says, standing on the other side of him. "And then they repeat the cycle."

"Well, good news," my grandfather states. "You aren't rock stars." Max laughs and looks over at his son.

I shake my head and cast my fishing line and look out onto the water. The memory of the talk we had this morning replays in my head. When I walked out, and she said we had to talk, I thought she was going to come right out and tell me that she knew that I loved her. Last night when I brought her home, I made love to her. Every single time I touched her last night was me telling her I loved her in my own way. There was no way I was letting her get away from me.

My father stands beside me as we cast the fishing line, and he looks over at me. "What's up with you?" he asks with his chin going up. "You look worried."

"Just thinking," I say, and then I can feel his eyes still on me. "I'm going to fire Erika." I start with that and just saying it makes my stomach burn.

"What?" he asks, shocked and surprised. "Why the hell would you do something so stupid?"

"Because," I reply and turn to look at him. "I think I'm in love with her." I look at him as I wait for his reaction. I'm expecting him to be shocked, but what I'm not expecting is for him to throw his head back and laugh. Like full-on belly laugh as he shakes his head.

"Dumbass," he mumbles, and I just watch him as he puts the fishing pole in the hole in front of him. "You think you're in love with her?" He turns to me.

"Okay, fine," I fess up, ignoring the look he's giving me and look back out onto the water. "I'm in love with her," I say the words, and I can't believe how at peace I feel saying them. Like I've been made to say them. Like I've been saying them my whole life.

"I thought you were smarter than that," he says, and I look over at him angry.

"It just happened, Dad," I growl, not sure I can handle if he's disappointed in me again. The pit in my stomach is burning.

"It didn't just happen, Cooper." His voice is soft, and I look over at him. "You've been in love with her since forever," he says the words, and I just look at him.

"I was married," I remind him.

"Yeah, I was there." He shakes his head. "What I mean is that you've been in love with her forever. You've just figured it out."

"I have no idea what you are saying right now." I turn to him and put my hands on my hips.

"Think back," my father suggests. "Every single time she's in the room, do your eyes find her?"

"Um yeah, we are usually there together," I point out.

"Not the way you look at her," he shares. "And it wasn't overnight either." He doesn't say anything as I think back as far as I can remember. "Every single time you are around her, you have to touch her." He doesn't stop. "Whether it's your hand on her shoulder or her sitting next to you. You have to touch her."

"But she's my best friend," I remind him.

He laughs. "I'm assuming that you didn't just wake up this morning and decide that you love her?" I look out toward the water. "I'm also assuming that she doesn't make her bed every single morning."

"It just started a couple of months ago. I kissed her and …"

"And." He slaps my shoulder. "Things shifted." He smiles, and I nod at him.

I swallow the lump forming in my throat. "Things shifted," I confirm, understanding it. "It."

My father smiles. "It's the best feeling in the world." I smile. "Love is easy when it's right. I'm not saying it's an easy road, but loving someone shouldn't be hard. It should be just like breathing." I think about his words, and I'm shocked that he's right.

"It's always been easy with her," I say out loud, and I turn to look at him as he laughs.

He grabs his fishing pole, and all he can do is shake his head. His face beams with pride while he says, "Dumbass."

THIRTY

Erika

"CAN WE GO play in the sand?" Emma looks over at me as I fold the clothes I just took out of the dryer. When the girls complained of tummy aches, I didn't even think twice and opted to stay back. I knew how much spending the day with his family would mean to him.

"How is your tummy feeling?" I ask as she climbs onto the bed next to me. "Does it still hurt?" I left her downstairs while she played a game on the iPad. After I got her, her twelfth snack.

"No, it's better," she says, grabbing a shirt, trying to fold it. "Is this good?" She holds it up, and it falls to the bed.

"Here is a trick," I share, grabbing a shirt and shaking it out. "Put it down and then put one arm in." I fold the shirt. "Another arm in." I repeat it. "And then fold."

She picks up the shirt and does what I did, the smile filling her face. "I did it," she cheers, and I feel stirring beside me and look over to see Mia waking from her nap. She asked to watch television in the bed, so I brought her upstairs to the bed and laid her down. She was out before I even put a movie on. I cleaned up the house a bit and did a load of laundry before walking back downstairs and sitting with Emma.

"You did do it." I lean over and kiss her cheek. "It's perfect. Hi," I say to Mia, who sits up and comes over to crawl into my lap. "How was your nap?" I ask her as I rock her back and forth.

When we finish folding the laundry, I take the girls downstairs and make them both grilled cheese sandwiches and then finally give in and agree to go to the beach with them. We change back into our suits, and I make sure I put sunscreen on them here and not at the beach.

When I walk down the steps and head down to the beach, I'm shocked to see the girls. "What is this?" I ask when I see Karrie sitting with Allison, Vivienne, Caroline, Zara, Zoe, and Parker. Franny and Vivi, along with Alex, are sleeping on the daybeds.

Karrie looks up and smiles. "We decided that it would be a better day without the men." She smiles at me. "How are my girls?" She holds out her arms, and Mia runs to her.

"Apparently all better," I reply, sitting in the empty seat. "They wanted to get out and play in the sand."

"Can I wet my feet?" Emma asks me, and I just look at her while she giggles. "Just one time."

She holds up her finger, and she smirks exactly like

her father.

"Fine, I'm a sucker for the smirk," I admit, and everyone laughs.

"I'm not," Franny grumbles from her bed. "The key is not to look into the eyes."

"I'll remember that," I say, laughing as I watch the girls run in and out of the water.

"I can't believe that the vacation is almost over," Karrie voices from next to me. "I already miss them."

I smile at her. "They miss you, too. You need to come down and visit more."

"Can I come stay with you?" Vivi sits up on one of the beds. "And you can introduce me to Mr. Wilson?" She winks at me, and I shake my head.

"Your brother will not be happy with that," I say to her, knowing he would never be happy with her dating, especially someone like Wilson. He's known as the bad boy on and off the ice. He's been suspended five times already for fighting and illegal hits. "But you are welcome to come any time you want."

"Really?" Franny sits up from the bed. "We were never invited." She chuckles out.

My eyebrows pinch together. "What are you talking about? My door is always open. You don't even have to call," I invite, looking at both her and Vivi and then turning to Karrie and his aunts. "You were all always invited," I confirm, my heart pounding in my chest.

"Oh, I know your door is always open," Franny replies, getting up and coming over to us, sitting down on the sand beside my chair. "But Cooper's door was sealed shut."

"Frances," Karrie scolds. "The girls."

"Oh, they don't even know what I'm talking about," Franny says. "It's not like I'm saying her name."

"Okay, well, just in case," I say. "It's in the past, and he has a beautiful house with lots of extra rooms."

"The question is, who is he dating?" Zara says, and my back goes straight. Karrie's head flips to look at Zara. "Candace said that he showed up at practice with a mark very close to his man parts." I swallow, and my mouth is suddenly dry.

"Reminds me of someone I know." Karrie looks over at Allison.

"Can we please remember that people are here that don't want to hear any of that?" Alex whines, getting up and looking at Allison. "I'm going to go inside."

"You put a mark next to Uncle Max's junk?" Vivi asks, coming over and sitting down next to Franny.

"Your father threw your mother's vibrators in the middle of the street," Allison blurts out, and my mouth opens wide.

"Of course he did," Franny says, shaking her head. "He's a caveman."

"I remember that," Vivienne says, laughing. "And then he cuffed you to the bed."

"He did not," Franny denies, and I can't help but slap my leg and laugh.

"He did when she was going to go on vacation without him," Vivienne shares. "Four days as his sex slave."

"That's illegal," Zoe gasps.

"And fucking gross," Franny says. "He showed up in LA and was like what are you guys doing here." She mimics Matthew, and we are all laughing.

"I didn't know you guys would be here at this hotel." Vivi shakes her head.

"You guys weren't saying that when he handed you his credit card," Karrie says to Franny and Vivi, who just shrug.

"Auntie Erika," Emma says, coming over. "Can you make us mermaid tails?"

"Of course I can." I get up and walk away from the girls and go to the side.

"Can I help?" Karrie asks, and I just smile at her.

"Of course you can," I reply as we work side by side to cover the girls' legs.

"Those have to be the cutest little mermaids I've ever seen," Karrie coos, standing up. "We should take a picture." She runs over to her chair and grabs a picture of the girls, and then they break free from it.

"Do you want to go for a walk?" Karrie asks me, and I look at her, the knots in my stomach forming. The only thing going through my mind is that she knows I was the one who left a mark next to her son's dick. "We are going for a walk," Karrie says. "Who wants to come with?"

"I'm going to take the girls into the house," Franny informs us, picking up Mia. "And paint their nails."

"Nothing crazy. Your brother did not like the black last time." I remind them of when they came down the last time.

We turn and walk down the beach. "You are really

good with them," Karrie observes, and I look over at her, and I swear tears sting my eyes.

"They are good kids," I respond honestly. "And I love them." *And their father*, my head screams, but I don't say it out loud.

"I wanted to talk with you," Karrie says, and I look over at her when her voice cracks. She looks down at the sand as we walk, and I see her wipe away a tear. "I wanted to thank you," she declares and finally looks over at me.

"For what?" I ask, not sure what to say at this point.

"For taking care of him," she says, her smile filling her face, and tears running down her cheeks. I reach out and hold her hand.

"He's my best friend," I remind her. "And it's my job to take care of him." The guilt of not being honest with her creeps up.

"No," she says, shaking her head. "It's more than that." I don't say anything while she talks. I'm afraid that if I open my mouth, all the words will come out, and I don't know if we are both ready for this. "What you two share, it's something special." I swallow. "And I know that he's going to start dating, and I just hope that it doesn't change what the two of you share."

I try to make a joke. "We made it through his marriage," I admit. "And that was rough."

"What do you mean?" she asks, and I look at her and then the sand.

"I don't want to gossip," I add honestly. "But it was not all easy with Julianne and there was a point when being friends was a secret of sorts." I swallow, thinking back to the days when he first got to Dallas, when he would only call me when he was in the car and the texts would stop at four o'clock, and if I messaged him, he wouldn't answer until the next day. I would never have him choose between her and me. I would still not make him choose today. "I don't know what happened," I say softly. "I never asked him because, to be honest, I don't care. Whatever it was brought his friendship back." It changed one day when he called me at eight o'clock at night and then the next night the same thing, and I guess maybe Julianne realized that I didn't want anything from him. Maybe she realized that I was his friend and nothing more. But slowly, we started to hang out together more, and sometimes, Julianne would come also, very rarely, but she would.

"I know you mean the world to him," Karrie shares as we turn to walk back toward the houses.

"He means the world to me," I admit, smiling, leaving out that he means the whole fucking world to me as my heart beats so fast in my chest.

"I know he does," she says, and I stop walking. "There is no one else I would want by his side." I look at her, and I know she isn't talking about me being his friend.

"Thank you," I say as we get closer to the house. "For making such an amazing man." I smile at her, and she smirks at me.

"Look, the guys are back," she says, pointing at the men walking down the steps. She takes a step forward and then turns around, coming back to me and smiling. "Just make sure if he ties you to the bed, you enjoy every second of it."

THIRTY-ONE

Cooper

"That is the last of it," I confirm, putting the last of the luggage in the back of the SUV. My father and mother stand to the side with the girls in their arms as they say goodbye.

"I'm going to miss my two girls." My mother blinks away tears. My father puts his arm around her and brings her to him. She walks to the SUV and puts Emma in the back seat and then kisses her goodbye again. She's been kissing them goodbye since last night at supper.

My father puts Mia in her seat and then leans over to kiss Emma. "We will come and see you two in a couple of weeks."

"Oh, goodie," I mumble under my breath, and Erika wraps her arm around my waist. He closes the door and then comes to me.

"Be good," he reminds me when he grabs me in a hug. I hug him a bit tighter than I did last night, knowing

I won't see him.

"Thanks, Dad, for everything." Releasing me, he puts his arms on my shoulders and squeezes. Then he goes to hug Erika while my mother comes over to me.

"Call me when you land," she says. We are leaving today instead of tomorrow like everyone else because the girls have to get back to Julianne. I hug her, and she puts her head in the middle of my chest. "I love you," she adds, sniffling, and I rub her shoulders.

"I love you, too, Mom," I reply, and then my father leads her away from me.

I get in the SUV and make our way to the private plane. No one really says anything as I unload the SUV. Erika walks up the stairs with both girls while I wait for them to load the luggage, then I join them.

"I can't believe that two weeks is over already," I say, looking out the window as the plane takes off down the runway.

"I can't believe I'm going to say this," Erika says from her seat in front of me next to Emma, "but I'm going to miss them."

I look over at her and smile. "Really?" One eyebrow goes up. "All of them?" Not reminding her of two nights ago when Dylan thought our house was his and he tried to break in and then was yelling Mom and Dad, scaring the shit out of us. It didn't help that we were both naked, and I had to run downstairs and drag him inside to keep him from yelling.

"Yes." She folds her arms over her chest. "Even those two." She shakes her head. "I thought Max was going to kill him when he called him in the middle of the night. After he fell asleep on the couch." She shakes her head. We told Max it would be okay if he stayed, but he came over and threw water on him. I think he enjoyed it more than he should have. "I swear, if they are anything like that during the season …"

I laugh. "You know they won't be. Max and Justin will have their asses served to you on a platter."

"I should have gotten that in writing," she says, and I reach out my hand for hers. She smiles and holds out her hand for me. Even though I'm happy to be going home, I'm going to miss being with her all the time. "Your sisters want to come and visit," she shares, and I shrug, not caring. "Franny wants an introduction to Wilson." I shake my head.

"Not a chance in hell," I snort, laughing. "He showed up at my divorce party with two girls."

"Maybe he brought one as a gift," she jokes, laughing, and all I can do is stare at her and take in her beauty.

"Why the hell would she want to meet him?" I ask, and she smirks.

"The whole bad-boy persona," she replies, and I just look at her.

"Introducing them is like me throwing her to the wolves. Can you even imagine what my father would do to me?" I shake my head, thinking about it. "He would kill me." She laughs, thinking I'm joking, but I know he would not be okay with that union. "When do you go back to work?" I ask.

She closes her eyes and lets out a deep sigh. "Three

days," she says when the flight attendant comes over and places water down for us and then a basket of snacks for the girls. "When do you start training?"

"Tomorrow morning, I should start some cardio," I note, grabbing the basket before Mia pulls it down on her. She grabs the bag of chips, and then I hold it out for Emma, who grabs the cookies. "But in three days, I start ice training with AJ," I say of my off-season trainer. I started using him when I got to town, and as soon as July comes, I start training with him to get ready for the season. He is always challenging me, which is what I look forward to.

"Daddy," Emma says, and I look over at her. "Are we going to Mommy's house?"

"Yes," I answer softly. "And I'm going to miss you so much."

"It's okay, Daddy," Mia says. "Auntie Erika can stay with you."

I laugh. "Maybe she can." Erika shakes her head.

We land, and when we get up, I kiss her on the lips. We both look to see if the girls are watching us, and luckily, they aren't. She wipes the lip gloss off my lips, and I walk out after her with Mia in my arms.

I load the bags while Erika puts the kids in their seats, and when she closes the door, I shut the trunk. "You are dropping me off first," she says, getting on her tippy-toes and kissing my chin and I glare at her, and she laughs. "You go home, unpack, get the girls settled, and then call me."

"Call you," I say when she walks away from me.

"Call you." I shake my head.

"It's this thing where you pick up a phone, and you call the person. When they answer, you say hi," she jokes, getting into the SUV, and I get into the SUV with her.

When we pull up to her street, I already have this weird feeling in my chest, and I don't really know what to do about it or what to say. I pull into her driveway, and she turns and looks at the girls. "I'm home," she tells them, getting out and then opening the back door to kiss Mia and then walking around the other side to kiss Emma. I grab her bag out of the trunk, and she stands in front of me. My heart beats irregularly when she hugs my waist. "Call me after you drop off the girls." I hug her tighter than I have the past two weeks. I kiss her lips softly, pushing her hair back from her face. "See you later, kid," she says, winking at me and then grabbing her bag and rolling it away from me.

I walk back, getting into the SUV, and look back to see the girls. "Are you ready for the next stop?" I pull out, and I make my way over to Julianne's house or, better yet, the house we lived in as a family. When she served me with divorce papers, she asked that she stay in the family home. I didn't want to uproot the girls, so I gave her that. I pull up in the driveway next to the white Range Rover I bought her right before she served me papers. Again, I let her have it for the girls.

"Mommy!" Mia screams, and I smile at them. I open the back door, getting Mia out, and Emma is already standing to jump out of the SUV. I hold her hand as we walk up the pathway I've walked a thousand times before. Stopping in front of the brown door, I ring the doorbell. I take a deep breath when I hear the locks turning and the door opening and see Julianne standing there with a huge smile on her face. She's wearing shorts and a shirt, her blonde hair styled right down the middle and going down in perfect curls on both sides.

"There are my babies." She holds out her arms for them. Emma jumps into her arms as Mia squirms to get out of my arms. She grabs Mia and then bends as the three of them share a hug. "I've missed you guys." I watch her, and I wait for it, waiting for me to remember what it was that pushed me to her. "You guys got so big," she notes and looks up at me with a huge smile on her face, her brown eyes blinking away the tears.

"Come in," she invites me in and moves away from the door.

"I'm going to go get the girls' stuff," I reply, pointing over my shoulder, and she just nods as she turns, and the girls run into the house. Walking back to the SUV, I grab the girls' backpacks and then walk back into the house, feeling like a stranger in the same home we brought the girls home to. The same house we shared and that had family pictures hanging.

I walk down the hallway to the family room and see the family picture is still hanging, but there are lots more with just Julianne and the girls. "The girls went upstairs," Julianne informs me, coming down the stairs. "It's like everything is new for them."

I don't know what to say to her. "Here are the bags."

I hold up my hand.

"Do you want something to drink?" she asks, and I shake my head.

"How was the vacation?" she asks, and all I can wonder is what was I thinking?

"It was good. Relaxing," I share. "The girls had a great time and spent most of it on the beach."

"I'm sure your parents were thrilled to spend time with them," she says, standing there awkwardly.

"It's always fun when they are around. I'm going to go," I say, and I see something in her face. I'm not sure what that look is, but I also realize I don't care.

"Girls!" she yells. "Come say goodbye to your dad." I hear the footsteps as they run to the steps and hold the railing as they walk downstairs. I get down in front of the step and hold out my hands. They each pick a side and hug me.

"Be good for Mom," I say, kissing first Mia and then Emma. "And I'll see you in three days," I tell them, and I already miss them. "And I'll call you guys tonight before bed." I get up and look over at Julianne, and I nod at her.

Walking out of the house, I close the door softly behind me and get into the SUV. Taking my phone out, I call Erika right away. "Hello," she answers on the second ring, and it sounds like she ran to the phone.

"Hi," I say, smiling, and there it is, the feeling I was looking for. The speeding up of my heart and the smile on my face regardless if I want to smile.

"Oh, so you got the whole phone thing settled." She laughs, and all I can do is chuckle.

"What are you doing?" I ask as I make my way over to her house.

"I'm putting away my laundry," she says. "Luckily, I don't have anything to wash."

"Do you want to have dinner with me?" I ask.

"Did you even go home?" she asks.

"Not yet. I just left the girls," I share as I turn on to her street, and she laughs. "I figured that before I went home, I would pick you up."

"I've been home for thirty minutes," she says as she chuckles. "I didn't even pee yet."

"Well," I say to her, parking in her driveway. "Go pee and come outside when you're done."

"Oh my god." She laughs, and I hear her moving. "You aren't really here." I hear her unlocking her door, and then I see her walking out of her house. She stops, shaking her head. "Seriously."

I smile at her and roll down my window, waving. "Oh, and pack a bag."

THIRTY-TWO

Erika

"WHEN YOU SAID come and work out with me," I say while on the treadmill in front of Cooper. "I didn't think you meant you would get on the treadmill with me." I laugh as he slows the treadmill down to zero. "The girls are going to be up any minute," I remind him when he starts kissing my neck. "Cooper." I turn in his arms, and he kisses me. His kisses just get better and better. Just like the sex, fuck, all the sex. I'm waiting for the day that it's not going to feel like the first time all over again.

"Then we have to make it quick," he suggests between kisses, and I shake my head.

"No way." I push him from me. "Go to your corner," I order, and he rolls his eyes. "And put a shirt on."

"Does it bother you?" he asks, looking at me through the mirror. We've been back from the beach for a week, and I haven't slept a night without him. I had thirty-two minutes at my house the first day, and the second day, he showed up with his own bag. He called it compromising. I've slept at his house the past three nights, but I was out of the house before the girls woke up, except for this morning when he asked me to work out with him.

"Well," I reply, putting the speed up on the treadmill. "Would you be able to work out if I took off my sports bra?"

"I'd work out all over you." He smirks at me, and I shake my head. I run on the treadmill for forty-five minutes before I leave. The kids wake up and come downstairs right as he is handing me a protein shake to go. I kiss the girls, and then he walks me to the door and kisses me.

"I'll call you later," he says, and I walk out of his house and head for my SUV. I get home and shower, picking out my outfit. I slide on my tan pants that hug my hips, then flare out just a bit at the knee all the way down to my ankle. I grab a tight pink top with embroidered cream flowers all over it and slide on my nude-colored shoes.

Thirty-five minutes later, I'm walking into the office with a bounce in my step. "Good morning, Shauna." I smile and walk into my office. Pink roses are in the middle of the table on the side. Roses he sent me yesterday because he was thinking of me.

I set my purse down on the table and bend to smell the flowers, the smile coming to my face. This past week has just cemented what I thought I felt for him. I am without a doubt in love with him. Like stick-a-fork-in-me in love with him. Of course, I have yet to tell him or even have this discussion with him because how does one even start that?

"Becca is going to be in tomorrow," Shauna shares, and my heart sinks. When I got back to work last week, the first thing I wanted to do was tell her about Cooper, but she was whisked away on a week vacation by Nico. My stomach starts to rise and then fall, thinking about how I'm going to tell her. Hoping like fuck I don't see the disappointment in her face. She handed me her baby, and I made sure that I handled it with all the love in the world.

"We have a couple of calls today," Shauna says, and I nod, sitting down and checking my schedule.

"I want to reach out to a couple of people," I add, turning on my computer. "There are also a couple of contracts I want to look at."

"Let me know if you need me," she says, turning and walking out of the room.

I spent most of the day on the phone and look up when I hear a knock on my door. The smile on my face is almost forced when I see who is standing there. "Hi," Julianne says, dressed in jeans and a T-shirt with ballerina shoes. "Sorry to come unannounced," she apologizes, and I can tell she is nervous, and she is not the only one.

We haven't told the kids that we are together, but there have been times he's kissed me in front of them. "Come in," I invite, my hands starting to get clammy as she walks in.

"Is it okay if I shut the door?" she asks, and I stand.

"Of course," I reply, walking around the desk. As she

turns to close the door, I take a second to look at her. We couldn't be more opposite. She is shorter than me with blonde hair, and her hair and makeup are perfectly put together. I know from the past that she wouldn't even think about going out if she didn't have herself all put together.

I stand here looking at the woman who gave him a family. Looking at the woman he married and vowed to spend the rest of his life with. The woman who made his dreams come true for a while. "Do you want something to drink?" I ask her when she turns back to me.

"No, this won't take long," she assures me. "I'm sure you're probably wondering why I'm here." She laughs nervously.

"I am curious," I admit.

"Well, I won't beat around the bush, I know that you've always had Cooper's best interest at heart," she starts, and my heart flies to my throat. "So I'm hoping you can help me."

"I will help in any way I can," I say, and I wonder if she can hear my heart beating in my chest. I wonder if she can see how much I love him and not just as my best friend anymore.

"There is no easy way to say this," she admits. "But I had a lot of time to think over the last two weeks when the girls were away." She looks down and then looks up again, saying four words that cut me to the core. "I want him back." She blinks away tears. "I see how wrong I was."

I swallow, trying not to show how shaken this is

leaving me. "You should be having this conversation with Cooper and not with me," I say, the heat rising in my neck as I wonder what he would say.

"I did," she says, and if I thought I was cut to the core before, I was wrong. I expect to look down and see blood seeping out of my chest. I want to ask what he said, but it is not my place. "He said he would think about it." The hurt that goes through me is not a pain I think I could ever describe. It's hurt that he had this conversation with her and didn't tell me and hurt that he said he would have to think about it. Meaning that what we shared meant nothing to him. I don't say anything because there is no way I would even know what to say. "I was hoping that you could put in a good word for me." Her voice trails off. "I know we haven't had the best relationship, but I know that you mean the world to him. And I know if he had your support behind him, he would maybe give it another chance. For the girls."

I blink away the tears that threaten to come, the sting in my nose, and the pain in my chest. "I'll see what I can do," I reply, and she smiles at me.

"Thank you," she says, "for always putting him before anyone and anything." She turns and walks out of my office. Only when I see her turn the corner do I put my hand back on my desk and then my legs give out. I bend forward for a second, catching my breath and thinking I'm going to be sick.

"Shauna." I call her name, and she comes into my office, and I can see from the reaction on her face that I don't look good. "Can I get some water, please?" I ask as

I start to pant. I turn around and sit in one of the chairs that face my desk. A lone tear escapes, and I brush it away quickly before Shauna comes back.

"Here you are," Shauna says. Coming running into the room, she hands me the cold bottle of water. "What do you feel?"

Pain, I want to say. Pain in my whole body. But instead, I shake my head. "I just felt light-headed." I bring the water to my lips and take a sip of the cold liquid. "I skipped lunch," I lie, and she looks at me with her eyebrows together because I usually skip lunch anyway.

"Do you want a cold rag?" she asks, and I just shake my head.

"No, I'll be fine." I force a smile at her. "If you can shut the door," I say, and she nods, knowing I want to be alone.

"Let me know if you need anything," she offers, walking to the door and closing it softly behind her.

As I bring the bottle of water to my lips again, the phone rings on my desk, and I look up to see Cooper's face fill the screen. I get up and press the red button, my hand shaking.

When I sit back in the chair and close my eyes, the conversation replays in my head. "He said he would think about it." I repeat her words out loud at the same time a text comes in.

Cooper: I was thinking we could go out for dinner.
Cooper: Call me when you can.

I don't even open the messages, and I spend the rest of the day avoiding his calls. He even calls the office line, and Shauna knocks on my door to tell me. "I'm busy. I'll call him when I can," I say, pretending that everything is okay. Pretending I'm okay when all along I'm broken inside.

THIRTY-THREE

COOPER

"Do you two want to go swimming?" I ask. "Or do you want to go to the park?" I put their grilled cheese sandwiches on their plate right next to their carrots and celery. Then turn to place it in front of them on the counter. Both of them look at the plate to see if I passed the test.

"Can we go swimming and then to the park?" Emma says, and I want to laugh. Of course she would spin it so they could do both. I look over at the clock on the stove and see that it's just after one. I look down at my phone and see that Erika hasn't texted me all day. Usually, we exchange texts in the morning. Sometimes, it's only one word, but we keep the lines of communication open. It's been a week since we've been back from the beach, and I know without a doubt I love her.

"I think we can," I tell them. I was getting them dressed to go to daycare when I got a call that the daycare is closed because of a broken water valve. I thought about calling Julianne, but I knew it was my day and my problem, so I brought them with me to the ice training since they had a drop-in daycare service there, but I had to cancel the off-ice workout that I had planned outside. No way would they have been quiet for two hours. "If you guys eat all your food," I tell them, grabbing my phone, "then we can go to the pool, and we can swing by the park before I drop you off at your mom's."

I dial Erika's number as I pick up my protein shake and watch the girls. After two rings, it goes to voice mail, and hearing her voice just makes my face fill with a smile. "You've reached Erika." I wait for the beep and then turn.

"It's me," I say. "Just wanted to hear your voice." I walk to the living room in case the girls are listening. "Call me back." I hang up and then text her.

Me: I was thinking we could go out for dinner.
Me: Call me when you can.

I wait a couple of seconds for her to answer, and nothing comes in. The girls finish their lunch, and we get into the pool. The whole time, my phone never rings, nor does she text me back, which is beyond weird. Even if she was in a meeting, she would usually text me back that she was busy.

When the girls get out of the pool, I carry them inside to take a shower, and then I get them dressed. "Okay," I say when Emma gets out of the shower. The phone sits on the counter as I will it to ring. "What do you want to wear?" I ask, and she holds the towel to her chest as she runs to her bedroom and comes back with pink jean shorts and a white shirt.

"You get dressed," I suggest and put Mia in the tub as I wash her hair. Emma gets dressed in the bathroom with us. I grab Mia out of the tub and wrap a towel around her before turning and walking into her room. "Emma, you can go read a story in your room. I'll come and get you when it's time to do your hair." She skips to her bedroom as I walk into Mia's.

I place her in the middle of her pink carpet and dry her off. "Go pick what you want to wear," I say, walking back into the bathroom and picking my phone up.

Me: Can you call me, please?

I give her five minutes to call me before caving and calling her office line. Shauna answers after one ring. "Hi, Shauna, it's Cooper Grant," I announce.

"Oh, hi, Cooper," she replies. "How are you?"

"Good, thanks," I say, walking back to Mia's room. "I was trying to reach Erika, and I can't seem to get ahold of her," I add, my heart pounding in my chest.

"Give me a second," she says as she places me on hold. I'm expecting to hear Erika's voice next, but instead, it's Shauna again. "Hi, sorry, she's a little tied up at the moment," she shares, and I stop in my tracks. "She said she'll call you when she has a minute."

"Oh, okay," I respond, and something in me doesn't sit right. "I'll wait for her call." I hang up the phone, but instead, I call her cell, and when I hear the beep, I talk. "Can you give me a call, please?" I say and then walk into the room to find Mia dressed in a white skirt and a

Dallas shirt.

"Look at my shirt," she says, arching her back as she rubs the front of the shirt. "It's like yours."

I smile at her. "It is like mine," I agree and then walk back into Emma's room. She sits in the little nook that Erika did for her two days ago. A white plush carpet is pushed in the corner with six little pillows for her to lean back on. A basket of books are right next to her. A pink canopy is over her with big white and pink flowers all over the wall. "Ready to do your hair," I say as she puts the book back into the basket and gets up.

"Dad, can Auntie Erika take me to buy more books?" she asks as we walk back into the bathroom.

"I'm sure she can take you," I confirm, grabbing the brush and brushing her hair. She wants me to do a braid while Mia wants two ponytails. She says this holding up five fingers. I bend and kiss her neck, making her giggle.

When they are both settled, I walk to my bedroom to take a shower, leaving the door open in case they need me. I grab my phone again to call Erika, and it goes straight to voice mail. I don't even leave a message. Instead, I text her.

Me: Erika, you call me back.
Me: Now.

I take my shower, and all I can do is think about her. Something is off. I feel it in my bones. When I get out of the shower, I look around my bathroom. Seeing her stuff on the counter mixed with mine makes my chest ache. I walk into my closet, grabbing a pair of boxers and then tossing the towel in the basket. I slip on a pair of shorts and a Dallas shirt. I grab a baseball cap and walk to the room, finding the girls watching a movie.

I clap my hands. "Who wants to go to the park?" I ask them, and they both jump up. I pack their bags while they put on their shoes. I check my phone for the hundredth time, seeing all my texts delivered but no answer.

Parking my SUV at the park, I see that the park is full. I hold their hands as we walk across the grass, and then Emma runs to the jungle gym. I watch her climb up and stand behind Mia while she tries to copy Emma.

I hold Emma and Mia up as they try to make their way across the monkey bars. My phone buzzes in my pocket, and I grab it quickly and see it's just Julianne.

Julianne: Was wondering what time you'll bring the girls over.

Me: I'm at the park. We'll be by after this.

Julianne: See you then.

She ends it with a smiley face emoji, and I just put the phone back in my pocket. After an hour and a half, the girls are out of steam, so we walk back to the SUV. I turn on the air-conditioning while putting them into their seats. Once I get behind the wheel, Emma calls my name. "Can we go to the green lady shop?" I look into my mirror as I watch her. "The one that Auntie Erika always goes to." I smile and take my phone and call Erika, missing her voice. It goes straight to voice mail again, and at this point, I'm ready to drive over to her office.

"Yeah," I reply as we go through the drive-through, grabbing them the drink Erika always gets for them and make my way over to Julianne's house. I call Erika again two more times, and I'm freaking out.

Once I pull into the driveway, I unbuckle the kids and grab their bags so I can drop them and go. They run ahead of me and open the door, running in and yelling for Julianne. I step in and close the door behind me. The smell of cooking fills the air, and I find Julianne in the kitchen. She is squatting down in front of the girls kissing them, and then when she looks up at me, her smile gets even bigger.

"Hi," she says, getting up and walking over to me. "How did it go at the park?" she asks, grabbing the bags from me.

"It was good. Girls, come give me a kiss," I say, itching to get out of here so I can go and find Erika.

"Oh," Julianne says. "I made chicken parm. I was thinking maybe we could have dinner together." She smiles up at me. "It's been a while since we had a family dinner."

"Um, sorry, I have something I have to do," I say and walk over to the girls, bending and kissing them.

"If you want, you can do your errand and we can wait for you," she suggests, and I look at the girls, who are just looking at us.

"Maybe next time," I say, nodding as she hides her disappointment with a smile on her face.

"Let's walk Daddy out," she says, and I look over my shoulder as she walks to the front door with me. I want to ask her what the fuck is going on. I want to stand here and get to the bottom of this, but right now, I need to find

Erika.

"I'll call you guys later," I promise, walking out of the house. Jogging to my SUV, I call Erika and she doesn't answer. I leave a voice mail. "I'm going to your house right now." I hang up and make my way over to her house. I turn on her street and ignore the disappointment in me when her driveway is empty. "Of course it wouldn't be this easy," I say to myself.

Parking my car, I press the code to the door and walk in. "Erika!" I shout, running up the stairs two at a time to go to her room, but I don't know why I expect her to be here. I grab my phone, taking it out of my pocket.

Me: I'm at your house, and I'm going to come to your office.

I press send and know that if she doesn't want me showing up, she'll text me back. Thirty seconds later, the text comes, and my heart speeds up.

Erika: Go home, Cooper.

I shake my head. Something is definitely wrong.

Me: Erika, if I have to drive around all night, I'm not going to stop until I find you.

THIRTY-FOUR

Erika

The phone buzzes in my hand, and I open my eyes, looking down in my lap.

Cooper: Erika, I'm not going anywhere, so the faster you call me, the faster we can talk about this.

I put my head back against the headrest in my car. I left the office not long after Julianne and when Cooper called the office, I knew that he might come by, and I wasn't having my personal life be the talk of the office.

The phone rings in my hand, and I look down, seeing his face staring back at me. My hand shakes as I answer the phone. "Hello," I murmur softly, and I hear his voice.

"Erika," he says breathlessly. I can hear the worry in his voice. "I've been calling you all day."

"Yeah," I reply. Closing my eyes, I try not to let the hurt come, but just hearing his voice makes it hurt. "I saw."

"What the fuck is going on?" he questions. "Where

are you?"

"I'm in my car," I share, and I hear him groan.

"And where is your car located, Erika?" he asks, and I can hear him running.

"Where are you?" I ask him.

"Your house," he says. "Now, where are you?"

I look up at the house. "I'm at the last place I knew you would be at. I'm at your house," I say quietly and then hear a door slam shut.

"I'll be there in four minutes," he says, and he disconnects. I get out of the SUV and walk to his backyard. I sit on the couch as I wait for him. I can hear his SUV arrive, and then I hear the SUV door slam.

"Erika!" I hear him yelling my name, and I brace myself. He walks into the kitchen, and his eyes meet mine, and he comes outside. His blue eyes cloud over, and when he opens the door and comes to me, he gets down in front of me. He pushes my hair behind my ear. "I was so worried," he says, kissing my lips, and I close my eyes as he wraps his arms around my waist and pulls me to him.

"What the fuck is going on?" he asks, sitting on the table in front of me and holding my hands. "Like what happened?"

"I think we need to talk." My heart is beating so hard in my chest it is hard to breathe. I just need to get it out and go home. Just rip it off like a bandage, go home, and pretend you didn't have the best month or so of your life. "This thing between us," I start to say. "Maybe we should re-evaluate."

"The fuck?" he says with confusion on his face. He takes his baseball hat off and throws it on the table beside him, and then takes my hands back into his.

I watch his eyes as I say the next words. "Julianne came to see me," I share. His hands drop from mine, and I wonder if he feels caught. "She told me."

"What the fuck did she tell you exactly?" he asks, getting up and moving away from me. I can see that he's angry, but I just don't know why he's angry. "When you left me this morning, everything was good. So you are going to have to give me more than Julianne told me."

"Well, she told me what you guys discussed," I reply, and he throws his hands up in the air.

"Erika," he says my name between clenched teeth. "I'm teetering on the edge right now. I've just spent all day chasing you down."

I hold up my hand and then cross my arms over my chest and lean back on the couch. "I wasn't running," I say, annoyed he is totally right. "I think there is a difference. Would I be at your house if I was running?" I ask.

He glares at me, and he bites his teeth together. "You need to tell me exactly what was said." I get up, angry that I'm doing this. Angry that I put myself in this position when I knew being with him would kill me. What I didn't know was how much it would hurt.

"Can we not do this?" I demand. He shakes his head and grabs his phone.

"If you are not going to tell me what she said, then I'm going to get her on the phone." He looks down at his phone, and I can see his hands moving so fast. I step to him and snatch the phone from him.

"She said that she made a mistake and she finally realized how much she loves you. She told me she wants you back," I voice. His mouth opens, and I can tell the shock that fills his face. "And she wants me to put in a good word for her since you respect what I say."

"What the fuck?" he growls, and I roll my eyes.

"She said she told you," I relay, looking at him, and for the first time today, I think about the conversation. "She said she wanted you back and that she told you." I shake my head. "You said you would think about it."

"I most certainly did not say I would think about it," he objects, looking into my eyes. "This conversation she had with you is the first I've even heard that she wants me back." He comes to me. "And if she did have this conversation with me, I would have told her that this wasn't ever going to be an option." My hands come up, and I place them on his chest. "It's not an option," he says softly. "How could you think that?"

"I didn't know what to think," I say honestly. "She caught me off guard," I answer him

and put my hand to my head. "I thought she was there because the girls told her about us."

"She's going to hear about us," he says. "She is definitely going to know about us."

"I'm sorry," I say, shaking my head.

"What you mean to say is I'm sorry, Cooper, for not coming to you and talking to you and ignoring your phone calls all day long," he pushes, and I glare at him.

"She came to my office and asked to close the door." I throw my hands up. "What was I supposed to think?"

"You were supposed to think that Cooper would have told me had he had this conversation with Julianne," he points out, putting his hands on his hips. "You were supposed to come to me."

"Well, I know," I mutter, turning and starting to walk out of the yard.

"Where do you think you're going?" he shouts at my back.

"Away from you," I throw over my shoulder. "Because I'm pissed, and you're an asshole."

"Now this," he declares, his voice almost with laughter in it, "this I can deal with." His voice feels like he's right behind me, and when I take one more step, his arm wraps around my waist, stopping me from taking another step. "This," he says beside my ear as he presses his front to my back. "You being pissed at me I can deal with," he whispers softly, and he turns me in his arms. "What I can't deal with is you not answering me." His fingers come out and touch my face. "You need to answer me."

"I was scared," I finally admit it to him, but I leave out the part that I was scared she was telling me the truth. Instead, I lean my head up so he can kiss me, and kiss me he does. He kisses me until I don't remember what I said five seconds ago. He picks me up, and my legs wrap around his hips and I bury my face in his neck. I kiss him softly as he walks through his house and upstairs to his bedroom. The bed is still unmade from this morning when we woke up. The shirt I wore to bed last night is thrown on the chair. I lean back and put one hand on his face, and my eyes look into his. "Thank you," I express, kissing his lips softly, "for coming to find me."

"I would have searched under every fucking rock all over this world to find you," he assures me, and all I want to do is sob out because I'm so fucking happy. "Also, I hate when you wear pants." I throw my head back and laugh. "Your ass looks amazing in them, but it just takes me that much longer to get in you," he explains. I pull the shirt over my head, and he takes his own shirt off. I reach out to touch him, my fingertips rubbing up and down as his hands unclip my bra, and he peels the straps off my shoulder, then bends to suck a nipple into his mouth. The bra falls from my arms when my hands go to the side of my pants as I pull the zipper down. He stands up, watching me as I move my hips side to side to get the pants down. I kick my shoes off, leaving me in my white thong. He pulls his shorts down over his boxers. I can see his hard cock shape as he kicks off his shoes. I walk to him, getting on my tippy-toes, and his finger rubs up and down my slit through the panties. His tongue slips into my mouth when my hand finds his cock. Our hands move in sync as he slides his fingers into my panties and into me.

I let go of his mouth for a second to moan. "Cooper," I say his name as his fingers pick up the pace. "I need you," I plead, and it's the three words I know that make him snap. He picks me up and brings me to the bed, placing me down in the middle. My legs open for him when he crawls on the bed. He peels the panties down my legs, and he tosses them over his shoulder. He bends down and sucks my clit for a second and then gets back on his knees, taking his boxers off and tossing them aside. Grabbing his cock, he rubs it up and down my slit before pushing it slowly inside me. Both of our eyes watch my pussy take him all the way to his balls.

He falls forward on his hands by my shoulders, then starts moving again. Softly this time, in and out as my legs spread wider for him. One hand rubs his arm up and down, and the other hand comes up to his head, bringing it to my lips. I slide my tongue into his mouth as he fucks me over and over again. I let go of his mouth to moan out when I come, his forehead on mine. He doesn't stop, and he doesn't speed up. He keeps fucking me with the same softness that he did when he slipped into me. He kisses me again, and my hand rubs up and down his arm as I try to get closer to him. He lets go of my lips, his nose rubbing mine while he moans as my pussy squeezes him again. "I'm right there," I admit again, and he just keeps going. Nothing is going to get him to go faster. He takes his sweet time fucking me between taking my breath away with kisses. He slows down when I know he's close because, like me, he doesn't want this to end. "Don't stop," I whisper. "Never stop." I look into his eyes when I say this. The words I love you are on the tip of my tongue, but the fear in me stops me from saying them. He picks up his pace again, and when he slides his tongue into me this time, he plants himself all the way inside until his balls slap against my ass and he empties himself inside me.

THIRTY-FIVE

Cooper

MY HEAD FALLS back against the cold tile, and my eyes close as she takes me into her throat. The waterfall shower is falling behind her. "Fuck," I hiss, my eyes opening slowly as I see her bob her head over my cock. Her eyes are closed as her hand works my shaft up and down, and her other hand is between her legs. Her wet hair falls in front of her face. I move it to the side, and her eyes open as she looks at me, her mouth full of my cock. All night we didn't let each other go. Each of us secretly seeking out each other. She twirls her tongue around my cock, and I pull her up to me. Her mouth meets mine as she bends over. My hand comes up to feel how wet she is.

My fingers slide in her, and I swallow her moan, but after a couple of thrusts, she pulls back from my lips to moan my name. "Cooper."

"Climb on," I invite as she moves over to me, and

I think she is going to face me, but she turns around, placing her legs outside of mine. She reaches between her legs to hold my cock and slides down on it. My hands grasp her hips as she rolls her hips, trying to get me in deeper. Her head falls on my shoulder, and she looks over at me, and my chest twinges. I'm so fucking in love with her. I almost told her yesterday, but I don't want her to think I said it because of Julianne or just to calm her. When I say I love her, I don't want her to doubt that I'm telling her just because. I want her to know that I'm doing it because of her and her alone.

I move my head to hers and slide my tongue into her mouth, and she starts to ride me. My hands move to her tits and I tweak her nipples and then one hand slides down to her clit, wet from the shower water. My middle finger goes round and round on her clit as my other hand pinches her nipples, and she picks up her pace. I can tell she's close because she's not moving her tongue in my mouth. She lets go of my mouth to pant out and close her eyes. "Want to come together?" I ask between clenched teeth because if she squeezes my dick anymore, only one of us will be coming this time. Her eyes open as she looks at me. Both our mouths open as we both fucking come together, my hand on her clit rubbing even faster. When she finishes coming on my cock, she slumps on me. I kiss her neck, holding her hips again. "Happy Saturday," I announce, and she laughs.

I get out of the shower before she does, wrapping myself in a towel. I walk to the closet and pull out a pair of shorts. "I'm going to start the coffee." I stick my head back into the bathroom, seeing her step out. She wraps her hair in a towel and smiles at me.

"You read my mind," she says, winking at me. I turn and shake my head, walking down the steps to the kitchen. I take out the coffee and start hers, walking over to the fridge and grabbing the flavored creamer she likes.

Walking back over, I put the creamer on the counter. Her arms wrap around my waist, and she places little kisses on my back. "You smell better than the coffee," she teases, laughing, and I look over my shoulder, seeing her hair hanging wet as she's wearing one of my big T-shirts.

"Is that so?" I turn and kiss her lips. "Nothing sexier," I say softly, looking down at her, "than you in my clothes."

She laughs. "Really?" She looks up, and her green eyes sparkle with mischief. "Well, maybe I might be inclined to wear one of your shirts and let you fuck me from the back so you can see your name on me." My cock springs to action as she pushes away from me and goes to grab the coffee. She makes her coffee and then mine as I walk to the fridge and take out some fresh fruit for her.

"Look at this." I pick up the can of whipped cream in my fridge. "I see this in your future," I state, and she rolls her eyes at me, bringing her coffee cup to her mouth.

"You can eat it off my pussy, only if I get to lick it off your cock."

"You know that with either of those options, I don't lose." I close the fridge door. "And neither do you."

She laughs as we make breakfast side by side, and I wrap my arm around her shoulder when the doorbell rings. I look at the clock on the stove and see it's just after nine in the morning. "Expecting anyone?" she asks, and I shake my head and leave her in the kitchen to walk to the door.

I unlock the door and open it, stunned and shocked to see Julianne and the girls. "Daddy!" Emma shrieks, and I literally just blink.

"I'm sorry. I should have called," Julianne apologizes, and I look at her. She stands there in shorts and a T-shirt. "But the girls and I were wondering if you would like to come on a bike ride with us," she says at the same time that I hear Erika behind me.

"So who was it?" she asks, coming into sight, and Julianne looks at me and then at Erika, and there is no denying we spent the night together. She stands there, taking in the scene at the door and stopping in her tracks as Emma runs past me toward Erika.

"Auntie Erika!" Emma says, stopping in front of her and jumping up and down. "Daddy and Mommy are going to take me on a bike ride," she says, and I can see Erika's shield come down. She takes in the whole scene and then turns to her. "It's family time."

A smile fills her face. "Really?" she replies, bending and tapping her nose. "That sounds like so much fun."

"Um, I should have called," Julianne says. I know this conversation has to happen, but I just wish I didn't have to leave Erika to do it.

"Erika," I say, grabbing Mia and turning to walk back

to her. "Can you take the kids for a second while I talk to Julianne?" She avoids my eyes, and I see the struggle that she has to swallow.

I can see the tears forming in her eyes, and she looks at Emma. "Who wants a snack?" she asks, grabbing Mia from me and turning to walk into the house. I want to go after her, but first, I need to talk to Julianne.

"Why don't we step outside?" I tell Julianne, not ready for her to start shit in my house and twist it in front of the girls.

I step outside, and she looks at me. "What the fuck is going on?" she asks in almost a whisper. I walk over and sit down on the step and look over at her.

"I think we need to discuss a couple of things," I suggest, and she cocks her hip and looks at me.

"About you fucking Erika?" she asks, and this right here is why I didn't want to do this inside.

I look at her, and my tone is softer than I want it to be. "Julianne," I start, and she just shakes her head as she blinks away tears. "Trust me, the last thing I wanted was for you to find out like this," I say honestly. "I mean, you were going to find out today, that is for sure." I swallow. "But not like this."

"How can this be?" she asks. I knew it. Like deep down inside, I knew this day would eventually come. She rubs her hands over her face. "You said she was your best friend."

"And she is," I confirm to her. "She is my best friend and …" I stop talking because saying she's the love of my life will not go over well. "I think we need to start with what you told her yesterday," I add, and I see her face go a shade of white.

"I went to her for help," she defends. "Because I realized that I had everything I ever wanted, and I stupidly let it go," she admits to me. "And I wanted her to help me talk to you about it."

"Shouldn't you have been the one who talked to me about it?" I ask, and she comes over to me and sits next to me. "You didn't even tell me any of this. You went straight to Erika."

"I thought I would tell you today," she explains.

"You told her that I said I would think about it," I try to say as calmly as I can, but it comes out harsh and she looks down. "Julianne, I love you because you are the mother of my children," I say finally. "But I don't love you like that."

"How long has this been going on?" she asks, and I know she's really asking me if it was going on while we were married.

"A couple of months. Nothing started until after we were officially divorced."

She pffts. "You really expect me to believe you?"

"I expect you to believe me because it's the truth. I've never lied to you, and I never will. I was faithful to you the whole time." My voice goes soft. "I was with you the whole way. I gave you everything," I remind her, and she just looks at me.

"No, you weren't," she denies, wiping away the tear that comes out of her eyes. "The whole time we were married, you were always holding back," she says, and

I'm shocked. "You were married to me, and we had children, but there was always something missing." I listen to her words.

I swallow. "I'm sorry you feel that way. I'm sorry I wasn't the man you deserved."

"But we have a family. We have two girls. Shouldn't we try for them?"

I look at her, really look at her. "In the end, I think we were always going to end up here," I admit for the first time. "I think we were both swept up in what we were expected to be." She turns to look out onto the street. "Can you honestly say you were happy?" I ask, and she doesn't say anything. "Can you honestly say you love me?"

"We were happy," she says and then admits, "Sometimes." I put my arm around her. "This sucks," she says, and we both laugh.

"It does," I admit, getting up. "I don't know what to tell the girls."

"I'll tell them I forgot we have to go bake a cake or something." She gets up and stands next to me. "I'm sorry I showed up like this."

"I was going to call you later to tell you and have this conversation with you," I admit. "It was time."

She nods as I open the door, and we walk in. "I'm going to wait here," she states, and I nod. Walking into the kitchen, I see the girls sitting at the counter eating a plate of fruit.

I look around. "Hey," I tell the girls. "Where is Erika?"

"She said she had to go to the bathroom," Emma

offers, getting off her stool. "Are we going on the bike ride?"

"Um," I say, smiling down at her. "Maybe another time. I think Mommy said something about making a cake."

"I want cake," Mia says, pushing down as I walk them both to the door.

"I'll call you later," I promise the girls and then Julianne smiles at me. I watch them get into the SUV and pull out, turning and closing the door.

I walk up the steps two by two, and when I get into the room, I know nothing will be the same again.

THIRTY-SIX

ERIKA

"WHAT'S GOING ON?" I hear from the doorway, and I brace myself, sliding my pants up my hips and tucking my shirt in. My eyes never move from looking down.

"I'm getting dressed," I reply, zipping up my pants and walking over to the side of the bed where I just saw my shoe. Tossing the pillow off it, I grab it.

"I can see that," he says, and I can't look at him because I know if I do, I'll cave. I have to do this for him. "Care to tell me why?" His voice comes out calm, and I wonder if Julianne is still downstairs with the kids. When the doorbell rang, the last thing I expected was to see Julianne and the girls. It felt like the world was slipping away from me. As if my body was on the outside looking in.

"Family time, Emma said." If I thought my heart was shattered yesterday after Julianne, I was wrong. Nothing could have prepared me for the pain that I had looking into her baby blue eyes and seeing that I was the one standing in her way. I settled the girls on their stool as I handed them something to eat. The tears ran down my face as I wiped them away so they wouldn't see. I ran as fast as I could upstairs, making sure that I would be downstairs and ready to go when he came back in. I tore through the room like the Tasmanian devil, grabbing my clothes and dressing, and I rushed around the room. The tears made it hard to see in front of me. I thought I was doing good for time, but then I heard his voice.

"Well," I say, putting on my shoe and then walking around the bed to find the other one, tossing the pillows on the bed as I make my way through the room. I pick up his shirt from last night and then see the heel of the shoe sticking out from under his pants. "For one, I was trying to keep myself busy, and for two." I find the shoe and finally look at him. "I didn't know if Julianne was going to come back into the house, and well, I didn't want to be in just a T-shirt." I look into his eyes, and the tears sting my own. If I ever do anything for anyone in my life, it has to be for him. I have to give him this. The way Emma smiled at me and said she was going for a family bike ride, it broke me inside. Was I the one stopping him from having all of this?

"I see," he says, coming into the room, and all I can do is stay stuck to the floor. My feet are almost as if they are glued to this one spot.

"Listen," I start, swallowing down the words and bracing myself for what is to come. "I just want you to know that if you've changed your mind," I force out, my voice trailing off. "It's okay." I smile, and the one tear comes out. "I mean, I understand. Julianne and you, you have a family. There is a lot of history there." I leave out that he is the best thing to ever happen to me, as the sob threatens to return, I avoid his eyes. I can't look him in the eyes. My hands are shaking, so I walk back to the bed, and I sit. My head down, I close my eyes for just a second to gather all the strength I need to get this conversation over with.

I can hear him moving in the room, then I can see his feet in front of me. He squats down, taking my hand in his. "Erika." He calls my name, and my eyes come up to his. "What are you saying?" he asks softly, his hand coming up to hold my face.

"It's everything that you've ever wanted," I reply, knowing he deserves for me to be honest with him. "You can have everything that you've ever dreamed of having." I can feel the tears coming as I look at him. My whole chest is aching for him.

"And what do you think I've ever wanted?" he asks softly, his thumb rubbing my cheek.

"Family," I say, the tear escaping the corner of my eye, and I turn quickly to stop him from seeing. "The family you've always wanted. You've said your whole life that is what you wanted." I smile at him. "And I'm not going to stand in the way of that." I swallow, my heart is beating so hard in my chest it's all I can hear. He bends his head and kisses my hand. "The first time I met with you and asked you what you wanted, you answered a family." I look at him. "You said whatever I do in my career will be amazing, but I want a family to come home to." I remind him of the words he told me when he turned twenty. I look at him, my heart breaking that I won't be the one who gives him this. "So, I'm telling you that it's okay if you changed your mind." I smile at him. "We can still be friends," I start to say and stop when my voice trembles.

"I'm not interested in just being your friend," he insists and then pulls me in his arms. Arms that held me all night long. Arms that make me feel safer than I have ever felt. Arms that I would recognize blindfolded. "Is it my turn yet?" he asks softly, letting me go. "I'm just waiting for it to be my time to speak." His smell is all over me, making my chest ache. "I'm waiting for you to get it all out of your system."

"I know that it's not going to be an easy decision either way," I state.

"Erika." He calls my name, and I stop. "Before you leave and walk out of this room, there are a couple of things you need to know." I close my eyes and exhale a breath out. My head is telling me to walk out of the room, yet my heart is telling me to turn around. I hold the bag in both hands so he doesn't see them shaking.

"I didn't want to do this, this way," he explains, and my stomach flips even more. "When we were on vacation, I spoke with my father." I can't say anything because the lump in my throat won't even allow me to even breathe at this point. "I told him I was in love with you," he says the words, and I gasp out in shock. "Actually, to be honest, I told him I was firing you and then he called me a dumbass, so I had to admit I was in love with you." My hands come up to hold his face. "Which made him call me a bigger dumbass because you see, he's made me see that." He smirks. "I've been in love with you since I can remember. I've loved you for what feels like my whole life." He comes to me as the tears pour down my face.

"Do you really mean that?" I ask before blinking away what feels like the biggest tears I've ever had. My whole chest feels so full I put my hand on it.

"That night when I took you on a date, I wanted to tell you then," he admits to me, holding my face in his hands. "Then yesterday I got home, and I wanted to tell you then also." His thumbs rub my tears away. "But I knew you would think it was only because of Julianne."

He takes a breath. "It's always been you," he confirms. "Everything that has happened." He smirks. "Meeting Julianne, getting traded, getting divorced. It was all going to end up at the same place." I close my eyes as I listen to his words. "I love you with every single being of my body, Erika." He kisses my lips. "Like head over heels in love with you." He shrugs. "I guess I always have been."

I don't even stop the tears that come as he kisses my lips softly. "I have to say something."

"No, because I'm not done."

"Well, can you hurry up, please?" I ask, I can't stop the smile from filling my face.

"You asked me what I wanted most out of all this," he says. "And you're right, I did say family." I nod my head. "What if that family is with you?" I sob out. He takes me in his arms, and I smell him, and he smells of my home. He smells of me. He smells of everything that makes me happy.

"I love you," I whisper, admitting what my heart has known for a long time.

THIRTY-SEVEN

Cooper

"I LOVE YOU," she declares, smiling as my heart finally settles down. Watching her struggle with doing the right thing and stepping aside.

"You know you can't take it back, right?" Kissing her lips softly and tasting her tears. "Like it's out there. You can't come back and say I made a mistake."

She pushes me away. "I was doing what was best for you." She holds up her hands. "It's called sacrificing for the ones you love."

"What about you?" I ask. "What do you get in all of this?"

"You," she says. "Happy. That was my reward. Emma's eyes were so happy when she said family time. What was I supposed to do?"

"You were supposed to be like, wait a second, does Cooper want this?" I state, and she glares, making me laugh.

"Cooper Grant," she huffs, putting her hands on her hips. "You just declared your love for me and pissed me off in the same moment."

"You know what that means, right?" I question and laugh. "It means I really, really love you."

She shakes her head. "What are you going to tell the girls?" she asks, and this is another reason I love her so much. She refuses to think of herself before anyone, even someone who has not been that nice to her on the best of days.

"Well, for one, I don't know how much they will understand, but it's not like they don't know you. Or they haven't seen me kiss you," I point out to her. "So I think it'll be okay."

"I think you still need to tell them something," she decides, and I nod. "Cooper," she says, and I smirk at her. "I love you."

"I said it first," I reply, and she shrugs.

"Technically, I said it first while you were sleeping," she says, and I walk back to her, grabbing her face.

"You know what we do next, right?" I say. "Make-up sex."

"What we are going to do next," she says, "is go eat something, and then I have to call Becca and ask her to come over."

"Okay, so you call Becca," I concede, kissing her. "I'm going to go cook, and then we have make-up sex." She throws her head back and laughs. I kiss her before walking down the stairs, this time with the biggest smile on my face.

I walk back into the kitchen and clean up the plates the girls left and look up when I hear her running down the stairs. "They are going to be here in ten minutes!" she exclaims, looking at me with her face pale. "What the fuck? Who is out of the house at this time of the day on a Saturday?"

"They have kids," I remind her. "I think Phoenix goes skating."

"Well, whatever, she's going to be here in five minutes," she warns and then starts to pace. "Should I change my outfit?" She looks down at what she was wearing yesterday. "I mean, this is basically a walk of shame." She turns and runs back up the stairs. "I'm going to change."

I shake my head and make another coffee as I hear her yelling from the bedroom. "I don't even have time to go home and change!" she shouts, coming back into the kitchen wearing blue jeans and a long-sleeve sweater that goes off her shoulder. "Does this look like I didn't sleep here last night?"

"It's before noon, and she's meeting you here," I point out to her. "I think it's too late to ask that," I say as the doorbell rings.

"Fucking hell," she curses, putting her head back. "I haven't even thought about what I'm going to say to her."

"I can help," I assure, walking past her and toward the door.

"No," she whispers. "Don't say anything." She puts her hand on her stomach. "I think I'm going to throw up."

I unlock the door, and I'm stunned to see Nico with her. "Sorry, I told him to wait in the car," Becca apologizes. "But well, he's Nico."

"It's fine," I say, moving aside so they can come in. "This is better. We can get two conversations in one." Nico looks at me, and I can see his eyes are worried.

"I felt that I needed to be here," Nico states, "since it has to do with one of my players."

"Would you like some water or coffee?" I ask, and they both shake their heads.

"Where do you want to do this?" I ask Erika, who just smiles.

"Anywhere," she answers. "Why don't we go to the family room, so it's more conformable and less formal."

"Well, that's a good sign," Becca says, grabbing Nico's hand and telling him to relax.

I wait for them to sit down before taking a seat next to Erika. "Thank you for coming," Erika says. And I can tell she is really nervous, so I grab her hand in mine. "Becca." She turns to Becca. "I can't thank you enough for what you've done for me," she says and looks down, and I can see her struggling as she wipes away a tear. "Giving me a shot right out of the gate and putting your trust in me, it meant everything."

"Are you starting your own firm?" Becca asks, not giving her a chance to finish.

"God, no," Erika replies, and then she laughs nervously.

"What she is trying to say is that I want to fire her," I finally say, and Nico sits up. "I would like to have someone else represent me."

"Why the hell would you want that?" Nico asks. "She's bent over backward for you. She's brought you deals left, right, and center, and she squeezed my …" He stops before he says balls. "Neck the last time."

"I am thankful for everything she has done for me," I respond. "But I think that it would be a—"

"We're dating," Erika cuts in and says. "I'm dating Cooper." She looks at me. "Like a Band-Aid."

"Wait a second," Nico voices, sitting up and looking at us. "This meeting isn't about you wanting to be traded?" I just look at him.

"And it's not about you starting your own firm?" Becca reaffirms, and Erika just looks at her. "Oh, thank god." Becca looks at Nico. "Told you it was nothing serious."

"How was I supposed to know?" Nico defends, relaxing back onto the couch. "Who calls someone on a Saturday?" Shaking his head, he looks at us.

"Well, in my defense," Erika explains, "I wanted to tell you last week, but you were out of the office." I put my arm around her and bend down to kiss her shoulder. She looks at me, smiling shyly.

"Well, it's about time," Nico says, rubbing Becca's back. "It's been interesting watching the two of you."

I share a look with Erika. "It was like watching two hamsters in a cage both going around and around," Becca jokes. "I'm just happy you took the chance." She looks at me. "But if you hurt her." She smiles, and it's a friendly smile but looks almost like she is ready to stab me in the leg. "Well, let's just say it won't be pretty."

"Are you threatening my player?" Nico quizzes, chuckling.

"Me," she says, putting her hand to her chest. "I'm not threatening him; I'm informing him that if he hurts my girl, well …" She smiles at Nico, then turns back at me. "Shit is going to get very real."

I swear a shiver courses up my spine. "Duly noted," I concede and then look at Erika, making a mental note to ask her how serious she is.

Nico gets up. "Okay, I can breathe a little bit easier," he says, holding out his hand to Becca. "How about we head home?" She slides her hand in his, and we walk them out as they both wish us well.

Becca stops walking and turns around. "I'm going to send you an amended contract on Monday. Don't fuck up until then." She smirks at me.

"I'll be on my best behavior," I declare to her, and Erika wraps her arm around my waist. Only when they drive away do I look down at Erika.

"Define best behavior," she questions. "Because we have make-up sex to do, and then we have to have the I-love-you sex and then."

"And then we have to discuss you moving in here," I announce, turning and walking back into the house. I wait for her at the door as she walks in. "What do you want to do first?" I ask. "Make-up sex, I-love-you sex, or talk about moving in?" I ask, pulling her in my arms. "We can have this discussion with my cock in you." I bend and suck her neck. "You tend to give me what I want when you are underneath me." I smirk at her. "Or on top of me." I nip her lips. "Or in front of me." I pull her shirt off her and find her with her pink lace bra. "Hmmm," I appreciate, bending and I'm about to take her nipple in my mouth when my phone rings from somewhere in the house. "Hold that thought," I say, running to the kitchen and seeing that it's my father.

I press the connect button, and his face fills the screen. "Hey," he greets, and I can see that he's in the kitchen at home. "Your mom and I were just talking," he says, and I look up to see Erika coming into the room with her shirt back on.

"Yeah," I reply to him, walking to sit on the stool. "I'm here with Erika."

"Hi, Erika," my mother pipes in from somewhere in the kitchen, and then I see her face on the screen.

"Hi, Karrie," Erika says from beside me as she grabs a piece of strawberry and tosses it into her mouth.

"Anyway, your mother and I were thinking about coming to visit next weekend. Maybe for the week," he informs us. "We miss the girls."

I laugh. "They will be so excited to hear you are coming."

"Good. We are going to look at renting a house."

"Oh, don't bother, you can stay at Erika's place," I comment, and Erika just looks at me with her mouth hanging open.

"Oh, is she going away?" my father asks, and then my mother comes into the screen to see my face.

"What are you doing?" I hear Erika whisper at me.

"Ripping it off like a Band-Aid," I explain and then look at my parents. "We're moving in with each other."

"Oh my god," my mother and Erika say at the same time.

"Is that so?" my father says, smirking.

"Yeah, we were just discussing this," I reveal and look at Erika, who just shakes her head.

"We were not discussing anything," she finally says, taking the phone from me. "But you can stay at my house any time you want. I will be staying there as well." She glares at me and I take the phone.

"No, she won't," I tell them.

"Oh my," is the only thing my mother says.

"Send me the details," I tell my father, who just smiles.

"Proud of you," he praises, and my mother glares at him. "What?" he asks her.

"Matthew Grant," she scolds. "Did you not hear what Erika said? They were not discussing it."

"They weren't discussing it because it was already decided she's moving in with him," my father states, and I look at Erika, who just looks at me with huge beautiful eyes.

"I can't argue with that logic," I agree, laughing, and I grab her chair and pull her to me. "Give me a kiss," I say, and my parents stop talking to watch the screen. I bend and rub her nose with mine. "Love you," I whisper right before I kiss her softly.

"See," I hear my father speak. "She's moving in with him."

THIRTY-EIGHT

Erika

"Hey." I answer the phone as soon as I see it's him. A smile comes to my face even though I don't want it to.

"Hi," he says softly. "Where are you?" I can tell he's getting into the SUV after hearing the door slam.

"I'm at my house," I reply, looking around the closet. "Where are you?"

"Just left the rink. I was dragging my ass out there," he shares, and I laugh.

"Why would you book a training session on a Sunday?" I ask him. This morning when his alarm went off, the only thing I could open was one eye. He spent all night trying to get me to agree to move in. And I mean all night. "It's Sunday, rest day," I remind him.

"In my defense," he says, laughing, "I didn't think I would be up all night trying to convince you to move in with me."

"You definitely worked really hard," I say, folding my

stuff. I got up about forty minutes after he left and came here to think.

"Where in your house are you?" he asks, and I hear a car door slamming.

"I'm sure you can find me," I tease. Tossing the phone beside me on the floor, I look around at the pile of clothes surrounding me. I hear the front door close, and then I can hear him coming up the steps.

"Erika." He says my name, and then I see him standing in the doorway to the closet. He is wearing gym shorts and a Dallas shirt. His hair is wet at his neck but a baseball cap is on his head.

"Did you shower?" I ask before he takes a step into the closet and shakes his head. "You do not step one foot closer to me until you shower." I point at him, and he kicks off his shoes and gets naked in front of me.

"Do you want to join me?" He smirks at me, and I shake my head.

"As much as I'd love to," I say, "I can smell you from here." He laughs, walking to the bathroom.

My stomach is in knots as I look around and make piles. It takes him ten minutes, and he comes out with a towel around his hips. He comes to me and bends to kiss my lips. "Better?" he asks, and I smile.

"It would be better if you brought me a coffee," I say, looking at my watch and seeing that it's just after ten.

"Do you want me to go make coffee?" he asks, getting dressed in front of me. He looks around and sees the piles of clothes all around me. "What are you doing?"

"I came home after you left to think," I explain,

folding another one of my silk shirts. I don't even know what I'm folding or why. I was just keeping my mind busy while I worked through things in my head.

He sits behind me, putting his arms around my waist and kissing my neck. "What are you thinking about?" he asks softly, resting his chin on my shoulder.

"I'm thinking about this whole moving in," I reply, my hand going up to his face.

"Why don't we talk about it?" he says, and I chuckle.

"The last time you said that, you pushed my shirt up and ate me on the couch," I remind him.

"You were sitting in front of me with a white shirt on and no bra. And your nipples were teasing me." I side-eye him. "And it was a tight shirt."

"And you dragging my legs off the couch and burying your head between my legs?" I ask.

"That was you again, opening your legs while sitting on the couch," he declares, and I can't help but laugh.

"Do you think this moving in with you is a little bit too fast?" I ask, turning in his arms. "We just started dating."

"We've been living with each other for over a month," he reminds me, and I tilt my head.

"We were on vacation for two weeks." I laugh. "Things don't count when you're on vacation because everyone is happy."

"Okay, fine. But I want to know that you'll be there when I come home." He looks down. "I want to go to bed knowing that you will be going to bed with me." His eyes find mine. "Is it the house you don't like? Do you want me to move in here?" He shrugs. "I don't have a problem with that. I don't care where we live as long as it's together. Are you okay with making two rooms for the girls?" I smile at him. "I'm sure they'll be okay if they can move all their stuff here."

"Why are you so amazing?" I ask, rolling my eyes. "It's your most annoying quality."

He laughs. "It's just stuff," he relays. "It's all just material stuff. What matters is that you and the girls are there. None of the rest means anything to me."

"What if we get on each other's nerves?"

"What if we don't?" he asks, and I roll my eyes.

"Living together doesn't mean you're going to prison. It means that we share a home. We share a bed and our lives. I'm not expecting to be handcuffed to you."

I laugh. "That might be fun." I lean over and kiss his lips.

"Can we do a trial run?" I ask, and he smirks.

"We can call it whatever you want to call it," he confirms. "We can call it a vacation if you want. As long as you are there when I go to bed and wake up, I don't care what label you put on it." He pulls me to him, folding his legs around me. "So what do you say, Erika? Want to vacation with me?"

I put my hand up to his cheek, his scruff on his face pricking my fingertips, but I love it. "Okay." I kiss him. "Let's vacation together at your house."

It takes us six hours to pack up most of my clothes, and that included an hour when he buried his face between my legs. It takes his SUV and my SUV to transport all the hanging clothes, and when I walk into his closet that night, I see him standing there looking around. He is dressed in boxers, and that is it.

"Change your mind?" I ask, leaning against the doorway. My hair is piled on top of my head after getting out of the shower. He looks over at me and smirks.

"Nope." I walk to him and wrap my arms around his waist. "I don't think I've ever been this happy to share a closet with someone." He puts his arm around me, and I look down to see the towel he had around his waist on the floor.

"Well, if you leave wet towels on the floor …" I joke with him, not even caring, and he knows it. "When are you going to tell the girls?"

"When they get here tomorrow," he says. "I'm going to tell Julianne." I nod. "Then the girls." My heart speeds up because, at the end of the day, his main commitment is to his kids. And I love him more for it. "Can you relax?" he asks, and I look up at him. "You've been here pretty much the whole month, and they haven't even said anything."

"Me being here when they wake up is one thing," I share, walking over and picking up the towel. "My stuff being everywhere is another thing."

"Are you going to change and treat the girls differently?" he asks, and I gasp. "Exactly. So as long as nothing changes, it's going to be fine."

"You're being annoying," I accuse, rolling my eyes at him.

The next day, I get home from work, and I already have shaky hands. The sounds of my gold sandals click on the pathway as I look down at my outfit one last time before stepping in. This morning, I chose the pink pencil skirt with white flowers that Mia loves and a long-sleeve, sheer, high-collared silk shirt that Emma loves. I open the door and it all feels strange as I walk into the house putting my purse on the stairs and then walking into the house. "Hello?" I call out to them. I find them in the kitchen.

"Hi," I greet, walking in, the girls looking over at me. I walk to Emma first and kiss her head like I always do and then to Mia. "How was your day?" I ask, talking to Cooper. He bends and kisses my lips, my eyes going to the girls to see that they don't even care.

"Told you," Cooper says, grabbing the salmon out of the oven. "Now, do you want to change before dinner?"

"Yeah," I state. Walking upstairs to the bedroom, I grab a pair of shorts and a tank top to change. When I walk back downstairs, I hear Cooper.

"She went to change her clothes. Remember you saw all her clothes in Daddy's closet?" I watch from afar to see if they will say anything.

"Did she bring all her clothes?" Emma asks, and he nods. "And her shoes?"

"Yes," he says, preparing the plates. "Just like I have all my stuff here, so does Erika."

"But I have stuff at Mommy's house," Emma says, and I put my hand to my stomach.

"That's because you get two houses." He smiles at her. "You have clothes at Mommy's and at my house. But when you live at one house, all your stuff stays at the one house.”

She doesn't ask any more questions, and when I walk back into the room, she looks over at me. “You have to share a bed with Daddy,” she declares. “He takes all the covers.”

I chuckle. “Maybe he'll learn to share.” I walk over to him and put my arm around his waist. “Will you share your covers with me?” I ask him with a smile.

“I'll share everything with you,” he confirms, and his eyes say so much more. That night, the routine changes a bit. Usually, he's the one doing everything, but I ask the girls if I could read them a bedtime story, and just like that, another routine is created.

EPILOGUE ONE

Cooper

One year later

I WALK INTO the house and slam the door behind me. "Erika!" I yell her name, and I can hear her moving around upstairs.

"What?" she shouts back, and I run up the steps two at a time. "Where are you?"

"In the closet packing," she states, and I see her on the floor in front of her luggage. "How many days are we going to be at the beach?" she asks, and I put my hands on my hips.

"Is there something you need to tell me?" I take off my baseball hat and toss it on the custom-made island thing she said she just had to have.

She looks at me confused. "Not that I know of," she says, looking down at her bag. She's dressed in shorts and a T-shirt with her hair piled on her head. "Why, what happened?" She places another shirt in her luggage. We leave tomorrow to go on a two-week family vacation. This time, we are going to Mexico and even more of us are going since Dylan just beat our grandfather's rookie record.

"Oh, I can think of two point six million things you have to talk to me about." I look at her, my cock unaffected by my anger toward her.

"Oh, that," she glosses over. "Glad it finally came through."

"One," I say to her, holding up my finger. "How did you get my account number?" I hold up another finger. "And two, what the fuck, Erika?"

She chuckles. "Well, one …" She holds up her finger, and she is so fucking gorgeous. I'm already over whatever it was that bothered me. "I have your account number from your checks that you have in that top drawer, but also, I was your agent. And two"—she holds up the other finger—"it's half the house." She smiles at me. "Since my house sold and you put my name on this house, it was only fair I paid you for it." We have been living together for a year, and she finally put her house on the market. It sold in four days.

"You aren't paying me for the house, Erika," I insist, walking out of the closet. "I'm going to tell them to send it back."

"Don't be a dumbass," she says, and I see her walking out of the closet. "Now, can you please pack your stuff while I get the things for the girls ready?" Walking to me, she gets on her tippy-toes and kisses me under my chin.

She heads to the girls' bedrooms. Ever since she moved in, things couldn't be better. The girls are thriving as they have their girls' nights out. Hockey games are so much different. She comes to most of the games with the girls, and the three of them wear my jersey. I walk down the hallway to Emma's room, passing the pictures on the walls of us with the girls.

"Erika," I say her name, and she looks up at me, unfazed by what I said. "I'm not kidding."

"Fine," she concedes. "Then I'm paying rent."

I put my hands on my hips. "Is that so?"

She stands up and puts her hands on her hips. "I suggest you pick your battles, Mr. Grant."

My cock gets even harder when she calls me Mr. Grant. "And why is that?"

"Well, I went to the doctor today," she shares, and I look at her weirdly as she walks out of the room with the girls' luggage.

"Okay. Are you okay?" I see she has tears in her eyes. "Why would you go to the doctor?"

"Well, I was feeling a little sluggish," she explains, and my heart sinks, thinking the worst. "And I felt sick for like that whole month you were in the playoffs. I thought it was my nerves," she reminds me and then walks back into the bedroom. I follow her and see all the little changes she's made. The picture of us by the bed, the chairs that she brought from her house. The throw pillows with a matching blanket that gets tossed to the floor every night. She turns. "I'll tell you, but you can't freak out."

"Okay," I agree, and she holds up her hand.

"And you keep the money." She walks over to the white envelope on the bedside table.

"Erika," I grit out between clenched teeth as she hands me the envelope, and I can see tears in her eyes.

I grab the envelope from her and open it, taking out the small piece of paper inside. My heart goes to my throat as I look up at her. "We're having a baby," she announces, looking up at me. I look down at the ultrasound picture.

"How?" I ask, my heart feeling so full in my chest it's making it hard to breathe.

"Well, if you pull the goalie and then shoot a million pucks at it, one is bound to score," she jokes. Three months ago, she took out her IUD and decided to go on the pill in case we wanted to start trying. If truth be told, I started trying that night. "Plus, it takes a month for your body to get used to the pill, and well, your pull-out method sucks."

The only thing I can look at is the picture. "We're having a baby," I whisper and look down at her. This woman, who is my best friend and has been by my side through thick and thin, is making all of my dreams come true.

"We are having a baby," she confirms, putting her hand on her stomach as the tears stream down her cheeks.

I grab her face and kiss her softly. "Well, just one more thing to do," I declare, and she looks at me. "We're getting married."

EPILOGUE TWO

ERIKA

Five years later

"YOUR DAUGHTER JUST said 'I will cut you off at the knees,'" I tell Cooper when he walks into the house. Our daughter is sitting on the stool with her brown hair and blue eyes, looking all angelic, but with her father's smirk.

He looks over at her as she tries to hide the smile, knowing that. "To who?" he asks, smirking.

"To a little boy at daycare," I inform him, and he shrugs.

"Serves him right," he replies, and I just shake my head. "Maybe he went into her bubble."

"He did, Daddy," she says, and I just glare at my husband. He was not kidding. When we got to Mexico, he told his father that I was pregnant, and then I swear within a week, I was walking down the aisle. I really didn't care as long as he was by my side, and I walked down the aisle with Emma and Mia holding my hand. "He came into the bubble," she states, her hands around her head.

"Go wash your hands," I say. She nods and gets down, running to the bathroom. "Last time she was with your father, she went to school and told the boys to keep their penises in their pants."

He tries to hide the laughter, but he can't. "That was bad."

"For the whole vacation, he was like when you have a boy, you worry about one penis. When you have a girl …" I start to repeat what Matthew said.

"You worry about every penis out there," he finishes. "He's not wrong."

"Cooper Grant," I scold, putting my hands on my hips that have grown so wide with this pregnancy. "Do not test me right now."

He sets his glass down and comes over to me, grabbing my face. "I'm sorry. I will talk to him."

I let the kiss linger. "I already called him," I explain, waddling to the fridge and grabbing the plate of strawberries. "He said he would have a talk with her." I look at him. "That is not going to happen. The last time he did that, she called the boys predators." I close my eyes. "Why is he like this?"

"You should thank god I'm not like that," he says, and I look at him.

"You are going to get a vasectomy," I vow. "I'm making the appointment."

"Are you insane?" he questions, blocking his junk with his hand. "You said you wanted three kids."

"Well, we have four." I put up my hand. "One more and it's our own hockey team."

He comes over to me and puts his hands on my stomach. "Two more and we even have a full line, including a goalie."

I'm about to tell him not a chance in hell when my cell phone rings, and I walk over to it, seeing that it's Michael.

"Hello?" I answer the phone. "How is my favorite client?"

"Miserable," he responds, and I close my eyes and walk out of the room. "I'm being benched. Last night, I played three minutes and fifty-five seconds in the first period, and that's it."

I close my eyes and sit down on the step. "Who told you that you were being benched?"

"Who do you think?" he says of the coach that has been riding his ass harder than any other player on the team. He's a coach who has no problems going to the media and calling out his players for fucking up, and he has mentioned Michael a lot lately. "I can't do this, Erika," he declares, his voice going soft and sounding broken. "I can't keep doing this. Erks," he repeats, using the nickname he gave me five years ago. "Get me out of here."

"Let me make a call," I reply, hanging up the phone and calling the GM of Columbus.

"I thought you were on maternity leave," he says, not

even saying hello.

"I thought you said the bullshit with Michael was over." I repeat what he told me at the end of last year when things were getting rocky. "It'll blow over, Erika, is what you said."

"I'm standing by my coach," he confirms, and I stand.

"Yeah, well, get ready to trade him," I express, my stomach cramping when I hang up the phone and call the one person I know will take Michael and has cap space.

"Did you have the baby?" he asks, and I close my eyes, ignoring the pain I feel.

"Not yet," I say, not adding that I've been having contractions all day. "I just got off the phone with Michael Horton," I lead with, and he lets out a huge breath.

"Funny you should say that name," he responds, and I listen to him. "Ten minutes ago, the GM of Columbus called me up."

"Nico," I hiss his name. "Do not toy with me."

He laughs. "I'm making it happen," he affirms, and then his voice goes low. "But if he pulls any shit like he is pulling in Columbus …"

"I'll talk to him," I reassure him.

"Tell him to pack his bags. I don't want him on the ice tonight," he says, and I close my eyes.

"Thank you," I say and hang up the phone. I call Michael back, and as soon as he answers, the pain rips through me, and I yelp out.

Cooper walks out of the kitchen, looking at me. "It's me," I say to Michael between clenched teeth. "Pack your bags," I pant. "You're coming to Dallas." I don't even hear what he says before I hang up the phone and look at Cooper.

"What's happening?" he asks, looking at me as I stand here crouched over with my hand on the railing.

"Michael is being traded to Dallas," I share, and then a splash stops him from coming to me. "And my water just broke."

Four hours later, our son is born just as the news hits the hockey world.

Michael Horton is traded to Dallas.